Devlin—

I need you—your help. **Please.**

My daughter is missing, and you're the only one I can turn to. I hope we can put the past behind us and save my Jessica. She's all I have.

You're the only one who can bring her home safely.

Please call me.

Amanda

Please address questions and book requests to: Silhouette Reader Service
U.S.: 3010 Walden Ave., P.O. Box 1325, Buffalo, NY 14269
Canadian: P.O. Box 609, Fort Erie, Ont. L2A 5X3

NEW MEXICO

PAULA DETMER RIGGS

Desperate Measures

Published by Silhouette Books

America's Publisher of Contemporary Romance

SILHOUETTE BOOKS
300 East 42nd St.,
New York, N.Y. 10017

ISBN 0-373-47181-5

DESPERATE MEASURES

Copyright © 1989 by Paula Detmer Riggs

Printed in U.S.A.

Dear Reader,

New Mexico. Land of Enchantment. What a great place for an adventure! Or to raise a child. For Judge Amanda Wainwright in *Desperate Measures*, it became both.

Though Mandy lived and worked in the city, she loved the wild beauty of the Sangre de Cristo Mountains and the magical serenity of the high desert landscape. And as mothers will, she passed on that love to her daughter, Jessica—along with a passion for the colorful history of the state.

Tucked into a rugged corner of the Southwest, New Mexico has a way of demanding the best from those who dare to live there. Mother Nature has been generous in her gifts, but her largesse comes with a price. The weather can turn from balmy to blustery in a blink of an eye. Lightning zigzags through an endless sky, arrowing toward the unwary. In summer, heat blisters the mind as well as the skin. In winter, snow rages in the mountains.

The men and women who first came to the Land of Enchantment were strong and independent and brave. Some came to build intricate pueblos of adobe, others came searching for gold. More followed, eager for land and freedom. For two centuries, survival was a never-ending struggle. The legacy of these early inhabitants is a strong one.

Even in modern times, however, the risks can be great—as Amanda Wainwright and her daughter, Jessica, have discovered. From Amanda, Jessie has learned the power of a quiet assurance and tenacity. From the man who risks everything to save them both, they learn about sacrifice.

All three learn the power of love. Which is to me the greatest enchantment of all.

Paula Detmer Riggs

Chapter 1

WE HAVE YOUR DAUGHTER. FOLLOW THESE INSTRUCTIONS EXACTLY OR THE CHILD WILL DIE.

"Another crank letter, Your Honor?"

Judge Amanda Wainwright nibbled on the end of her gold pen and nodded absently, her green eyes sparking with disgust. She'd been on the bench all day, and she was tired and hot and out of patience.

"How many is that this month, Juana?" she asked her clerk, who was diligently searching through the oak filing cabinet in the corner for the thick folder that contained similar messages.

"Four. Not counting the man who sent you the dead fish."

Amanda wrinkled her nose at the memory and leaned forward to inhale the spicy fragrance of the pink tea roses she'd brought from home that morning.

"I'll be glad when the Santalucci case is over. Every time we have a trial with mob overtones, the mafia freaks come out of the woodwork."

Juana glanced up from the files. "I'll say. They seem to think it's a party."

Amanda laughed, then sobered immediately. The Santalucci trial wasn't funny, not when two good men were dead, allegedly at his command.

"Get used to the sick jokes. This trial has already gotten more publicity than most." She glanced again at the crudely printed block letters meandering across the page. The words were printed in an erratic hand on a single sheet torn from a lined legal pad. The letters were crudely formed and several words had been misspelled, but awkwardly, as though the inaccuracies had been deliberate.

Amanda threw the note aside and rubbed her aching temples. Threatening letters like this one were an occupational hazard, one of the drawbacks of being a New Mexico district court judge assigned to major cases.

"You'd think after five years on the bench I'd get used to trash like this, but I still get upset every time." She shook her head. "Sometimes I think I should have gone into social work instead of the law."

Juana's sunny round face drooped into a frown of apology. "I don't know how this got by me, Your Honor. Someone must have slipped it under the door of your chambers while I was down the hall in Records."

Petite and pretty, Juana Mendoza was thirty-three, a mother of two daughters and, in the judge's opinion, the best administrative assistant in the entire city of Albuquerque.

"You'd better talk to security. No one is supposed to be on this floor without authorization." Absently Amanda smoothed the thick fall of dark brown hair away from her neck.

The air-conditioning in the courthouse was always erratic, sometimes too hot, sometimes too cold. Today it had been barely detectable, and she'd sweltered in her formal black robe.

"Yes, ma'am. I'll do that right now—on my way out. Anything else I can do for you before I leave?" She pulled a file from the drawer and then shut it.

"Nothing, thanks, Juana. You might as well leave early, get a jump on the long weekend."

Juana rolled her liquid brown eyes and grinned. "The fireworks at the fairgrounds aren't going to be the only ones I intend to see."

"Better you than me," Amanda commented, and Juana laughed.

"You could take that new assistant DA up on his offer of dinner, Your Honor. You know the one I mean, the tall Viking type with the great buns?"

Amanda shook her head. "Granted, he's got a terrific body, but his mind is like a map of Nevada. Great empty spaces, populated here and there by an occasional discernible thought.''

Juana grinned. ''You're a tough lady to please.''

''I'm afraid so.'' Amanda wasn't especially concerned. Her life was exactly the way she liked it—orderly, predictable, pleasant. As long as she had her daughter, her work and her roses, she was happy.

Juana opened the file and riffled through it. ''I'd forgotten about a lot of these. Some of them are really sick.''

''Just don't forget to be back here bright and early Monday morning—ready for the trial. All of us have to be on our toes for this one.'' Amanda's dimpled smile took the sting out of the gentle warning, and Juana nodded. She placed the file on the blotter in front of the judge and whisked a piece of lint from the gleaming desktop.

''Well, I'm off. Have a terrific weekend, Your Honor.''

''Thanks. Jessie and I are spending it in Las Cruces with my brother-in-law and his family.'' She glanced at the framed photo of her daughter, then frowned as her gaze rested on the bulging folder.

A faint shadow of doubt crossed her mind, only to be immediately dismissed. This note fit the pattern precisely—melodramatic, badly punctuated, grandiose in its threats.

Still, it wouldn't hurt to call Jessica's sitter, just to put her mind at ease. Amanda kicked off her new pumps and wiggled her toes against the colorful Persian rug as she punched out the familiar number.

It was nearly five, and Jessie should have returned from her riding lesson by now. No doubt she was sitting in Elena's sunny kitchen, having her usual afternoon snack of *buñuelos* and milk.

Juana waved from the doorway, then pulled the door closed behind her. Amanda doodled on the blotter, listening to the ringing in her ear. She was looking forward to the holiday. She and Jessie needed to be together. As a single parent she had to work hard at finding time to spend with her only child.

Elena's faintly accented voice came over the wire, calm and easygoing as always, and Amanda relaxed. She was right. The letter was a hoax.

''Hi, Elena. This is is Judge Wainwright. May I speak with Jessica, please?''

The wire was silent, and Amanda frowned. ''Elena?''

''Uh, Jessie's not here, Mrs. Wainwright.''

''*Not...there?*''

Amanda experienced raw fear for the first time in her life. Her stomach lurched, and a stinging acid taste rose in her mouth. Stay calm, she commanded herself as she fought to keep her voice steady. Maybe she'd misunderstood. "You mean she...she hasn't returned from her riding lesson?"

"That's just it. When Jessie didn't come back at half past four like always, I phoned the stable, and the riding mistress said that she'd been picked up by someone driving a gray Volvo. I just assumed it was you, even though you hadn't said anything about picking her up early today." A sibilant edge of worry crept into the sitter's voice, thickening her accent as she added, "I figured you'd forgot to tell me, it being the beginning of the holiday weekend and all."

Amanda felt a terrible pressure in her chest as she struggled to suck enough air into her lungs. "Uh, right. Of course, I forgot that her...her uncle John was going to be picking her up." Amanda tried to force a note of apology into her voice. "I'll, uh, I'll pay you for a full day naturally, and I'm sorry I bothered you. I guess I'm just a little preoccupied right now."

Elena replied with a chirping note of understanding. "Who wouldn't be preoccupied with that horrible man coming to trial in your court? The TV says he had those two reporters tortured before he ordered them killed."

Tortured. Killed. The words hung in the air, deadly twisting snakes of poisonous sound that made Amanda shudder. She pressed a hand to her stomach in a vain attempt to stop the sickness spreading through her. Her fingers touched the ornate turquoise and silver belt that Jessie had given her only a few days ago for her thirty-fifth birthday, and she began to shake. *Dear God, please don't let her die. Don't let my baby die.*

"Mrs. Wainwright? Are you there?" Elena's anxious voice vibrated loudly in her ear, bringing Amanda back to reality.

Don't panic, she told herself over and over as she tried to control her frantic breathing. Think! She held her breath, then exhaled slowly.

Somehow she managed a few polite comments before she was finally able to hang up. Her hand was trembling so badly she missed the phone cradle and had to try again.

Panic clawed at her stomach as her eyes frantically skimmed the heavy black printing again, this time more slowly. The letters waved before her eyes, and she squeezed her long lashes together to block out the malevolent words that were suddenly all too real.

DO NOT GO THE POLECE, DO NOT GO THE FBI, DO NOT GO THE PRESS. DONT TELL ANYONE AT ALL, OR YOU'LL NEVER SEE THE GIRL AGAIN.

The demands were clear-cut. She was to slant her rulings and her instructions to the jury toward acquittal in the murder trial of George "The Saint" Santalucci. If she failed to comply, if she tried to have the trial postponed, or if she removed herself from the case for any reason, Jessie would die.

"This isn't happening," she said in a thin whisper. "It can't be happening."

Amanda twisted in her high-backed chair, trying to think, but her heart was pounding so furiously she felt faint. The framed diplomas and awards on the paneled walls blurred in front of her eyes, and her lungs burned from lack of oxygen. Jessie, her sweet little Jessie, was in trouble, and she didn't know what to do to save her.

"No! Damn it, I *won't* fall apart." Amanda beat her fist against the felt blotter, her teeth clenched. "That's what he wants, the bastard. He wants me to be a basket case, to be so scared I won't even think of fighting him."

Her mouth was as dry as the desert outside as she blotted the tears from her lashes with a tissue. Fury boiled in her brain as she thought about the man behind the kidnapping.

Santalucci was a native New Yorker who'd come to Albuquerque fifteen years ago after serving time for extortion. Now a suave gladhander with an oily grin who professed to be a legitimate businessman, he lived far beyond the income generated by his statewide chain of pizza parlors. His real money came from prostitution, drugs and gambling.

The *Albuquerque Sun* had been trying to nail him for years, printing every scrap of incriminating evidence its reporters could dredge up. And then, just when rumors of a scoop were the hottest, the two reporters heading the investigation had been found dead in a drainage ditch near the Rio Grande, their throats cut.

Through patient and exhaustive work the police and the district attorney had finally pieced together a largely circumstantial case, and Santalucci had been indicted by the grand jury. His trial was to begin in three days.

Three days in which to find Jessie. Seventy-two precious hours.

Amanda's composure wavered, and a dry sob shook her slim frame. Her baby, her dearest Jessie, a sweet trusting little girl barely seven years old was somewhere alone with monstrous criminals who maimed and killed without guilt, a tiny pawn in a deadly game.

"Oh, Jessie. Mommy's so sorry," she moaned, and her throat

clogged with horror as her mind replayed in terrible, vivid detail the twisted torture other innocent victims had endured.

Her nails dug into the leather armrests of her chair as she forced her mind away from the dreadful stories she'd heard in her courtroom over the years. That kind of thinking would only lead to mistakes. She had to remain calm, had to put aside her emotions to stay in control, just as she'd done three years ago, when her husband had suddenly died of a heart attack while she was in the middle of an important murder trial.

Her rulings in that case had already been cited as precedent in several other trials in the state. She was a professional, and had been an experienced attorney before she'd been appointed to the bench. She knew what had to be done.

An icy detachment spread through her as she snatched up the phone and punched out the number for information. "I need the regional office of the FBI," she managed to say calmly when the operator answered.

She wrote down the number, then stabbed the button impatiently and redialed. "Cyrus Tanner," she said crisply when the receptionist answered.

"One moment."

Cyrus Tanner had been the FBI station chief in Albuquerque for as long as Amanda could remember. Big and shambling, with a homely face and heavy Southern accent, he reminded her of a friendly basset hound.

Amanda had always liked Cy, and more important, she had always trusted him. His reputation as a straight shooter was one of the reasons she'd decided to call him. In spite of the note's blunt demands, she had no intention of trying to fight a monster like Santalucci alone.

"It's an emergency, Cy," she told him when he answered. "But I can't talk about it over the phone. It's…highly sensitive."

There was a short pause. "I understand, Your Honor," he said in no-nonsense tones. "Tell me where and when, and I'll be there."

Not here in the courthouse, Amanda thought quickly, and not at his office, but where? She had to be so careful, in case Santalucci was having her watched.

Oh God, she thought. Her eyes darted around the room, looking for bugs. Was that horrible man even now listening to her as she defied his instructions? She hadn't thought about that. Frustrated and angry at her own stupidity, she moaned aloud, a thin, desperate thread of sound that reverberated around the empty office.

"Your Honor? Judge Wainwright? Is something wrong?" Tanner's slow drawl roughened with urgency.

Suddenly her frozen detachment splintered as fear cascaded over her. She should have called from the pay phone in the lobby. From now on she had to be more careful, more logical. It was Jessie's only hope.

"I...we—need someplace safe. Where...where no one will see us together, but I...can't think of a spot."

"Mm. Give me a minute...." His voice trailed off as he thought, then came back on the line almost immediately. "Write down this address. I'll meet you there in two hours."

Amanda bit her lip as she scribbled the house number and street on her pad. It was an address near the University of New Mexico, in an older part of town that was only ten minutes from the courthouse. The homes there were small and comfortable, the residents a mixture of blue-collar workers and young couples just starting out.

"This isn't your house, is it?" she asked quickly, not bothering to hide the concern in her voice.

"No, it belongs to a friend, the widow of one of my former agents. It'll be safe to meet there. I'll call her and tell her to expect us at seven. Her name is Rosalie."

On the stroke of seven Amanda rang the bell at the address Tanner had given her. The house was one of many nearly identical pueblo-style bungalows dotting the wide, tree-lined street.

In the summer twilight, the aspens looked like dark, brooding sentries mutely standing watch over the quiet neighborhood, their branches skeletal and twisted against the purpling sky.

Amanda's heart began to race as she heard the sharp staccato of footsteps approaching the door. She looked over her shoulder one more time, scanning the street. Her charcoal Volvo was parked at the curb, solid and reassuring, and there was no other traffic to be seen in either direction.

She breathed a sigh of relief; she hadn't been followed. Perhaps the circuitous route she'd taken had paid off, or maybe Santalucci was so confident of her complicity that he hadn't bothered to have her tailed. It didn't really matter. She'd managed to arrive without being seen.

The door opened wide, creaking shrilly on its hinges, and Amanda flinched.

The woman in the doorway was in her late twenties and strikingly beautiful, with an aura of sensuality.

"Judge Wainwright?" she asked with a hesitant smile. "Cy's already here. Come in, please."

A memory of another woman, similar in looks, but younger and in some kind of difficulty, arose in Amanda's mind, then faded quickly as she forced a polite smile and stepped inside.

Cy Tanner was waiting in the pastel living room, his seamed face wreathed with curiosity. He was in his shirtsleeves, which were still buttoned at his hairy wrists, and his white shirt, once starched to executive stiffness, had wilted in the scalding July heat.

"Your Honor," he said in a low rumble, lowering his bald head in a courtly nod.

"Hello, Cy. It's good to see you again." Their last meeting had been at her husband's funeral. Cy had been part of a law-enforcement contingent paying respects to Judge Justin Wainwright, the man many had considered the most brilliant jurist in the Southwest.

Amanda sat down on the plush turquoise sofa, and the other two found seats opposite.

"My daughter Jessica's being held for ransom," she said without preamble. Maybe if she said the words quickly, they might not hurt so much.

Her fingers felt cold and clammy and were shaking noticeably as she took the folded note from her briefcase and handed it across the coffee table to Tanner. "This was under my door when I returned from court this afternoon."

There was a flare of interest in Tanner's muddy brown eyes as he took the note in his large hand and began to read. With swift efficiency, he skimmed the words, muttering a violent expletive under his breath as he handed it back to her. He didn't quite meet Amanda's eyes as he slid his gaze toward Rosalie.

"It's Santalucci. He's angling for an acquittal."

"Oh my God! That awful man." The younger woman looked at Amanda with sympathy. "You must be going through hell."

A nagging memory tugged at Amanda as she managed a polite nod of thanks. Who was this woman? She looked so familiar, and yet Amanda was certain that they had never met.

"Once I know the FBI is looking for her, I'll be okay," she said. It was hard forcing herself to be calm and composed, when all she wanted to do was scream in pain.

Tanner stood up and shambled over to the window, his bearlike back to the two women. He said nothing.

In the awkward silence, Amanda tried to ignore the nausea churning in her stomach. "I'm prepared to do whatever you say," she said urgently as the silence lengthened. "Anything. Just tell me, and I'll do it. My daughter means everything to me." Unshed tears thickened her voice, and she faltered. "I'm sorry. I know it doesn't help to lose control."

She bit her lip as Rosalie reached over to touch her hand. "Go ahead and cry. It helped me a lot when my husband was murdered."

Murdered? Oh God, did they think Jessie was already dead?

Amanda groped in her purse for a tissue and wiped the puddled tears from her lashes. She compressed the tissue into a damp wad as she looked from Rosalie to Cy. He was still staring out into the deepening darkness, his shoulders hunched.

They do, she thought. They think she's dead!

Her heart began to pound as she leaped to her feet and crossed the room to grab Cy's arm, which jerked under her frantic, clutching fingers.

"There's something you're not telling me, isn't there?" she cried, her body trembling. "You know something about Jessie. Something terrible." Her voice rose to a shrill crescendo before she managed to control it. "Tell me. I want to know." Her heart thudded loudly in her ears, the beats coming so quickly they blended into one pounding roar.

"No, that's not it," Cy responded quickly, his big hand covering hers protectively. "I swear on the heads of my kids."

Amanda could hear the truth ringing in his words, and she felt light-headed with relief. "Then what...why...?"

Tanner led her over to the sofa and gently pushed her down onto the fat cushions. When she was settled, he returned to his seat. His hands circled the peeled pine armrests of the chair as though he wanted to twist them from their moorings. His expression was grim.

"We have a problem," he said, and Amanda could feel his frustration permeating the air. "I'm not sure I can give you the kind of help you need."

"*What?*" Her disbelief exploded into the room. "But you *have* to help me. There's no one else." Her spine tightened painfully as she sat forward on the sofa cushions. He *was* going to help her, she vowed in silent determination. It was his job, and she would see that he did it.

Tanner's eyes avoided her angry glance as he clawed at his tight collar with stiff fingers, loosening the silk tie and fumbling with the tiny button beneath the knot. His lips pursed as he slowly raised his head.

"We've had the devil's own problem with leaks," he said curtly, "especially after those two reporters were murdered." His drawl flattened in anger. "Santalucci always seems to know what we're doing before we do it. The odds are, he'd find out about this, too, and probably well before we turned up any solid leads. If you insist, I'll do all that I can, but—" His voice roughened defensively. "Your daughter might be dead by the time we found her." He shot to his feet and began pacing nervously.

Amanda watched his agitated movements in rising dismay. "What about using agents from Santa Fe or even Phoenix? You could meet them someplace where no one knew you. And if you didn't tell anyone in your office, no one could leak the information."

Suddenly Tanner froze in midstride and turned to face her. "It's a damned long shot, but it might work." He gnawed his drooping lower lip, his brow knotted in thought.

"You mean using outside agents?" Amanda asked quickly, her hopes rising.

"Just one. Devlin Buchanan. He knows this town, and he knows Santalucci. If anyone can find Jessica, he can."

Amanda paled. "But...but he's dead!"

Who could forget the sight of Special Agent Devlin Buchanan's mangled, blood-soaked black Corvette wrapped around a cement bridge abutment on the interstate? Every TV station in the city had carried the grisly pictures.

"Yeah, what's the matter with you, Cy?" Rosalie challenged, her smooth ivory complexion now dotted with splotches of pale pink. "We were at the funeral, you and me. It was awful, all those pushy reporters and that terrible man, Santalucci, grinning all over his face."

Of course, Amanda thought with a rush of chagrin. *That's* where she'd seen Rosalie before. In her courtroom.

Devlin Buchanan had been the defendant, accused of deliberately stalking and killing the man who'd murdered his partner, Special Agent Antonio Cruz. Rosalie's husband.

A deep sigh rumbled from Tanner's throat as he looked from one woman to the other. "I can't tell you the details. Just take it from me, the man's alive."

He shoved his hands into his pockets and retraced his steps to the front window where he peered through the gauzy white curtains into the black vista.

The blue van, the one that had pulled up just after the judge had entered the house, was still there, parked near the corner. The windows were dark, but the red pinpoint of a cigarette told him that someone was inside—waiting for her to emerge.

He dropped his head to his chest for a moment before turning to face the two women staring at him. At times like this he hated his job.

"Is he a fugitive, Cy?" Amanda demanded. "Maybe wanted for another revenge killing we haven't been told about?" She didn't bother to hide her disdain.

Buchanan was a renegade, a man with an attitude, who gave decent cops a bad reputation. From the moment she'd convened court on the first day of his trial, she'd actively disliked him.

He'd been arrogant, unrepentant and definitely annoying in the way he'd stared at her so intently. He had incredible eyes, she remembered now. Light gray and rimmed with black, and his lashes had been amazingly dark for so blond a man.

Tanner's lined face colored deeply. "I realize you don't have the greatest opinion of Agent Buchanan," he said formally. "A lot of people, some of them right here in the local office, thought he was guilty. I'm not one of them."

Buchanan had sworn under oath that the other man had pulled a gun first, and the jury had believed him. But the press, intrigued by the wild West image of a solitary lawman fighting for right against impossible odds, hadn't let the story die.

His angular face had been plastered all over the state, his cover blown, his career as an agent destroyed.

Two months after the conclusion of the trial his car had smashed into that freeway overpass, and the story of the maverick agent had been buried with the simple coffin that had supposedly contained his remains.

"I can't believe it—Dev, alive." Rosalie sounded stunned, and her eyes were round with bewilderment.

Amanda's brow puckered as she remembered the groupies, strident and pushy and dressed in outrageously sexy outfits, who'd waited outside the courthouse daily to catch a glimpse of the rangy agent with an arrogant disregard for the rules and conventions of civilized society—and the sex appeal of a rock star.

"Where is he now?" Her controlled voice sliced through the tension, drawing a startled look from Rosalie.

"In Mexico. In a tiny village near Rosita, about two hundred and ninety miles straight south of here. Place called La Placita."

Rosalie picked nervously at a loose thread on the narrow cuff of her pink blouse and tried to smile. "I liked Dev, but, well, sometimes he scared me. He's cold inside, like a machine. When Tony died, Dev wouldn't even talk about him, like Tony hadn't even existed.'' Sudden anger gave her lovely features a harsh cast. "They were partners for eight years, and he never even sent flowers to the funeral.''

Tanner passed a hand over his bald head, and a heavy sigh escaped his lips. He suddenly looked older than the fifty or so Amanda imagined him to be.

"Dev took Tony's death hard. He just has his own way of handling things.''

"Yes, with his gun," Amanda said with open disapproval.

"Sometimes that's the only way.''

"I don't agree.''

"I realize that.'' He frowned. "You ripped into him pretty good at the conclusion of his trial.''

"He deserved it.'' Amanda refused to back down. Devlin Buchanan symbolized all that was wrong in the field of law enforcement, and as an attorney himself, he should have known better.

Tanner arranged his face into a persuasive smile. "Look, Your Honor. It takes a special kind of person to go undercover. It's the toughest job I know, working without a net out there on the streets where one mistake can result in a knife between your ribs.

"Dev was out there a long time, maybe too long, I don't know. But I do know he did a hell of a job. And we let him down, you and me and the citizens of this state. Instead of giving him the medal he deserved, we destroyed his career and nearly cost him his life.''

He glanced down at the holster attached to his belt. "I wish I had a dozen men like Devlin Buchanan.''

Amanda let the tense silence settle around her. Cy was wrong. She had appreciated the former agent's dedication. It'd been his methods she hadn't been able to condone.

"Judge?'' Rosalie's hesitant voice caught Amanda's attention. "Cy's right. Dev's awful bitter about the trial and all. I don't think he'll help you, even if you ask him to. Tony said he was a bad man to cross.''

Amanda nodded, Rosalie's words repeating silently in her brain. A bad man to cross. A man who attracted violence like blood attracts sharks. A man who made his own rules. How could she possibly trust her daughter's life to someone like that? And yet, what choice did she have?

A heavy pressure constricted her chest, making it difficult to breathe as her questioning gaze fastened on Tanner's homely face.

"Tell me how to find him.''

Amanda was on the road south before dawn the next morning, driving a small tan pickup that had once belonged to Tony Cruz. It'd been Tanner's idea to take the truck.

"Just in case that blue van parked down the block belongs to one of Santalucci's men," he'd told her with a grim nod toward the window. "Leave the Volvo here and drive east down the back alley. You won't be followed." And she hadn't been.

So far, so good, she thought, as she glanced into her rearview mirror again. Nothing but the twisting ribbon of the rutted dirt road behind her was visible.

Everyone who mattered, her neighbors, her Friday cleaning lady, Juana, all thought she and Jessie had gone to Las Cruces to visit Justin's younger brother, John. Not that Santalucci would check, she prayed, but just in case, she'd tried to cover her tracks.

Tanner had given her detailed directions to the village where Buchanan made his home. "There aren't many signs," he'd explained dryly. "In fact, none at all, so you'll have to watch your odometer carefully, or you'll miss the turnoff."

The sun was directly overhead as she entered the sleepy village of La Placita, which was little more than a ragged cluster of drab adobes lining two rutted, pockmarked streets.

It was siesta time. Most of the houses had their shutters drawn against the noontime heat, and even the sprawling cantina on the edge of the weed-strewn plaza looked uninhabited.

Amanda fought off an eerie feeling of loneliness as she drove slowly toward the boxlike church that stood on a small rise at the outskirts of the village.

A quarter mile past the church was Buchanan's house, the last building on the road. Low and sprawling, it was a compact adobe with whitewashed walls and heavy sun-bleached shutters at each window. A deep portico formed by the overhanging eaves ran along the front, casting a deep shadow on the weathered exterior.

Amanda parked behind a dusty Jeep with Chihuahua plates and hopped out. A blast of superheated air hit her, plastering her white cotton shirt to her body like a shroud.

She could smell the heat, acrid and stinging, as it radiated off the parched earth. Behind her sunglasses her eyes began to water from the dust driven into her face by the dry southern breeze.

Her denim skirt felt heavy and hot against her bare legs as she walked toward the dense shade of the porch, her large canvas tote clutched tightly in front of her like a shield.

In the distance a dog barked loudly, a frantic crescendo of sound that ended abruptly in a shrill yelp. Nearby, a bird called, its song haunting and lonely and unanswered. From the church below came the sound of faint, somber organ music.

At least I'm not all alone in this place, Amanda thought uneasily as she knocked on the heavy door.

There was no sound from within, and she tried again, hammering on the rough panel with the heel of her hand. Nothing. No sound, no movement from behind the shuttered windows, no sign of life.

"Hello? Mr. Buchanan? Are you there?" Her voice echoed off the thick walls to mock her. What would she do if he really wasn't home?

Amanda caught her lower lip between her teeth and stared at the bleak landscape. It was a place for lizards and rattlesnakes and cactus, a desolate, barren plot baking under the relentless sun. She shivered suddenly in spite of the merciless heat and started toward the side of the house. Perhaps there was a side entrance.

Her sandals slid on the pebbly soil as she stepped off the porch and rounded the corner. She glanced down at the hard surface in front of her, only to gasp aloud as an angular shadow darted across her path.

Before she could react, Amanda was seized from behind by hard hands. A sinewy forearm as solid as an oak staff pressed against her throat, constricting her windpipe, and her right arm was twisted into the small of her back with a force so punishing tears welled in her eyes.

Her breath came in ragged, suffocating gasps as her body was pulled upward until she was standing on her toes. The landscape blurred into a shimmering, surrealistic white panorama as she kicked out wildly, fighting to breathe. Her last thought, as she lost consciousness, was for her daughter.

Chapter 2

Amanda felt strange, disoriented, her body heavy and weighted with numbness as though she were caught in the deadened sleep of early morning. The blackness shrouding her slowly receded, leaving her trapped in the dense gray fog she could see swirling beyond her closed lids.

A callused hand brushed her forehead, smoothing back the tangle of hair that lay damp and matted against the hot skin.

"Judge Wainwright. Wake up." It was a commanding voice, resonant with masculine sensuality and with an unexpected gentleness that drew her like a lonely dove to a safe haven.

"I feel so dizzy." She started to open her eyes, but the room began to spin, and she closed them quickly.

"The dizziness will be gone in a minute. Just relax."

Amanda nuzzled her cheek against the hard fingers that trailed lightly along her hairline. The clean smell of soap teased her nostrils as her mouth rested against his racing pulse.

"Mmm," she murmured. The fog was thinning, whirling in whitening eddies around her, and she turned her head, her eyelids fluttering.

The man was leaning over her, his face partially hidden by the shadows, but she could see his lips. They were firm, wide enough to fit his strong chin and there was a sensuous fullness to the bottom curve. Sexy, she decided in drowsy detachment as her eyes slowly closed again. That was definitely a sexy mouth.

She felt him move closer until his breath warmed her skin. Was that a kiss brushing across her lips? Her heart fluttered as a warm wave of pleasure slowly washed through her. A smile curved her lips as she slid her tongue along her bottom lip. She could taste tequila.

Tequila? Her fuzzy brain rejected the idea as impossible. She was hallucinating.

Amanda sighed and opened her eyes slowly. Through her lashes, she saw rugged male features, bronzed and unsmiling. His forehead was broad, his cheeks angular, with a strong jaw forming the apex of a blunt triangle that gave added emphasis to those impossibly vivid silver eyes.

"Buchanan?" He couldn't have kissed her. Not this hard-faced man. She'd been trapped in a dream, that was all. A very realistic dream.

"Yes. Don't try to sit up too fast. You've been out for nearly an hour."

Amanda slowly turned her head, fighting the dizziness that still gripped her. She was lying on a couch of some kind, upholstered in material with a rough texture that prickled the skin of her cheek where it brushed against the back cushion. A shaft of dusty sunshine bathed her face in light, and she squinted in pain.

"How do you feel?"

"Rotten. I...you attacked me!"

"Yes."

Scalding heat rose from the V of her blouse, spreading upward to bloom in her cheeks. No wonder she felt so lousy. He'd choked her into unconsciousness!

She glared up at him, a steady roaring in her head. "Don't you ever do that again!"

The lips that she'd found so fascinating only seconds before slanted upward on one side as his gaze dropped to her mouth. "We're not in your courtroom now, Your Honor. I make the rules here."

She opened her mouth to blast him, but the words caught in her throat, emerging only as a weak croak. She challenged him with her eyes, and he chuckled. "Don't get all riled up, now. You're just beginning to get some color back in those white cheeks."

He stood up and crossed his arms over his broad chest, long well-muscled arms that were deeply tanned and corded with ropes of taut sinew.

He was dressed as she'd never seen him in court, in a red T-shirt and cutoff jeans that barely covered the top of his hard, hair-roughened thighs. Before she could stop herself, her eyes had followed those long bronzed legs all the way down to his bare feet, braced wide apart on the scuffed terra-cotta floor.

"If you'd like, I'd be glad to peel down to give you a better look."

Amanda jerked her gaze to his face. He was laughing at her.

"No, thank you," she said in frosty tones. "I'm not in the least curious."

"Liar." ·

Amanda glared at him. Already she was off guard and at a disadvantage with this man, and she hated the feeling.

"*Ella es muy bello, Señor Dev.* Very beautiful, your lady friend." It was a child's voice, high pitched and excited, speaking rapid Spanish.

Amanda looked around hurriedly. A small boy had come in, dressed in thin cotton shorts and a ragged T-shirt, both of which were several sizes too big. His big brown eyes and hesitant grin reminded her of Jessica, and her burgeoning smile faltered as pain sliced through her.

"She's no friend of mine, Pepe," Buchanan answered, grinning at the boy who approached slowly, a frown puckering the olive-skinned smoothness of his face. "If this lady had had her way, I'd be doing twenty to life in prison right now." His Spanish was accented but grammatically correct and he spoke with an impatient cadence.

"Right, Judge?" he asked in English.

"Right," she shot back before she realized what she was saying.

To her surprise, Buchanan chuckled. "At least you're honest, although I sure as hell can't figure out what you're doing here. I could have killed you with that choke hold before I recognized you." The lazy amusement faded from his eyes. "That was a very foolish thing you did, coming down here alone and without notice. I don't like snoops."

At the harsh note in the man's voice the boy called Pepe winced noticeably, and Buchanan gave him a hasty smile.

"*Está bien,*" he muttered, draping a big hand over the boy's bony shoulder. Pepe snuggled trustingly against Buchanan's long lean torso and stared at Amanda with wide eyes.

"Cy didn't tell me I'd be risking attack, just by knocking on your front door," she said astringently, then stopped as she realized that her throat hurt abominably and her neck was stiff. Gingerly she touched the spot a scant inch above her collarbone where his hard forearm had pressed against her throat.

His eyes narrowed in disbelief. "Cy? You mean Cy Tanner?"

"Yes, Cy Tanner—remember him?" she asked pointedly. "Your former boss. He sent me to you." She threw her legs over the side of the couch and sat up. Her head ached, and her tongue felt like used sandpaper. "If you had a telephone, I would have called first— or he would have. But you don't, so I had to come unannounced."

"You want me to believe that Cy actually gave you directions to my house?" A thunderous frown punctuated his urgent question. "Why the hell would he do that?"

His words whipped toward her, raw with suspicion. There was no hint of amusement in his eyes now, only angry menace that stripped her bare.

But she didn't intend to let him know how much he was upsetting her, no matter how hard he glared at her. She'd gotten used to his intimidating stares before.

"Because I need your help. Very badly." Her throat was raspy and sore, and her voice came out hoarse and strained.

Buchanan muttered something abrupt and angry in Spanish, but Amanda didn't catch the words. "Entertain the lady while I fetch her something to drink, Pepito," he ordered, giving the boy a gentle shove in Amanda's direction before turning abruptly to walk toward the kitchen she could see through an open door to the right.

He walked with loose-jointed assurance, spine straight, shoulders back, hips barely moving. His legs were long and muscular with the thick calves of a sprinter, and his buttocks bunched with latent power beneath the torn pockets of the faded denim cutoffs.

Fast and unbeatable in the dashes, Amanda thought with a frown, remembering her days as a college track star, but would he have the staying power and stamina of a distance runner?

"*Señora, está bien?*" the boy asked softly, his small hands tucked behind him as he rocked back and forth on his bare feet and watched her from beneath his curly black lashes.

Amanda nodded. "I'm fine," she said in halting Spanish. She could understand the language better than she could speak it.

"Do you live here?" she asked Pepe slowly. "*Es tu casa?*"

The boy shook his head. "It belongs to Señor Dev. He's my best friend." Pepe ran over to a simple pine table under the front window and returned with a carved horse, which he hugged to his thin chest with obvious pride. "He made this for me. For my name day."

Shyly he extended the toy toward her, and Amanda took it from his hand as though it were of finest porcelain. Painted gray, the prancing animal had a black mane and tail and wore the distinctive spots of an Appaloosa on its hind quarters.

"He's beautiful, Pepe. What's his name?"

"Diablo." The boy spoke with pride, his brown eyes sparkling eagerly. "None of the others in the orphanage has one quite so fine."

"You are a very lucky boy," she said solemnly, handing the horse back to him. "My little girl collects bears, but she doesn't have anything as special as this."

Pepe's shy smile broadened into gamin delight. "You have a child?"

Amanda nodded, pain rippling through her at the thought of the desperate danger threatening her baby. "Her name is Jessica Marie."

The kitchen was stiflingly hot. Devlin had forgotten to close the shutters against the morning sun, and he felt the heat that had collected in the floor tiles beneath his feet. He clenched his big fists on the counter and stared down at the stained surface.

What the hell was going on here? The last time he'd seen Amanda Wainwright, she'd been lecturing him on due process, a cold and disapproving glint in her big green eyes. He'd been emotionally raw that last day of his trial, his defenses badly frayed after reliving Tony's death over and over, on the stand and off.

He muttered a ripe obscenity and dropped his head forward, feeling the weight of his thirty-nine years more strongly than ever. His ribs were sore where she'd got him with her elbow, and his shin was bruised and aching from the heel of her small sandal.

He didn't know which had been worse, when she'd been fighting him like a tough little dervish, or when she'd been smiling drowsily up at him. Both had nearly knocked him flat.

Devlin ran a hand through his hair and took a deep breath. He hadn't remembered how really beautiful she was.

Her hair had been shorter two years ago, worn in some kind of frizzy style that hadn't suited the classical lines of her profile, and her face had been too thin.

She was perfect now, softly rounded in all the right places, and her hair curved in a loose wave around the delicate line of her jaw and swept backward to brush her shoulders. In the shadowed light it shone with deep golden highlights instead of with the red he'd noticed earlier in the bright sun.

Sweet, sultry, sexy, with the delicate features of a thirteenth-century Madonna and the silky brown mane of a Las Vegas showgirl, she made a man's blood race just looking at her. But beneath the

tantalizing sensuality of those emerald eyes was a clear warning—
do not touch.

"Don't worry, lady," he muttered. "You're not my type." And
he wasn't interested in her problems, either.

He wasn't ever going back to the States, to that cesspool of the
streets that had nearly finished him. He was out of it now, and most
of his wounds had healed over.

But sometimes, at night, he could still hear the curses of the dope
dealers and the sound of Tony's last breath whistling through the
hole in his chest. Nothing or no one could ever get him to open
himself up to that kind of pain again. Not ever.

He thumped his fist gently against the counter, his brows pulled
together tightly over the crooked bridge of his nose. He'd send the
woman back to Albuquerque with a few well-chosen words and be
done with her.

He grabbed a glass from the dish drainer and filled it with tap
water. The sooner he got rid of Amanda Wainwright the better.

She was wiping tears from her long lashes with her fingertips when
he returned, and he sucked in his gut. Whatever sob story she intended to give him, he wasn't buying.

"Sorry I don't have any bottled water, Your Honor," he said curtly
as he handed her the glass.

"This is fine." Amanda felt the change in him immediately. It
wasn't anything tangible. But there was a subtle difference in his
demeanor and in the tone of his voice. He didn't seem angry, exactly,
just withdrawn.

Her throat felt slightly better as the water slid past the bruised
tissues. The water was cool, but not cold, and tasted slightly bitter.
She could feel his eyes on her as she drank, but she avoided his gaze.
Instead, her eyes searched the room as she swallowed.

She was in the living room, on the only couch. To her left was a
massive fireplace made of stone, to her right the heavy front door
she'd hammered at.

The adobe was strictly masculine, sparsely decorated in native,
handmade pine furniture stained dark and covered with drab homespun. It was not a homey place.

"A poor thing, but mine own." Buchanan's voice held a touch of
defensiveness, and Amanda flushed.

"Sorry, I didn't mean to be nosy," she said stiffly. Now that she
was actually here, face-to-face with the one man who could save
Jessie, she didn't know how to start. Especially now, after that dis-

astrous beginning. Her stomach fluttered with nervousness as the memory of the dream kiss that had seemed so real.

Her eyes shifted to the child. "Does he understand English?" she asked softly, giving Pepe another smile.

"Some. I've been teaching him." He lifted Pepe into his arms. The boy looked even smaller cradled against the man's huge chest. "I need to talk to the lady privately," Buchanan said in Spanish, carrying Pepe over to the table. "Why don't you practice your whittling?"

As he bent over to let the boy's bare feet touch the ground, Amanda noticed a black handgun tucked into the waistband of Buchanan's cutoffs, the handle snugly fitted into the hollow of his spine above his buttocks.

She inhaled sharply, feeling her throat tighten with distaste. Even in exile the man carried a weapon.

After settling Pepe with a shapeless hunk of wood and a small penknife, Buchanan returned to stand in front of her, arms crossed, his expression blank, his eyes watchful.

"Okay, you claim you came all this way just to see me. Why?" His gray gaze held her captive, warning her to tell him the truth. She could see the shrewd intelligence behind those smoky irises, could sense the leashed violence beneath the indolent stance. With only a few inches of dry Mexican air between them, Amanda felt the full force of the man's personality.

Over the years she'd seen bigger men, men with power and charisma and charm, some more muscular and others much taller, but she'd never before met a man who had the power to intimidate her, just by standing in front of her so calmly.

She stood up, wincing slightly as the blood rushed to her feet in a tingling surge. In her sandals she was a good ten inches shorter than he was, and as she straightened to her full height, she was forced to tilt her chin until she could look him in the eye.

"I told you," she said, imitating his brusque manner. "I need your help."

"For what?" His expression revealed nothing.

"George Santalucci has my daughter. He's going to kill her if I don't see that he's acquitted of killing two *Sun* reporters last August."

Buchanan's face darkened to a dusky red. "The bastard," he said in a quiet voice that was more menacing than one raised in anger. "How old is your little girl?" He sounded as though he were almost reluctant to ask.

"Seven," Amanda said with a soft tremor in her voice. "She's about the size of your friend Pepe." Her voice faltered, and she bit her lip. She wasn't going to break down, not in front of this impassive man, not in front of anyone. She had to be strong for Jessie. When this terrible nightmare was over, she'd let go, but not now.

Her sandals slapped the tiles as she began pacing the room, suddenly too nervous to stand still. Swiftly, in the logical, economical sentences of the trial attorney she'd once been, she told Buchanan everything that had happened since she'd found the plain white envelope on the floor of her chambers yesterday afternoon.

Buchanan leaned against the back of the sofa, his hands gripping the wooden frame under his heavy thighs, his feet crossed at the ankles, and watched her. His big body didn't move, only his eyes. Like a hawk stalking his prey, Amanda thought when she'd finished.

"I know the kind of hell you're going through, Judge," he said slowly. "And I'm truly sorry about your daughter, but I'm out of the people-helping business these days." A muscle twitched beneath the weathered skin of his jaw, and he dropped his gaze to the floor beneath his bare feet. Leashed tension seemed to radiate from him like a tangible aura.

"Just like that, you're turning me down?" She stared at him in disbelief. "You can't do that! You're the only hope I have." Please help me, she wanted to plead, but the words wouldn't come. This man wouldn't respect weakness, not in her or anyone.

His body jerked, but his face remained impassive. "I doubt that, Your Honor," he said finally in a silky, quiet voice that raised shivery bumps on her skin. "You're a very powerful woman in Albuquerque with a lot more contacts than I have." One side of his mouth raised in a sardonic twist as he added, "In case you've forgotten, I've been out of touch for nearly two years. I wouldn't be any good to you."

Amanda blinked back hot tears of frustration and disbelief. "She's only a baby," she cried in a strangled voice, barely able to get the words out. "She's never even been to Disneyland or seen the Pacific or learned to ski. She should grow up to go to parties, have a career, get married—whatever she wants." The tears overflowed, wetting her cheeks before she dashed them away. "She's too young to die."

His jaw clenched so tightly the cords of his neck were clearly visible beneath the shaggy tendrils of the sun-bleached blond hair curling around his ears.

"Judge, I don't have any more to give, not to you, not to her. I'm burned out."

"But she's an innocent victim!"

Buchanan's heavy sigh was ragged. "They were all victims, the kids who were drug addicts before they could shave, the teenage hookers who tried to quit and ended up beaten to a bloody pulp, the poor suckers who thought they were getting a loan and ended up with a meat hook in the chest when they couldn't pay." A savage look of anger slashed across his hard features. "I tried to send that bastard a warning he couldn't ignore and almost ended up in state prison."

"You acted outside the law," she said, her voice rising. "You know and I know you deliberately went after that man D'Amato. You stalked him for days until you finally found a reason to confront him."

"He killed Tony."

"And the law would have punished him, eventually."

"Yeah, sure, if the local cops *happened* to scare up enough hard evidence, after a year or two of delays and legal maneuvering, *maybe* he would have come to trial. *If* the arresting officer hadn't violated the poor man's rights, and *if* the bastard hadn't skipped the country by that time." He pushed a hand through his thick hair, then shook his head. "Those laws you're so crazy about protect the criminals damn well."

She could feel the turbulent undercurrent of emotion buffeting him, and she backed up until her spine touched the rough wall behind her. Rosalie was wrong. He wasn't cold inside. He was filled with white-hot rage.

"You hate this, don't you?" he said in a flat voice. "Having to come here and beg for my help."

"I'm not begging," she said in a heated voice. "But...but she's all I have. I love her so much." She hugged her arms to her chest and tried not to shiver. She was nearly exhausted after a sleepless night and her long, hot drive, and she felt slightly sick. But she'd do anything, say anything, even promise anything to save Jessie.

In silence he watched, measuring her, judging her. An emotion she couldn't decipher flashed in the black pupils for an instant before his lashes swept it away. His shoulders bunched angrily, then straightened as a cynical smile slowly took over his hard features.

"But you would beg, wouldn't you, Judge Wainwright? If I asked you to?" His voice held a steel purr of triumph.

Amanda forced herself to remain motionless. She'd never struck another person in her life, but now, suddenly, she had a furious need to lash out, to vent her anger in physical violence. *No!* she thought fervently. Violence is never justified. Never.

"Yes, Mr. Buchanan," she said with as much dignity as she could muster. "I'd beg for my daughter—on my knees, if that's what you want." She held her head high, her features stiff, her hands twisted together in front of her.

Buchanan bit off a harsh expletive and pushed himself to his feet. "Forget I said that. I was...out of line." Amanda noticed a slight thawing in his cold expression, as though her words had struck a deeply buried vein of feeling.

He took a step toward her, then stopped abruptly as though the movement had been involuntary. "Look, even if I wanted to, there's really nothing I can do to help you. I just don't have the heart for it anymore."

He crossed the room and opened the door. "If you start now, you can make it back to Albuquerque before dark." His expression was implacable, his shoulders set. He'd made up his mind, and nothing Amanda could say was going to change it.

She picked up her canvas tote with shaking fingers and started toward the door, feeling more and more empty with each step she took.

"If you change your mind—" she began softly, only to be interrupted by a curt shake of his head.

"I won't."

Amanda nodded unhappily. She started to walk past him, then stopped as she caught sight of a late model black Blazer parked diagonally in front of his Jeep. As she watched, the driver's door opened and a man emerged, his body partially hidden by the door. "For a recluse, you certainly have a lot of company," she said caustically. "I'm sorry I disturbed your solitude."

"Damn it to hell!"

Buchanan shoved her aside and slammed the door, bolting it with one hand while reaching for his gun with the other.

"Get down," he shouted in English and then in Spanish. He pulled Pepe from his seat and shoved him behind the couch.

Amanda had a glimpse of Buchanan's hard features contorted in furious concentration as he upset the heavy pine table and crouched behind it. Pepe's carving crashed to the floor and slid across the tile to land near the door.

She started to protest the rough treatment when the room erupted in sound. Bullets crashed through the door, splintering the wood like soft cheese, and ricocheting off the fireplace and the walls. Sparks flew from the stone, and the metal casings pinged on the tile as Amanda stared in horror at Buchanan, her heart racing so ferociously she was forced to gasp for air.

She was terrified, so terrified she was numb as she folded her torso around Pepe's trembling body. The noise was deafening, violent explosions of hissing hot metal pounding painfully against her eardrums.

There was a sudden lull, a silence so complete it was palpable, and tension snaked down Buchanan's body in a visible line. Amanda watched in horrible fascination as he wrapped both large hands around the butt of the automatic and rested the barrel on the edge of the upturned table, taking aim. In profile he looked even more dangerous, the angular planes of his face frozen, his eyes unmoving.

A heavy constriction in her chest reminded her that she was holding her breath, and she exhaled slowly, her body tensing in anticipation. But of what? She was afraid even to guess.

Suddenly the door exploded inward, the bullet-riddled panels giving way easily to a booted foot. Two men rushed in, spraying the room with bullets from their hideously effective weapons.

As Amanda watched in horror, Buchanan raised his head and emptied his gun, shooting rapidly but without haste. There was a sharp cry of pain, followed by a clatter of metal on tile and a vicious curse spoken in unaccented English. Footsteps clattered on the porch outside, then the sound of a car door slamming echoed across the courtyard.

The next thing she knew, Buchanan had leaped to his feet and disappeared. In the startling stillness, Amanda risked a quick look around the edge of the couch.

He was bending over a muscular black-haired man in combat fatigues who appeared to be unconscious and who was bleeding profusely from a wound in his shoulder. Buchanan was gripping the man's weapon, a stubby black machine pistol that was still smoking.

Amanda tried to speak, but her voice came out in a useless squeak. She cleared her throat and tried again. "Is he dead?"

He gave her a quick glance. "No, not yet. His buddy'll be back for him soon. We'd better get the hell out of here."

A faint movement beneath her breast reminded her that she was crushing Pepe beneath her weight, and she leaned back, only to gasp in horror as she spied dark red blood pooling on the floor next to them.

"Buchanan," she cried in an urgent whisper. "Pepe's been shot." Her voice had a hollow quality, as though it came from a very great distance, and her head was becoming heavy, too heavy for her neck to support. Her eyes began to blink rapidly as her vision blurred.

"Don't you dare faint," Buchanan hissed next to her ear, shaking her sharply with one hand. "I need you."

Slowly his words penetrated, and she managed to fight down the cloying grayness that was tugging at her so seductively.

"I'm okay," she said in a strangled voice, and he gave her a curt nod. Together they searched Pepe's body for wounds. The boy was unconscious, his long lashes lying still on his bloodless cheeks, and he was breathing deeply through his mouth.

"One wound, right through the fleshy part of his thigh," Buchanan muttered as though to himself. "Looks clean, but he might be in shock. We have to get help."

He glanced around the ruined room, his brows knit ferociously. "We'll have to risk it," he said suddenly, lifting the boy into his arms with so little effort that Amanda was startled.

She scrambled to her feet, her eyes darting from Buchanan's face to the gaping door. The Blazer was still there, but there was no sight of the other man who'd attacked them.

Buchanan hoisted Pepe to his shoulder, holding the boy steady with his right hand while he levered the gun toward the door with his left. Blood from the child's wound dripped down his shirt, spreading into a ragged maroon stain above his belt.

"Let's go. This way." He began pushing Amanda toward the door leading to the hallway at the far end of the room.

"Wait," she cried, trying to hold on to Pepe's thin leg to keep it from being jarred. "Let me wrap something around the wound."

"No time. That bastard will be back any minute now."

Amanda glanced over her shoulder as Buchanan pushed her through the thick doorway. "Last door to the left," he ordered, walking backward to keep watch.

The door opened in, and Amanda nearly stumbled as she looked down into nothing. Beyond the threshold was a dark cellar, rank with the smell of stale air. There was a stairway hacked into the dirt, the risers made of rough unpainted pine.

"You go first," he ordered impatiently, his eyes alive with worry. "Use the flashlight. In that niche to the left."

Buchanan shifted Pepe to a more comfortable position on his broad shoulder and cocked his head as though listening.

Amanda's gaze, fixed on the dark hole beyond the light, shifted to the left. A large lantern, one of those with a square housing and a large lens, sat in a jagged hole in the clay. Her hands shook as she fumbled for the switch.

"Hurry. Here he comes."

The sound of bullets slamming into the room they'd just left jarred her, and she smothered a cry as she hurried with frantic steps down the crude ladder.

Buchanan followed, closing the door behind him. The sound of shooting was muffled but still audible, and Amanda shivered.

"Wait," he ordered. "Shine the light up here."

Amanda complied, holding the lantern with both hands to keep it steady. The bright beam bounced off Pepe's limp body and zeroed in on Buchanan's face. In the eerie light the sharp planes of his cheeks stood out in bold relief. His eyes were shadowed, the irises silvery in the glare as he slammed a heavy iron bar into makeshift braces built into the door frame.

Amanda shone the light on the stairs as he descended, her body shaking with reaction. "Where are we?" she whispered as he pointed with the gun toward a narrow tunnel in the brown clay.

"Under the courtyard. This leads to the church. I had it dug right after I moved in here—just in case." The passageway was too low to accommodate his height, and he had to stoop to keep from banging his head against the uneven roof.

"What do you mean, just in case? Are you saying you *expected* this...this invasion?"

"Look, no more questions, okay? We're not out of this mess safely yet."

His terse growl was meant to discourage further conversation, and Amanda forced herself to be silent. Besides, she needed all of her concentration to keep from stumbling on the rough ground.

The air in the tunnel was chilled and musty, the darkness ahead complete. The light wavered in front of her, a lonely beacon in the suffocating tube, and she fought down a rising panic. She'd never really liked narrow spaces like this.

As though sensing her fear, Buchanan leaned forward to say in a surprisingly sympathetic tone, "It's not much farther. Only twenty yards or so."

Amanda twisted her head to thank him, only to have her cheek brush his. He smelled of spicy after-shave, and his skin felt faintly raspy against hers. A shiver of pleasure shot through her at the accidental contact, and she jerked back in surprise, causing her foot to slip on the loose dirt.

Buchanan's hand shot forward to grasp the curve of her hip, steadying her. A tremor of instant reaction jolted her, and she swallowed hard. His hand lingered, pressing into her side, and she could feel the strength in those long fingers.

"Watch out for loose rocks," she said faintly, intensely aware of his hand guiding her reassuringly.

Suddenly they were face-to-face with another door. As Amanda held the light, Buchanan reached over her shoulder and tugged on a leather thong dangling from a hole bored into the raw oak.

The door swung inward, creaking loudly on unoiled hinges. The opening was barely four feet tall and only wide enough for them to squeeze through sideways. Beyond the portal stretched a narrow room with a low ceiling, lined with empty shelves that had once contained wine bottles.

Buchanan took the lead, walking swiftly to a shadowed staircase at the far end of the cellar. Pepe moaned, and he slowed down. "It's okay, Tiger," he said in Spanish, rubbing the boy's back with his big hand. His eyes were dark with worry as they met Amanda's.

"Is there a doctor in the village?" she said, gripping the lantern tightly.

"No, just Padre Garza. He's trained as a medic."

His face tightened as he climbed the stairs, his bare feet silent on the steps. Amanda followed, trying to ignore a feeling of rising nausea churning in her stomach. Pepe looked so small and helpless slung over Buchanan's big shoulder.

At the top, the stairwell opened into a small office, sparsely furnished, its heavy shutters closed against the heat.

As Amanda followed Buchanan into the room, the outer door burst open and a tall, thin, middle-aged man hurried in. He wore a clerical collar over a black short-sleeved shirt and dark trousers, and his narrow pockmarked face was lined with worry.

"I heard the shots, and I saw a man running from your house," he said to Buchanan in a hurried voice that vibrated with anxiety. It took Amanda a second to realize that he was speaking perfect English.

"I called the *policia*, but Capitan Hernandez is in Rosita for the day, and his deputy is in the hospital in Juarez with a broken leg." The priest's black eyes darted to Amanda, lingered for a curious second, then fixed with open concern on Pepe's limp body.

"Pepe took a slug in the thigh," Buchanan told him quickly, shoving the gun he carried into Amanda's hands. With infinite gentleness, he lifted the boy from his shoulder and cradled him in brawny arms. "I think he's in shock."

"Take him into the sanctuary while I get my bag. The light's better there."

The two men hurried out of the room, leaving Amanda standing, awkwardly juggling the lantern and the gun. Hastily she followed and found herself in the main part of the church.

Long and narrow with a high, vaulted ceiling, the sanctuary was quiet and cool, its thick walls screening the heat as well as the noise from the street.

Two gray-haired, matronly women were huddled over the child's still body, which Buchanan had laid on one of the pews. The older of the two crooned softly to the boy as she tucked her *rebozo* around Pepe's frail chest, while the other clutched wooden rosary beads and looked on anxiously.

Buchanan was standing by the front door, which he'd opened a crack. "The Blazer's gone," he said over his shoulder, and Amanda heaved a deep sigh of relief.

"Thank God," she muttered, her voice shaking like an aspen leaf in a high wind. She was feeling very strange all of a sudden, as though she'd stepped through a portal into another dimension.

This was not her life she was living; how could it be? The only time she'd ever held a gun before was in court, and even then she'd hated the feel of the weapon in her hand.

She set the lantern on the nearest pew and stared down at the snub-nosed automatic. It was very heavy, and its steel casing felt surprisingly warm against her palms.

A tremor of reaction shook her, and she took a deep breath. The child could have died. She could have died. All of them could be lying on Buchanan's floor at this moment, riddled with bullets. Her breath shuddered through her parted lips as she struggled to blink away the horrible images streaking across the screen of her imagination.

Buchanan's steady nerves and skill with a gun had saved them, she had no doubt about that. But who were those men? And why had they invaded his house like storm troopers?

Maybe Cy was wrong. Maybe Buchanan *was* involved in some kind of illegal activity, and this was part of it. She shivered and put the gun down next to the lantern. She never wanted to see it again.

Closing the big door, Buchanan walked rapidly up the wide center aisle. Standing next to the pew where Pepe lay, he looked like a volcano ready to erupt, with his clenched fists planted on his hips, and his legs planted wide apart on the tiles. A thin film of sweat dotted his brow as he hovered over Pepe like an anxious father, his eyes fixed on the boy's inert form.

The priest was swift and sure, his hands gentle as he dressed the boy's wound. The bullet had entered cleanly and exited the same way, leaving a tiny purpling hole in the tanned flesh. Amanda was relieved to see that the bleeding had slowed to a thin dark trickle.

As the priest worked, Pepe's eyes opened and he groaned. The *padre* murmured reassurance to the boy in a soft voice, and the panic left Pepito's eyes.

"Señor Dev?" he asked in reedy voice. "Did those bad men hurt him?"

"No, Pepito," the priest answered with a smile in his voice. "Your friend is safe. Both your friends." Garza's eyes met Amanda's, warmly friendly, but with a hint of curiosity in their black depths.

Almost against her will, she went to stand next to Buchanan. "Diablo is waiting for you, Pepe," she said softly. "He needs you to take care of him."

"Diablo wants his ice cream, like Señor Dev promised us," the boy said with an eager smile. "Chocolate. *Por favor.*" His brown eyes sparkled with childish greed, and Buchanan laughed.

His eyes crinkled at the corners, and a deep crease slid into his right cheek as his laughter faded to an affectionate smile. But Amanda saw the clenching of his jaw and the dusky wash of color darkening his skin as he reached over to touch the boy's damp forehead with gentle fingers.

"I promise, *muchacho*," he said in a thick voice. "As soon as Padre Garza says it's okay."

Pepe's gaze shifted to the priest. "Now, *padre*," he wheedled in a surprisingly strong voice.

Father Garza shook his head. "Tomorrow. Right now you need some nice hot soup and then sleep." He gave rapid orders for the two women to watch the boy while he talked with Buchanan.

The two men walked a few paces down the aisle, and Amanda followed. "He'll be fine," Garza said in English. "He just fainted; there's no sign of shock."

Buchanan's chest lifted in a deep sigh. "Thank God," he said in a low tone, and the priest nodded.

Listening in silence, Amanda began to feel very unsteady, and she started to weave. Her resilience was rapidly reaching its limit. More than anything she wanted to stretch out for a few minutes of peace and quiet before she began the long drive home. Just...a...few...minutes. Her lashes fluttered, and the voices wavered in and out of her hearing.

"Who's the woman?" The priest's voice was nearly inaudible.

Buchanan scowled and tossed a quick look over his shoulder. "A lady judge from Albuquerque, and right now it looks like she's about to pass out on us," he muttered, taking a step backward.

Amanda stared at him uncomprehendingly as he slipped an arm around her waist. "Sit down a minute and catch your breath. You're as white as the walls." He helped her into the nearest pew.

Devlin was afraid to let go of her hand. She looked so forlorn and fragile with Pepe's blood spattered over her white shirt and staining her slim palms.

He could feel her pulse racing beneath the bones of her small wrist, a steady urgent beat that was surprisingly strong. Her eyes carried a wounded horror that tore at the boarded-up place inside him where he'd dumped his pain over the years. No more, he thought in silent rage. No more pain.

He dropped her hand and stepped back, wiping the beads of sweat from his forehead with the back of his wrist. She wasn't going to get to him. He wouldn't let her. He was retired—for good.

Amanda let her spine sink against the hard back of the pew and tried to breathe strength into her shaky legs. She hated to feel so damned helpless like this.

The priest bent toward her in concern. "I have some brandy, *señora*. Perhaps a small glass?"

"No...no thank you. I'll be fine." She offered her hand. "I'm Amanda Wainwright," she said with a numb smile. "I'm happy to meet you, Father, although I wish it could have been under less stressful circumstances."

"And I, *señora*. This is not a pleasant way to experience the hospitality of La Placita."

She shook her head. "It certainly wasn't what I expected, I admit." She slumped against the curved backrest and tried not to think of the last ten minutes.

The priest looked at her anxiously, then shifted his gaze to Buchanan. "Those men were not *bandidos*," he said, his voice lowered.

"No."

"Did you recognize them?"

"One of them I did."

"From the States?"

"Yes." Buchanan glanced at Amanda, his expression dark with speculation. "I think they were following her."

"They were not!" Amanda protested loudly, then sat up, her heart pounding in furious chorus against her ribs. "This time I was checking my rearview mirror the whole time. There was no one behind me

from the time I left the main road. I would have seen them if they'd been there.''

"Not these guys, Your Honor. They're pros." Buchanan's hand gripped the top of the nearest pew and the knuckles whitened.

"Remember the guy I shot, blond hair, scar on his right cheek? Name's Steck. He's a professional killer, a high-priced hit man." He hesitated, then said tersely, "He works for Santalucci."

Chapter 3

"Why would they want to kill me? That doesn't make any sense. I can't do anything for Santalucci if I'm dead."

Devlin could see the shock in her eyes and on her face. He relaxed slightly, one important question answered. She had no idea that she'd been leading Santalucci's paid killers directly to his door.

"They weren't after you. They were after me."

Amanda didn't hear him. She was caught by a wave of rising panic. She'd made a mistake, a terrible, deadly mistake. In her blind determination to get Jessie back, she'd practically dared Santalucci to carry out his threats.

"There's only one explanation," she whispered harshly, her hand cupping her throat. "He knows I came here for help and that's why he tried to kill me. And now he'll kill Jessie because of it." Her voice grew shrill, her rapid words twisting together until they were nearly unintelligible. "My baby's dead, and it's all my fault."

Her body began to tremble, tiny shivers at first and then, as she stood hugging her arms to her chest, violent shudders began to shake her.

Devlin gripped her arms tightly and shook her. "She's not dead," he said forcefully. "Do you hear me, Judge Wainwright? Your little girl isn't dead. That would be a stupid move at this stage of the game, and Santalucci isn't stupid."

She stared at him, her eyes unfocused, her breathing becoming more and more irregular. It was a classic case of delayed reaction. He'd seen it dozens of times.

"I don't...know...what's wrong with me," she whispered, her teeth beginning to chatter. Tears welled in her eyes, spilling over to collect on her long lashes.

"Damn," he muttered under his breath as he roughly hauled her to her feet and into his arms. She stiffened, pushing against him.

"I have to find her, Buchanan. She's all alone, someplace...in the hands of those...those killers." Her lips trembled and she began to sob, quietly, without hysteria, a kind of desperate weeping that Devlin knew was coming from the depths of her soul.

He could feel her slight body shudder as she clung to him, her cheek pressed tightly against his chest. Hot tears dampened his shirt and seeped through to wet his skin.

Like a mother lioness fighting for her cub, he thought, she was willing to take on any adversary, to fight to the death to protect her child.

A killing rage shot through him. Santalucci deserved to suffer the fires of hell for putting her through this kind of torture. He deserved to die for all the pain he'd inflicted on other innocent victims.

"Your little girl is okay," Devlin murmured, awkwardly rubbing her back. "She's okay."

He closed his eyes and took a deep breath. He'd never been good with words. His tongue always seemed to put a hard edge on everything he said, no matter how diplomatic he tried to be. But even if he'd been a master of tact, there was nothing more he could say, nothing he could do to take away the horror that was filling her mind. All he could offer was his human warmth, his body, as unspoken support.

He stood quietly, letting her rest against him. She was so tiny, her head barely coming to his chin, and her body was surprisingly voluptuous without the camouflage of the voluminous black robe she'd worn in the courtroom. She felt like a delicate butterfly in his arms, so dainty and light, and she smelled of flowers, the kind that filled the air in the spring.

It had been months since he'd been with a woman. Over a year, in fact, and he hadn't really missed the actual sex. It was the warmth of a woman's body next to his that he wanted. And the smell and the taste and the soft laughter. All the sweet things that a man needed in a woman.

His body began to quicken in sharp male desire, and he jerked away from her. What was the matter with him? He'd damn well better remember who this woman was and why she'd come to him.

It was his gun and his willingness to fight dirty that she wanted, and that was *all*. That was all anyone had ever wanted. But maybe, this time, with the tacit sanction of a district court judge, he could take Santalucci down and not have to worry about another trumped-up indictment. It was something to think about, anyway.

Amanda blinked up at him, her tear-filled eyes dark with confusion. He shoved his hands in his pockets and jerked his head toward the door. "Let's get out of here. I think we could both use a good stiff drink."

"Yes, a drink," she repeated in a hollow voice. She wiped the tears from her cheeks and took a deep breath as though armoring herself against the world. Or maybe she was shielding herself only against him.

Doesn't matter much, either way, he told himself as he walked over to say goodbye to Pepe and the *padre*. The only thing he and the Honorable Judge Wainwright would ever share was their hatred of George Santalucci.

The house was a mess. The front door hung from one hinge with most of its panels shredded and lying in a heap of jagged splinters.

A pool of blood had congealed on the tile just inside the door, marking the spot where the man Buchanan had called Steck had fallen.

Amanda inhaled sharply, her mind racing through a brutal replay of the gun battle that had almost killed her. She could still see the blood and hear the bullets.

"What do you think his friend did with him?" Her voice sounded tinny and tentative, and she cleared her throat.

At her side Buchanan shrugged. "Probably took him to Juarez, or maybe El Paso. Scum like that always have a place to hide."

She nodded. She didn't really care *where* those horrible men had gone, just as long as she never saw them again.

Inside, the house had become appreciably hotter, the result, Amanda thought, of having the front door wide open during the warmest part of the afternoon.

Buchanan headed for the kitchen. "I'm having tequila, but there's wine if you'd prefer." He paused at the doorway, waiting for her decision.

"Uh, wine would be nice, thank you." His brow quirked sardonically at the polite words, but he only nodded curtly before disappearing from her sight.

Anything to dull the pain, she thought wearily, sitting down on the couch where she'd awakened earlier. Only two hours ago, she thought in exhausted amazement as she glanced at her watch. She'd been caught in a dream then, not realizing what kind of nightmare actually awaited her.

She felt a strange lassitude come over her. For some reason she was finding it hard to concentrate. She had to make plans, to figure out what she was going to do next, now that Buchanan had turned her down, but her usually logical brain patterns were unaccountably scattered.

"It's a local vintage, but I think you'll like it." Buchanan set a glass of white wine along with the bottle on the table in front of her and sat down in the chair opposite. He'd stripped off his bloodstained shirt and replaced it with a faded black tank top that partially revealed a broad, muscular chest as darkly tanned as the rest of him.

Amanda's breath quickened involuntarily. The man had the kind of body women loved to touch, with wide shoulders that sloped away from a strong neck at just the right angle, sharply defined pectoral muscles covered in soft-looking, sun-bleached hair, and a hard torso that showed not a wrinkle of fat. She deliberately dropped her gaze. Buchanan's manly assets were no concern of hers.

Without looking at her, he picked up an open bottle of tequila and a glass that had been tucked under the coffee table, pouring himself a generous measure.

"*Salud,*" he said brusquely as he lifted the glass and drank. The fiery liquor disappeared in three swallows, and he poured the same amount again. This time he seemed content to sip more slowly.

Amanda tasted the wine. It was very dry and cool on her tongue. The taste made her think of ripe peaches.

The alcohol hit her system with a rush, reminding her that she hadn't eaten since five that morning, and she inhaled deeply in an attempt to clear her head.

"Looks like you'll have quite a story to tell back home, Your Honor," he said in a flattened voice that reminded her of a famous attorney she'd once known. It was the tone the wily old lawyer had used just before he went for the jugular.

"No story, Mr. Buchanan. I just want to forget it ever happened."

One thick brow lifted sardonically. "Some things you can never forget, Judge. I know. I've tried."

The cynical gleam was back in his eye, and his body radiated tension.

"Or maybe you just tried to run away from your memories."

Amanda held her breath. She expected him to explode, but he merely shrugged. "Maybe. Either way I doubt you'll lose sleep over it."

Amanda ignored the sarcasm. "Why did you let everyone think you were dead?"

"Seemed like a good idea at the time."

"You don't talk much, do you?"

"You and I don't have a whole lot to talk about."

"We have Santalucci."

He lifted his glass and drank, then licked the moisture from his lips with his tongue. "You don't give up, do you?"

She searched his face for a sign that he'd changed his mind, but the man was a rock. "I can't give up. You're the only one who can help me."

"Or maybe the only one who's expendable."

Amanda's jaw dropped. "No one's expendable."

"Don't kid yourself, Judge. We're all expendable, one way or another." He put one foot on the floor, the other against the heavy coffee table and tilted his chair backward onto two legs. The muscles of his thigh worked rhythmically as he rocked the chair gently back and forth.

Amanda averted her eyes from his bare legs. "Cy said you were bitter. I guess he was right."

"Cy still believes in the system. I don't."

"What do you believe in?"

He let the chair drop onto four legs and reached behind him with his left hand. The Beretta balanced easily on his palm, gleaming with the dull patina of oiled metal. He ran his thumb along the black grip. "Think about it, Your Honor. A few ounces of pressure, a good aim, and there's one less creep to worry about. Saves the taxpayers a lot of money, too." One tawny brow raised in a mocking salute. "That's what *I* believe in."

"Yes, I know. Too bad your gun can't tell the guilty from the innocent."

"After twelve years on the streets, I can."

"You're talking about vigilante justice, Buchanan," she countered impatiently. "We outgrew that a long time ago."

"Did we? How come crime statistics are sky-high, the jails are overcrowded and judges like you are freeing convicted criminals because their damned constitutional rights are being violated?''

''We're a country of laws. That's the only thing that gives us the necessary order to live the way we do.''

''Oh, yeah? Tell that to the poor suckers on the street who've sold their souls for a little of the so-called good life your precious laws guarantee.''

He put the gun on the table and picked up the wine bottle. ''More?'' he asked coldly. His hand was steady as he refilled her glass.

Amanda stared at the Beretta. How many times had it killed? She shuddered. Today it had saved her life. She had to concentrate on that.

A fleeting memory of Buchanan's warm hand stroking her cut through her troubled thoughts. His steady touch had brought her back from the edge of panic.

She hadn't come to debate ethics with Buchanan, and right now she didn't want to think about his methods. With Jessie's life in danger, she didn't have that luxury.

''What do you think the Saint'll do now?'' she asked as he slumped down in his seat, his legs fully extended in front of him. The sun had bleached the hair on his legs to platinum.

He shrugged. ''I'm not sure. Tell me again what that note said.''

Amanda recited the terrible words from memory, her voice faltering at times.

When she finished, he gave her a measured look. ''Are you going to do what he wants you to? Slant your rulings and your final charge to the jury toward acquittal?''

''Of course not,'' she exclaimed. ''That would be unconscionable.''

''I admire your guts, but I'm not sure you should make a snap decision like that. Santalucci is capable of carrying out his threats.''

''I...I know. Two dead reporters prove that.'' According to the DA, both men had received notes warning them to back off or face the consequences.

He refilled the tumbler with tequila and raised it to Amanda in a salute before drinking deeply.

The silence lengthened until Amanda wanted to scream. ''Talk to me, Buchanan. Tell me what you think he'll do now,'' she ordered when she couldn't stand the quiet another second.

He lifted one foot to the edge of his chair and rested his elbow on his raised knee. ''I don't think he'll do anything to your daughter until the trial starts. Right now, she's his ace. He's not going to waste it before the game starts.''

His hawklike eyes studied her in silence. There was a lot he wasn't telling her, she could feel it.

''But he...he could hurt her. To show me he's not bluffing. He could do that, couldn't he?''

Terrible pictures clicked through her mind, images that she couldn't bear to face. She leaned forward, silently beseeching him to say the words of denial that she so desperately needed to hear.

Dusky color rose like a tidal wave, darkening his skin from his corded neck to his ragged hairline, but his expression remained unreadable.

''He could do that, yes,'' he said with steely quiet. ''But right now we've got time on our side. I figure it'll take me a few weeks to find out where they're holding her. That's the easy part. Getting her out safely is going to be a lot trickier, but we'll find a way.''

A shaft of late afternoon sun shone through the jagged hole in the door, slicing the distance between them like a glinting blade, and she stared unseeingly at the dust motes jerking crazily in the light.

''We?'' She could feel the hope blooming in her heart.

Buchanan dropped his foot to the floor and sat forward, tension radiating from the stiff line of his back. ''I thought I could just walk away from the stench, from the rotting mess that surrounds the man. Play dead and forget that the bastard who really killed Tony is still walking around free. But I was wrong. It's not over for me, not when Santalucci's goons come into my home and shoot a little boy whose only crime is being my friend.''

He stood up suddenly and with one powerful movement of his long arm, threw his glass into the fireplace where it shattered into jagged splinters. ''This time I'm going to bring him down,'' he vowed in a chilling whisper, ''and nothing or no one is going to stop me.''

Padre Garza arrived while Buchanan was emptying the contents of his desk drawers into his briefcase, and Amanda was cleaning up the kitchen after their hasty supper of beans and rice.

Devlin met the priest at the door. ''How's Pepe?'' he asked at once.

''Still asking for his ice cream.'' Garza chuckled, then added soberly, ''A few days in bed, and he'll be good as new.''

''Kid's stronger than he looks,'' Devlin muttered, relief cascading through him in a hot rush. He hated the feeling of impotence it gave him when he had to stand by helplessly and watch an innocent victim suffer. If he could have taken the bullet himself, he would have done so willingly, but nothing was ever that easy.

Garza walked slowly to the middle of the room and turned a complete circle, his brows drawn in disbelief. "Have the authorities been here yet?" he asked after his anxious eyes had swept every corner.

"Not yet," Buchanan said tersely. "I don't want to leave before dark, but I don't want to be hassled by the local law, either."

The priest gave him a questioning look, and Buchanan inclined his head toward the pistol lying on the coffee table. "I don't have a Mexican permit."

Garza smiled. "I'll vouch for you, Dev. They won't give you any trouble."

An answering smile briefly touched Buchanan's lips. "I have a feeling I'm not going to be very welcome around here after the word gets out." His gaze drifted through the open door to the kitchen where Amanda was drying dishes in front of the sink.

"How's she holding up?" the *padre* asked softly, watching his friend closely.

"Okay. A hot bath before supper helped, I guess. Anyway, she's not so pale and her eyes have more life in them."

"I have to tell you, Dev. She looks better in those old khaki shorts of yours than you ever did." The priest's black eyes twinkled.

Devlin felt heat brush his cheeks. "I guess," he muttered, sneaking another look toward the kitchen. Amanda was standing on tiptoe, her arms stretched up to return the plates to the overhead cabinet. The pale blue T-shirt he'd given her outlined the curve of her tiny waist and the pert swell of her breasts.

Devlin absorbed the sight without a word, and the priest chuckled. "Easy, boy. You've been living like a monk for too many months to be objective."

Buchanan's head swiveled around. Garza was regarding him with amused sympathy. "You want to tell me about it?" the *padre* asked quietly.

Devlin shoved his hands into the back pockets of his cutoffs. "Her daughter's been kidnapped. She came to ask for my help."

"You're going back with her? To New Mexico?"

"Yeah, I'm going back."

Garza's expression became serious. "You were in bad shape when you first came here, Dev. For a while I thought you were going to drink yourself to death."

Devlin flinched. "I gave it my best shot," he muttered with a wry grin. "Only you wouldn't leave me alone." The priest knew most of his history, at least the parts he could tell without risking the lives of others still in the field.

"I needed someone to beat at chess, that's all." Garza watched the troubled look return to his friend's eyes. "Don't do it, Dev. This time you might not be able to pull yourself out of that black pit that nearly killed you."

Devlin filled his chest with air, exhaling slowly. "I don't have a choice, Matt. I couldn't live with myself if the child died, and I could have prevented it."

"And if she dies anyway?"

Devlin's hand balled into fists. "I don't know. I guess I'll handle it, somehow."

Garza opened his mouth, then shut it again. Devlin already had too many ghosts haunting him. Another one might send him over the edge. But the former agent wasn't a man who listened to the advice of others. Not willingly, anyway.

"You think your...visitors will come back?" the priest asked quietly, deliberately changing the subject.

Devlin flexed his shoulders. He was feeling the old tension returning, pulling his muscles into tight bands of pain along his spine. "Eventually. That kind never gives up."

The priest looked uneasy. "Does she know why—"

"No," Buchanan interrupted swiftly, forgetting to keep his voice low. From the corner of his eye he could see Amanda's dark head jerk up in alarm, and he cursed silently as he led Garza out of her line of sight.

"There's no need for her to know," he said curtly. "She has enough to worry about."

The priest nodded. "I understand." He cleared his throat. "If anyone comes asking, I'll say that you've gone to Mexico City until your house is repaired."

"Thanks, but be careful. Those men are dangerous."

Only a slight dipping of Garza's head acknowledged the warning. "Can you stop by the orphanage and say goodbye to Pepito and the others before you go?" he asked.

Devlin shook his head. "There's no time."

Garza started to say something, thought better of it and simply nodded. His black eyes were troubled, and Devlin felt a pang of guilt. Mateo Garza had been a good friend, and he'd had few of those in his life.

"It'll be okay, Matt. Don't worry about me."

Devlin stuck out his hand and the priest took it. Their eyes met, Devlin's clear, Garza's filled with concern.

"God bless you, Dev."

Devlin hesitated. "And you, Matt," he said quietly.

The priest excused himself to say a few words to Amanda. Devlin carried his briefcase to his bedroom, extracted his ID card from the top of the pine highboy and tossed it into the case. As a retired agent he was authorized to carry a gun for his own protection. All nice and legal. The judge would appreciate the irony.

In silence he packed steadily until the drawers in his bureau were empty and his bags were nearly full.

"Need any help?"

Amanda was standing in the doorway, a dish towel in her hand, her face slightly flushed from the steamy heat in the kitchen.

"I'm nearly finished. Just a few more odds and ends to pack." It'd been a long time since a woman had cooked for him. Or smiled at him. Or even argued with him. He stifled a pang of loneliness. He'd chosen his life, and he was happy with it.

"You're very efficient," she said wearily, casting curious eyes around the narrow cubicle that contained a single bed, a dresser and a chair. There were no mementos, no pictures of loved ones, not even a painting on the rough white walls. Like a cell, she thought in sudden insight. A lonely, solitary cell.

Was Buchanan doing some kind of penance down here in this desolate place? She studied the muscular line of his back. Maybe those strong shoulders were carrying a heavier load than she knew.

He turned suddenly and caught her staring. A scowl tugged at his heavy brows.

"Father Garza said to tell you he would pray for us," she said quickly, feeling the chill of those gray eyes against her skin.

"Good. We can use all the help we can get."

He watched her eyes narrow at his abrupt tone. She wiped her forehead with the towel, her lips curving into a disapproving frown. Above the bow of her mouth a dewy line of perspiration caught the light from the setting sun, accenting the sensuous curve of her lips.

His breath quickened and he averted his gaze. Damn, he was hungry, he thought irreverently. Her skin would taste salty, like the intoxicating tang of a margarita, he decided, his tongue sliding along his teeth.

Damn, he thought again. He'd been in this godforsaken place too long.

He slammed the drawer shut and looked around him, forcing himself to concentrate on the list in his head of the things he would need. All that was left to pack was the gear stored in the battered wooden trunk at the foot of his bed.

Amanda draped the towel over the pine headboard and sat down on the edge of the mattress.

"I saw Father Garza's face when you two were talking. He looked extremely upset. I thought at first it was because of Pepe, but the *padre* said he's going to be just fine." There was an edge to her voice that he hadn't heard before.

"He was worried about those men coming back."

"I don't think so." She traced the coarse pattern of the homespun spread with an unpolished nail.

"Then your guess is as good as mine." He edged away from her and began pulling things from the trunk at random. The biker's boots and leather jacket, the battered Stetson with the rattlesnake hatband, the tiny Derringer with the ivory handle—everything had a history. Devlin felt a tightening in his belly as he thought about the drug subculture that had nearly finished him.

He could sleep through the night now. Most nights anyway. And the flashbacks of the night Tony died were gone. But the nightmares were there, waiting for him. Always waiting. He wiped the back of his thick wrist across his brow. God, it's hot in here, he thought angrily. It was always hot and dry and damned dusty.

"I'm not stupid, Buchanan. There's something you're not telling me, and I want to know what it is."

He started to close his suitcase, but a small hand clutched his wrist, stopping him. Her nails dug into his skin.

"Answer me! If it's something that might affect my daughter, I have a right to know."

Devlin shook off her fingers. He could break that fragile wrist easily. Too easily.

He shut the suitcase with a loud click and hoisted it effortlessly to the floor beside the narrow bed. "I want to leave around ten. That way we should hit the border while it's still dark." He needed to shower and change before they left.

He started toward the door, only to have her jump up from the bed to block his path. Her small fists rested firmly on the swell of her hips beneath the bunched waistband of his shorts, and her slender legs were planted purposefully. She wasn't going to give up.

"Leave it alone, Judge," he said in a voice that carried a stiletto warning. "It's private."

"No, I won't leave it alone, whatever it is. And I'm not leaving here until you tell me what's going on.'' Her perfect breasts pushed against the thin cotton of the oversized shirt as she took a determined breath.

Stubborn, he thought. Used to getting her way. "Suit yourself. There's food in the fridge.'' He lifted her out of the path and started toward the door.

Sputtering in protest, Amanda grabbed the tail of his tank top and yanked. He stopped short and uttered a frustrated curse under his breath.

"Tell me the truth, Buchanan. What was Father Garza so upset about?"

"None of your damned business.'' He spun around so suddenly she was jerked off balance, and her body crashed into his chest, her nails digging into his shoulder as she fought to stay on her feet.

Her breasts slid over his belly as he kept her from falling, and he gritted his teeth, his hands bracketing her small waist.

"Watch where you're going,'' she mumbled, a blush of confusion tinting her cheeks. A tingling awareness sizzled up her back and surged into her brain. His breathing was as irregular as hers, and his skin radiated a masculine heat that flowed through her pores and into her blood.

She took a deep breath and stepped back. Another second and she would have been in his arms. She knew it, and so did he.

"I need some answers, Buchanan,'' she said softly, trying to ignore the blush she could feel flooding.

Devlin rested his balled fists on his hips, his head cocked in impatience. Okay, he thought, the lady wants an answer. He'd give her one and see how she liked it.

He looked her straight in the eye. "After my acquittal, Santalucci put a price on my head. Two hundred thousand dollars—for the person who kills me.''

He watched her skin turn from a rosy tan to a sickly white, and guilt twisted inside him. He'd succeeded in shaking that amazing control of hers, just what he'd intended to do, he realized, but the victory wasn't nearly as sweet as he'd anticipated. In fact it wasn't sweet at all.

"That's why you attacked me. You thought I'd come to...to kill you." Her voice shook.

He nodded. "I thought you had a shotgun in that damned satchel of yours."

Amanda put a hand to her temple where the pain was starting.

"They weren't after me. They were after you, and I brought them right here. But how...how did they know?"

"That's the question, isn't it? Maybe it was a coincidence. Odds are it was."

She shook her head. "That's illogical. They followed me."

"Or someone else tailed you here who recognized me and called in the goons. That's what I think happened. It was just a bad break for both of us."

Amanda shook her head woodenly. "I can't let you do it. It's not fair to ask you to risk your life for a...a stranger. I'd never forgive myself if something happened to you."

Devlin absorbed her words, feeling as though they were a left hook to the jaw. She meant what she said; he could see the truth of her words mirrored in her tear-swollen eyes.

An unfamiliar emotion twisted inside him, nameless and unwelcome. No one had cared about him in a very long time. He didn't *want* anyone to care. It made him vulnerable, and that was something he couldn't afford.

Devlin turned away. "Don't worry about me, Judge," he said in a cold abrupt voice. "I can take care of myself."

Chapter 4

They left a few minutes before ten. Buchanan drove. He'd showered and shaved and changed into faded jeans and a worn chambray shirt, rolled to the elbows. His feet were encased in dusty boots that showed heavy wear.

He'd been surprised, and a little disconcerted, Amanda had noticed, to discover that she'd arrived in a truck that had once belonged to his partner.

To keep awake, and because he seemed genuinely interested, she launched into a detailed description of her meeting at Rosalie's. "I didn't recognize her at first," she concluded. "She's lost a lot of weight since...since your trial, and she's lightened her hair. She looks really beautiful."

A half smile of memory, faintly visible in the green glow from the dashboard, creased his left cheek. "Rosa always was a pretty little thing. Tony was crazy about her." He slowed for a particularly wicked pothole in the middle of the narrow road, slanting her a side-long look as he braked. "Has she remarried?"

"No, at least I don't think so."

"Did she tell you she blamed me for Tony's death?"

Amanda shot him a startled glance. "No. Does she?"

He shrugged. "Maybe she's gotten over it, but right after it happened, she came to visit me in the hospital. Said it was all my fault.

Seemed to think I had some kind of a death wish and that Tony had paid the price for it instead of me.''

She didn't know what to say so she remained silent. Buchanan didn't seem angry with Rosalie, only sad.

After a quick look in her direction he lapsed into silence, his brows drawn together in a jagged V. Beneath the taut skin of his jaw, his muscles jerked rhythmically as though he were clenching and unclenching his back teeth.

His hands seemed relaxed on the wheel, but the tendons cording his forearm were tight and bulging beneath the tanned skin.

His focus was inward, his concentration complete. Like a skilled attorney preparing to try a critical case in court, she realized suddenly. Or an actor getting ready for a particularly demanding role.

But wasn't that exactly what he was doing? Preparing for a role? But what role? she asked herself urgently. Savior or spoiler? That was the question.

She shifted uneasily on the bench seat. Both windows were open, and the night air whipped through the small cab in a refreshing stream, ruffling her hair and filling her lungs with the pungent scents of sage and sand.

"What's your plan?" she asked when the silence yawned uncomfortably between them. "What will you do first?"

He braked sharply to avoid a jackrabbit loping across the rutted track. "First thing I'll do is move into your spare room. You do have a spare room, don't you?"

She gaped at him. "Wait a minute. You can't move in with me."

"I can't?" His eyes remained on the road, but Amanda had a feeling his peripheral vision was as acute as if he were looking at her directly.

"Of course not. That would be like waving a red flag in Santalucci's face." A vivid image of Buchanan's ravaged living room passed in front of her eyes, and she thought of the quiet, family-oriented neighborhood where she lived. The two seemed as different as fire and ice and about as compatible.

"Are you afraid to have me in your house, Judge?"

"No. I'm afraid of dying." She clutched her seat belt tightly. "And I'm afraid of causing the death of others. Innocent people, who might be in the wrong place at the wrong time."

His jaw tightened, then relaxed. "It happens. It could easily have happened this afternoon." His hand slid off the wheel to rest on top of the gearshift. His wrist was relaxed, his long fingers dangling loose, but there was a tautness about his mouth that belied the casual pose.

"I can't stand violence, Buchanan. It makes me sick inside." She thought about the blood and Pepe's pinched white face, and sudden nausea pushed against her throat. "It all seems so…so futile, all the killing and bloodshed." Her green eyes challenged him across the dim interior. "I suppose you think that's naive of me."

His sigh was weary. "No, I think it's dangerous, Your Honor. Because, like it or not, the bad guys aren't playing by Marquis of Queensberry rules." He slowed down and looked at her, his harsh expression easing slightly. "I won't kid you. Steck or someone like him could come after me again, even in the house of a district judge. But the odds are they won't, not while Santalucci needs you alive."

Amanda swallowed. Her mind was sluggish and her body was exhausted, making it difficult to think. "So he needs me alive, I understand that. But what's to keep him from killing you?"

"You will."

She stared across the darkened cab. "How can I do that?"

"Let me rephrase that. I need to make him believe that keeping you under his control and keeping me alive are linked together somehow." A cynical smile appeared on his face. "How to make him buy that particular myth is the problem. I have a few ideas, but I need to think them through first."

His smile faded as he ran his fingers down his right cheek. "Maybe I should have accepted the new face and identity the government wanted to give me, but I didn't; and it's too late now."

She tried to think about Buchanan with a new face, but she found she rather liked the old one. His harshly chiseled features had character and strength, even if he wasn't particularly handsome. During the trial she'd seen the uncompromising stubbornness in those austere lines but not the compassion he'd displayed for Pepe—and for her. Or maybe she'd seen only what she had wanted to see.

For the first time she doubted her objectivity when it came to Devlin Buchanan. She might have made a very bad mistake. The sudden thought made her uneasy inside. Prejudice was one of the things she hated most—in herself as well as others.

"So what do we do about it?" she asked slowly, seeing his distinctive features in a new light.

"Somehow we have to outthink him. Take the offensive and keep it. Stay one move ahead of him. Be unpredictable." He grunted. "One thing's already in our favor; my coming back is sure to shake him up but good."

He shifted in the seat. "One thing the Saint isn't, and that's impulsive. He won't do anything until he figures out what the hell I'm doing living in your house." He eyed her speculatively.

Amanda took a deep breath and exhaled slowly, trying to banish the nerves clawing at her stomach. "Did that man D'Amato really draw his gun first? I need to know."

"Why?" The word cracked like a whip.

"Because now that I've...I've spent some time with you, you don't seem like the man I thought you were." And because I need to know whether I was right about you, she added silently. Whether I deliberately closed my mind to a defendant in my court because of my personal aversion to violence.

"Who did you think I was?"

"A hard, unfeeling, brutal man who was waging a one-man war against drug pushers without regard to the will of the people who paid his salary."

"And now?" His voice was silky, expressionless.

"Now I'm not so sure. At least about the unfeeling part. Because I saw how much you care about Pepe."

His jaw clenched. "I have feelings, all right. Mostly I can hate."

"Did you kill an unarmed man?"

His cold gaze speared her. "I'll tell you about D'Amato, since you're obviously so concerned. He shot Tony at point-blank range, blew a hole the size of my fist in his chest. And then he turned his gun on me and laughed. He liked it, killing people. No, he *loved* it. It gave him a real high!" His voice shook, and he stopped, composing himself.

"Tony bled to death right in front of me. I tried, but there wasn't a damn thing I could do to stop the bleeding. He was a good, decent man who believed he was making a difference in this rotten world. Gus D'Amato was scum, and he deserved to die." His stoic expression broke for the briefest of moments, and even in the limited light, Amanda could see a terrible pain in his eyes.

"But I gave the cocky bastard a chance to kill me first. That's as fair as you can get in my book."

She shivered in the night air. She had her answer. He'd set out to provoke D'Amato into a violent confrontation, one that would result in the death of one of them. Technically he hadn't broken the law, but in her eyes he was as guilty as if D'Amato had been unarmed. And worse, he didn't regret taking a life, so in every way that mattered, she hadn't been wrong about him.

"I...appreciate your honesty," she said carefully, mindful of his harsh expression. "And I want to be completely honest with you. I want you to find Jessie, but..."

"But what?" He shot her a cold look.

"I can't condone unnecessary violence. I mean, I know you have to defend yourself, but I don't want anyone to...to die." Her fingers clenched tightly in her lap. This whole conversation was taking on an aura of unreality.

His face twisted and his palm hit the steering wheel. "Don't lay your high and mighty ideals on me, Judge. I won't have my hands tied, not by you. Not by anyone." His husky voice whipped toward her with deadly force. "I'll do whatever it takes to get your daughter back, and I'll do it my way. That's my bottom line. Take it or leave it."

Amanda felt trapped in the small cab. Buchanan's hard body was too close, his masculine power too strong. She'd never felt more alone.

Buchanan pulled the truck to the side of the road and shoved the gearshift into neutral. The four-cylinder engine idled rhythmically in the dense desert silence.

His big hands wrapped tightly around the wheel as he twisted on the narrow bench seat to face her.

"I want your word right now, your word of honor that I'm to have a free hand in this." He paused, his mouth compressed. "I need your complete trust; my life might well depend on it." His watchful gaze left her no escape.

But how could she trust a man who'd virtually admitted to killing in cold blood? Wouldn't that be tacitly condoning all that she abhorred? Wouldn't that be making a mockery of all that she'd ever stood for?

She was suddenly overwhelmed with weariness. Nothing seemed to make sense anymore. Twenty-four hours ago her principles and convictions had been firmly entrenched and inviolate.

The rule of law was supreme and powerful and must not be circumvented. Violence was intolerable, even in the name of justice. Hotshot cops who made their own rules were contemptible and should be punished to the full extent of the law.

She'd believed those things without reservation or exception. But that had been when her daughter slept safely in her own bed at night. Now she wasn't sure about anything—except that she had to fight for Jessie. And this man had promised to help her.

"I'm waiting, Judge Wainwright." His voice was cold, his expression colder. "Do you agree to do things my way, or do we go our separate ways once we reach the city?"

"I have no choice but to trust your judgment," she said in a stilted voice.

He studied her in silence for a heartbeat, unmoving, concentrating on her eyes. Then he nodded curtly. "That'll do—for now."

He put the truck in gear and slowly accelerated. He didn't seem angry. Just distant.

Amanda leaned back against the seat and turned her head toward the window. Beyond the confines of the cab, the desert darkness stretched in an endless black curtain, broken only by the piercing beams of the headlights.

The small engine droned monotonously through the stillness, and the tires hummed in a steady rhythm on the hard gravel, lulling her into a half slumber. Her thoughts began to fragment, darting in all directions, until they re-formed around the larger-than-life image of Devlin Buchanan.

He'd been rude and brutal and incredibly kind, all in the space of a few hours. He displayed the incredible bravery of a hero, and the cool callousness of a villain. Two different men in the same strong, masculine body.

And yet she could still see the look of anguish in his eyes when she'd fallen apart in the church. His touch had been comforting without being sexual, and he'd tried to keep her from finding out about the price on his head because he'd sensed how upset she would be if she knew. The tough cop wasn't quite as tough as he pretended to be.

A faint sigh whispered past her parted lips, and her lashes lowered wearily. She was so tired, so very tired. Her last memory as she drifted into an exhausted sleep was of Buchanan's face, the face she'd seen in the dream that hadn't been a dream. The face of the man who'd kissed her.

Something was wrong. The sudden silence was startling. Amanda struggled to escape.

The pit was so deep; the monstrous evil creature sinking poisonous talons into her flesh was so real. Her hand reached toward the light where a strong, sinewy man outlined in brilliant gold was holding a sword aloft, ready to strike. But which of them was his target? The creature or her?

"Amanda, wake up. We're home." The voice above her was a rumbling masculine growl tinged with impatience.

"G'way." She licked her lips and sighed.

Hard fingers shook her shoulder, but she shrugged them off. She didn't want to wake up. There was something terrible waiting for her in that pit, and she didn't want to face it.

"Judge Wainwright, it's almost six. In the morning. We made it."

Her lashes fluttered as she stirred reluctantly, rubbing her cheek against the pillow in protest.

"Mm." But this pillow was too hard, and the coarse cloth covering it hurt her skin.

Amanda's eyes popped open. Oh no! she thought as her mind focused. She was looking directly at the lower half of the steering wheel that framed a man's knee, Buchanan's knee, and the back of her head was nestled firmly against his fly.

Oh God, she protested silently, her cheeks flooding with heat. His body was hard and ready behind the heavy-duty zipper.

"I know you're awake, and if you don't sit up pretty soon, we're both going to regret it." The husky masculine rumble vibrated through his body into her ear.

She sat up with a jerk, her cheeks still aflame. "I...must have fallen asleep."

"Yes, you did—about six hours ago." His voice was extremely dry.

She avoided his eyes as she looked out the window. The sun was just climbing over the Sandia mountains, pushing away the darkness, and the faint breeze coming through the open windows still carried the chill of night.

They were sitting in her driveway in front of the closed garage door, the motor silent. From the front of the truck came the metallic ping of hot metal cooling.

"How did you know where I live?" she asked, sliding quickly along the seat to the passenger's side.

"I looked in your purse," he answered, glancing toward the shelf above the dashboard. Her wallet was there, along with the other contents of her handbag. He must have dumped everything out and sorted through it with one hand while she slept.

"Very ingenious," she muttered, oddly discomfited to imagine his big hands rifling through her personal things.

"I can't believe you actually need all that stuff," he said sardonically. "The thing must weigh fifteen pounds."

Her empty handbag lay on the floor, along with the canvas tote from which he'd removed it, and she picked up the purse, scraping everything back into it without worrying about order or neatness. She'd sort through everything later.

Buchanan opened the door and climbed out. In the morning light he looked as tough as rawhide seasoned by hard wear, but as if he were stronger and much more durable because of the rough handling.

Beneath the lowered brim of his sweat-soaked Stetson, his eyes searched the surrounding area. He did it subtly, without seeming to do so, but Amanda noticed, and her stomach lurched. Had they been followed?

Memories of yesterday shuddered through her, impelling her to move, and she left the cab quickly, nearly stumbling as her foot touched the cement.

"Watch it!" he called sharply from the back of the truck. "Don't sprain your ankle on me now." He sounded tired and short-tempered, and Amanda bit her lip.

"Uh, anything I can do to help?" she asked, determined to ignore the scowl on his face.

"You can open the front door." He slung a worn canvas duffel bag over his shoulder and with the other hand lifted a bulging garment bag over the tailgate.

She hurried ahead, practically running up the brick walk. On the porch she fumbled in her bag for her keys.

The string of dried peppers hanging from the porch light, the roses climbing on the balustrade, the mail sticking out of the box—all the commonplace things she took for granted—seemed so normal, so benign.

She started to look behind her to see if he was following when she felt his bag thump against her leg. She yelped in surprise, only to have that cry swallowed by his mouth as his lips came down hard on hers.

Stunned, she tried to turn her head away, but the pressure of his mouth was relentless. His hand clasped the back of her head, his fingers twining in her hair to hold her captive. His other hand folded like a chain-mail glove over hers, preventing her from pushing him away.

With one smooth movement he pressed her against the carved panel in the middle of the door, and she winced as the center rosette pressed into her buttocks.

"Stop fighting and kiss me back," he hissed against her lips. "Someone's watching. I don't want them to recognize me just yet."

Panic shot through her, followed immediately by relief that he wasn't truly assaulting her. She stopped struggling and let her body relax.

He braced both hands flat against the door, bracketing her head with brawny bronzed forearms that were covered with soft golden hair. His eyes were narrowed to slits, showing silver between dark brown lashes that were straight and thick.

His face seemed to blur as he bent his head and began kissing her again, this time more gently, his wide chest only an inch from her breasts. She felt the heat from his body flow over her, invading her senses and filling her with warmth.

Pretense, this is pretense, she reminded herself as she accepted the intimacy of his lean body against hers. His chest was hard beneath the blue cloth, and her nipples were crushed as he slowly eased against her, caressing her with his lean body like a big cat.

He moved sinuously, his lips never leaving hers. He growled deep in his throat as though he could feel the urgency racing through her.

Fierce, she thought. He's so fierce, and yet she wasn't frightened. She was—exhilarated.

An answering moan escaped her throat, and he jerked against her. His breathing changed, shortened, became more labored. His lips were soft, sliding over hers with a delectable friction that accelerated her own breathing until it matched his urgency.

A gasp of ecstasy shuddered through her, a breathy involuntary whisper of sound that he caught with his tongue.

"Sweet," he whispered, cupping her head between his hands. "I love the way you taste." His voice was ragged and insistent, and his jaw, flushed beneath the wheat-colored stubble, was tight. His eyes sought her lips, searing them with the brilliant light flaming in his dilated pupils.

His lips, warm and moist and provocative, began nibbling hers. He was tasting her, devouring her, filling her with unexpected sweetness. His tongue parted her mouth, and she sighed in welcome. The stark reality of her desperate situation dimmed under the tantalizing pressure of his tongue against hers.

Oh yes, *yes*, she thought silently, unable to form the words aloud. Her hands slid to his shoulders and then around to the back of his neck. He was so strong, so solid, so real, just like the newly awakened feelings shuddering through her, and his body felt warm and wonderful next to hers.

Her palms tingled from the contact with his faintly damp shirt, and she threaded her fingers through his hair to salve the delicious ache.

The tousled curls beneath the band of his hat felt like softest wool against her skin.

Devlin groaned and pulled her closer, his body hard and insistent against her abdomen. It felt good, too good. He'd pay for this later, but he couldn't make himself let her go. He'd lost control, and he couldn't seem to get it back.

So long. It had been so long, and she tasted so sweet.

The sound of a door slamming down the street shattered the sensuous cocoon surrounding them, and Amanda froze.

Cursing silently, he dropped his head to her shoulder and fought for control. He could feel her stiffening up on him, and he couldn't blame her.

"Give me a minute," he rasped.

"No, no," she whispered frantically, trying to push him away. "Let me go."

Her cheek was pressed against his temple, and she could feel the blood pounding through his veins. The same furious rhythm beat in her body, the rhythm of desire. But how could she be responding like a enraptured schoolgirl when she didn't even know if her daughter was alive or dead?

"Where're your keys?" His voice was thick, the syllables slurred.

"I...dropped them." She couldn't move. Her mind was numb, and her body felt disconnected and alien. When she didn't react, Buchanan muttered a curse under his breath and picked up the ring from the mat by her foot.

He kept his back to the street as he worked the lock and pushed the door inward. There was no sound from inside, and the air smelled stale against the early morning freshness.

Moving cautiously, he pushed his bag inside with his booted foot and stood back. Amanda, her senses swimming, started to enter, only to be stopped by his strong hand on her shoulder.

"Stand with your back against the wall, and keep the door open a crack until I tell you it's okay."

He followed her inside, pulled the door nearly closed, then reached into an outer pocket of the bag for the gun he had stashed there.

He checked the magazine, flicked off the safety, and gave her a warning look. "The keys are still in the truck. If anything happens, get out of here fast. And I mean *fast*. Run over anyone who tries to get in your way."

Devlin had forgotten the heady, intoxicating rush that came over him whenever he sensed danger. It was better than any drug, more stimulating than the most potent of liquors. And God help him, he loved it.

Walking quietly on the balls of his feet, his gun held ready in his left hand, he felt the adrenaline bathing his muscles. His breathing was quick and silent, his teeth clenched, his belly tight and aching.

It was always that way now. The very tightness that enabled him to move quickly enough to avoid a knife thrust or dodge a bullet put too much strain on muscles already badly shredded by the gelatin-tipped bullet that had exploded inside him. He hated the hot slicing pain that reminded him of his greatest failure, but he'd learned to live with it. Most of the time.

His heart slammed against his ribs in a furious rhythm at the dark memory, and he shoved the bleak thoughts out of his mind. He had a job to do here.

Silently, meticulously, he made his way from room to room, his eyes never still, his ears straining for the slightest sound.

The beautiful old house was arranged in the shape of an elongated L, with the bedrooms forming the shorter line. He searched the living area first, but there were no marks of illegal entry, no indications of intrusion. He began to breathe more easily.

The family room looked out onto the patio, the most likely place for entry, but the French doors were securely locked. Swiftly he checked the den and the bathrooms. Nothing was out of place. Amanda's house was very orderly and impeccably neat. Like her.

His fingers tightened on the butt of the pistol as he pushed open the door to the little girl's room. If Santalucci had left any sign, it would be here, where a frantic mother would go first.

Sooner or later the man would send some kind of warning, some grisly proof of his power. It was his style to use terror and force, and Devlin fully expected him to use both on Amanda.

He felt a curious tightening in his throat as he circled the airy room. Cute, he thought. Pretty and feminine. Frilly things and lots of yellow. He wasn't crazy about the canopied bed, but he supposed little girls liked that sort of thing.

His sisters had slept three to a room and had never had enough closet space. But then an army sergeant's pay hadn't stretched far enough to afford luxury.

So, little Jessica, you like bears, he thought, running his hand over a large teddy bear sitting plump and smiling in a corner. Around it were grouped bears of every shape, color and description, from a tiny polar bear eating an ice cream cone to a life-sized koala holding a shoot of eucalyptus.

"Hang in there, Jessica Marie. I'll get you back safely," he muttered, backing out of the room. The odds were ten to one against, but he'd never paid much attention to statistics. They were too much like rules.

In the guest room he examined the window looking out over the patio. The latch was barely adequate. Anyone could break in without much effort and without being seen. The house was anything but secure.

There was one possibility left. The master bedroom. But it, too, was empty. No sign of entry, nothing out of place. It was tidy and clean and smelled like Amanda. The seductive scent tantalized his nostrils, reminding him of the kiss on the porch. Somehow he'd lost control out there, and it damn well better not happen again.

He leaned against the wall and absently rubbed his jaw. Suddenly he yawned, feeling the tiredness tug at his tense body. No wonder he was beat, he realized wryly. He hadn't slept in over twenty-four hours.

Idly he contemplated the huge four-poster that dominated the frilly room. The pillows looked soft, the mattress plump and beckoning. That was some great bed, he thought wearily.

Amanda's bed.

If he closed his eyes, he could see her there with her hair tumbling around her slender shoulders, stretched out on satin sheets, dressed in some kind of silky, lacy thing that would show off her tiny waist and barely cover her breasts.

He would take his time undressing her, kissing each fascinating inch he uncovered. Her skin would be softer than the sheets and scented with flowers, the delicate fragile kind that grew on the mountain slopes after the first rain.

And then, when she was lying naked and warm beneath his hands, he would trace the intoxicating lines of her perfect body. He would—

Devlin felt a sharp pull in his groin, and he scowled. He was way out of line, thinking about Amanda Wainwright like that. He needed to stay alert, to keep his options wide open. He couldn't afford to get involved, especially not with her. One slip, one lapse of concentration, and he was a dead man.

He shoved the gun into his jeans and eased back the curtain that covered the window overlooking the street. Frowning, he studied the black Chrysler parked halfway down the block.

The driver's window was rolled down, revealing two burly men in shirtsleeves. One man appeared to be talking on a cellular phone.

He knew those two. They worked for Santalucci.

By now the Saint would know of the judge's return, and that she hadn't returned alone. Chew on that for a while, you bastard, Devlin thought with vicious satisfaction as he left the room.

Chapter 5

"It's okay. No one's been here," Devlin said as he rounded the corner from the bedroom wing and saw Amanda standing by the door where he'd left her.

She looked like a bedraggled waif, without makeup and with her hair wind-tossed into a brown cloud around her head. Her eyes were darkened to deepest jade by a mixture of worry and fear, and violet half-moons of fatigue bruised the thin skin beneath the sable lashes.

As he reached her side, she gave him a bewildered look. It was almost as though she'd forgotten who he was.

"The house feels so empty. I keep expecting Jessie to come running in from the back with a skinned knee to be kissed or with one of her treasures to show me."

She managed a shaky smile. "When I heard you coming down the hall, I...for a minute I thought it was her. That this was all a mistake, a grotesque joke." She bit her lip. "Maybe if I met with Santalucci, explained that what he was doing was only going to get him in deeper..." Her voice faded.

She looked so small, so brave, looking up at him with unshed tears glistening like tiny diamonds on her long lashes and her head tilted at a determined angle. He shoved his hands into his pockets to keep from hauling her into his arms again.

"You stay away from that creep," he said sharply, sidestepping his duffel bag to glance through the crack in the front door. Satisfied that the black car couldn't be seen from this part of the house, he turned to face her.

"Listen to me, Judge. This isn't a meeting of the Junior League or a country club cocktail party. This is life in the gutter. It's filthy and it's dangerous and one mistake can be your last. And threatening Santalucci directly would definitely be a mistake. A damned stupid mistake."

He schooled himself to ignore the flash of hurt in her green eyes as she stared at him unblinkingly, her mouth opened in shock. He had to make her understand what kind of desperate danger she was really in.

In spite of her experience on the bench, she was still a civilian when it came to the dirty grind of undercover police work, an amateur with a little bit of knowledge, and a lot of misplaced idealism. And she had enough legal authority to mess him up but good if he wasn't very careful.

He couldn't let her back Santalucci into a corner, where his only escape would be killing Jessica Wainwright and maybe even her mother as well.

"We've got one shot at that bastard, one chance to get your daughter back unhurt. If we screw up, if we underestimate his intelligence or determination or ruthlessness, Jessica could die." He gave her a hard look. "Remember that and we'll get along fine. Forget it, and we're all in trouble."

The slight dip of her head told him that she'd gotten his message loud and clear. His gut twisted as he jerked open the front door and walked out.

He kept his back straight as she banged the door behind him. He'd just delivered a brutal blow to her blind side, but he'd had no choice. He didn't have time to pull his punches.

He also didn't have time to wait for Santalucci to come to him. He was going to raise the stakes just enough to keep the bastard from feeling too confident.

With long deliberate strides, he passed the truck, turned right and kept going, walking toward the black sedan at an unhurried but steady pace. He kept both hands in front of him where they would be easily visible.

The burly man in the driver's seat had small mean eyes the color of putty. His name was Blades, and his specialty was cutting. Under his bulky, ill-fitting blue blazer was a bowie knife in a special sheath. Devlin had watched him use it once in a bar, and he was good. His victim, a jive-talking pimp who'd been short on his protection money, had ended up in intensive care.

"So Steck was right," Blades said in a sneering tenor as Devlin stopped a few feet from the heavy car and stood with his hands on his hips. "That broad shacked up with you in Mexico *was* the high and mighty Wainwright." His tiny pig eyes flashed lasciviously, and the squat, olive-skinned man in the passenger's seat tittered.

Devlin fought the urge to smash his fist into the slimy creep's mouth for even mentioning Amanda's name.

"Too bad about Steck. He's losing his touch." He made his voice cold and unconcerned.

Blades's face took on a mottled gray tone, giving his fat jowls the pasty look of a plucked week-old turkey. "He can still take you down, cop," he spit out viciously.

Devlin shook his head. "I'm retired, remember. Living the easy life in Old Mexico." He cocked his head. "One thing you're right about, though. The lady judge and I have a good thing going. Or we did, until the Saint messed it up." His smile was arrogant.

Blades smirked. "He'll be sorry to hear that," he said with heavy-handed sarcasm. A cunning look replaced the sneer in his eyes, and Devlin felt a jolt of satisfaction. The stupid jerk was buying it.

Devlin looked up and down the street, then lowered his voice. "Tell the man I want a meeting. Tell him the lady listens to me, only me. If he wants the judge's cooperation, he's going to have to make it worth my while."

Before Blades could reply, Devlin turned and walked back toward the house, more conscious with each step just how dangerous it was exposing his back to a man like him, even if it was in broad daylight.

By the time he reached the pickup and wrenched open the tailgate, his shirt was sticking to his back and the skin under his hatband was drenched in sweat.

"Damn," he muttered as he reached for his suitcase. He was playing a lone hand in a deadly game. He only hoped he hadn't lost his touch.

Amanda set the table and made them breakfast while Buchanan carried the rest of his things to the guest room. She needed to keep busy.

He was right, of course. She had very little practical expertise when it came to dealing one-on-one with a ruthless professional criminal. Maybe she was naive and foolish, but she was thankful she still had some illusions left. Without them, she might feel as alienated and alone as he did.

She took a deep breath and removed a carton of eggs from the refrigerator. A loud footfall startled her, and she nearly dropped the eggs as she whirled around quickly, her heart pounding.

"Sorry, I didn't mean to scare you," Buchanan said tersely. He took off his Stetson and wiped his brow with a red bandanna he'd taken from his back pocket. His face was lined with weariness, and his shirt was damp with sweat.

Amanda's stomach fluttered at his rough appearance. It was silly to be afraid, she told herself, and then she realized it wasn't fear that was shivering through her. She *liked* the way he looked. He was the most supremely masculine man she'd ever met.

"I've brought in my gear," he said, "and I'm going to take a quick shower." He nodded toward the eggs in her hand. "How much time do I have?"

"Fifteen minutes. After that the hollandaise will taste like glue."

He gave her a bland look. "As long as I don't have to cook it myself, I'll be satisfied."

He walked away from her, his head tilted to one side, moving in an athletic, loose-hipped stride that was almost but not quite a swagger.

Her body tingled all over as though she'd just stepped off a fast falling elevator, and her nails dug into the egg container. She'd seen sexy walks before. And perfect male buns. But never on the same body—until now.

"This is ridiculous," she muttered in a disgusted undertone as she ground her teeth and began separating the eggs, forcing herself to concentrate on the hollandaise sauce. If she wasn't careful, it would curdle; then she'd have to start all over again.

She beat the yolks furiously, venting her anxiety and anger. As she worked, her mind tumbled back to the scene on the porch when he'd pulled her into his arms and kissed her with such fire.

He'd been pretending, but somehow, in his arms, his lips teasing hers, she'd slipped over the line from make-believe to reality. She'd come alive, her body filled with a hungry primitive craving, the kind she'd only read about.

She'd loved Justin dearly, but that love had grown slowly and steadily over many years. She'd been twenty-two, he thirty-eight when they'd met at the University of New Mexico law school where he'd been a senior professor. He'd become first her mentor, then her best friend and finally, five years after they'd first met, her husband.

They'd been lovers, of course, but the physical side of their relationship, while warmly pleasurable, had never been of primary importance to either of them.

Smiling in fond memory, she poured the sauce over the poached eggs warming on the hot tray and ran water into the bowl.

Buchanan was raw and tough and rude, not at all the kind of man she usually found attractive. Her smile faded as she thought about the few serious relationships in her past.

Like her mother before her and the other gently bred women in her family, she liked men with finesse and gentility, gentlemen in every sense of the word. Men like her father, a *summa cum laude* graduate of Harvard Law School, and Justin, who'd no doubt written more books on the law than Buchanan had read.

So why did she find him so intriguing? Why, in spite of all she had to worry about, did her mind keep returning to that blasted kiss that meant nothing at all to him? Or to her.

Bracing her arms on the tiled counter, she stared through the wide window into her backyard. Her prize-winning roses were drooping from lack of water, and the oval swimming pool reflected the blistering sun like a turquoise lake, hurting her eyes. Sighing, she lowered her lashes and stared unseeingly at the hand-painted design on the kitchen tiles.

Because you need him, came the frustrated answer from someplace in the back of her mind. It was true, she admitted. She was dependent upon the man right now. He could do what she couldn't—fight Santalucci with his own weapons, and win. And because she needed him so desperately, she was uncommonly vulnerable to him, emotionally and physically, whether she wanted to be or not.

This feeling of dependency was alien to her. No, more than that. It was anathema. Since her early teens when her mother had died of cancer, she'd prided herself on being independent and self-assured. She liked being in control. She enjoyed the sense of confidence that control gave her. Cool and composed and professional, that's how she liked to be seen, because that's what she was. Until Thursday afternoon when she'd opened that plain white envelope.

She sighed, releasing some of the tension tightening the muscles of her face. Now that she knew what was going on in her brain, she could deal with it.

The sharp tap of approaching masculine footsteps interrupted her thoughts. He walked quickly, his back straight, his eyes narrowed. Arrogant, she thought, as though he knew he could handle anything that came his way—including Amanda Wainwright.

His hair was damp and combed back from his face into rough tidiness. He'd dressed in khaki cotton trousers and a short-sleeved rugby shirt of two-toned gray that turned his eyes to charcoal. He hadn't bothered to shave.

"Where do you want me?" he asked, glancing around the long narrow kitchen.

Where did she want him? she echoed involuntarily. Certainly not in her house, and especially not in the bedroom next to hers. Or anywhere else, if she had a choice. Which, at the moment, she didn't.

"In the breakfast room. The coffee's on the sideboard under the window." She carried the platter of eggs to the table.

Her stomach knotted as he pulled out the chair she indicated and sat down. She might be able to control herself and her actions, but controlling Devlin Buchanan might very well prove to be impossible.

"You're a good cook, Your Honor. I'm impressed." Buchanan took a final sip of coffee, holding the Wedgwood cup by the rim instead of the handle, which was too delicate for his long fingers. He replaced the cup in the saucer and pushed it to one side before leaning back and rubbing his lean belly. His square brown hand covered a large portion of his midriff.

"Thank you," she said with a dry look at the long, flat torso above his belt. He'd eaten all of his portion and half of hers, and she had a feeling he could have eaten the same again. She made a mental note to double the amount of food she normally fixed for two.

"I guess we've put it off long enough."

He glanced down at the empty dishes between them, his brow furrowed. He had a small scar on the left side of his forehead, a jagged comma at the tip of his bushy blond eyebrow that gave him a perpetually sardonic look. Funny, she hadn't noticed that before.

"Put off what?" she asked, berating herself for letting her mind wander. She was still worn out, she told herself. Resolutely she focused her attention on his face.

"Some tough decisions, Amanda. Last night, while you were, uh, sleeping, I was thinking about a cover story to explain my presence in your life."

The memory of *where* she'd slept stretched between them like a tunnel of intimacy, one which Amanda didn't want to enter.

"Uh, have you come up with anything promising?"

She worried her napkin with nervous fingers, folding and refolding the starched linen until it was a wrinkled lump.

"More than promising. I think it'll work."

He rested his bronzed arms on the table and leaned forward. A shaft of sunshine tangled in his hair, emphasizing the silver that was mixed with the blond.

"It's plausible enough to convince Santalucci I'm no threat, but flexible enough to allow me freedom of movement."

She's not going to like this, he realized, watching her eyes look everywhere but at his face. In her own home, she seemed more like the woman on the court bench, aloof and cold and untouchable. And yet she still had that same sultry, almost flirtatious pout to her mouth that had nearly driven him crazy all those weeks, thinking about what it would feel like to have that mouth pressed against his. And when she smiled, a tiny dimple popped into her left cheek, just above the corner of her mouth.

He caught the tip of his tongue between his teeth and tried not to think about kissing that pert little dimple. Right now he had to figure out the best way to tell her what he was going to do. But there was only one way with Amanda. Straight out.

"I'm going to be your bodyguard."

"You are not!"

It was out of the question. The last thing she wanted was Buchanan shadowing her every move. It was bad enough having him in her house.

"Oh, yes, I am."

He was right. She clearly hated the very idea. He rubbed his belly again, reminding himself of the life he used to lead. No wonder she looked at him like he was some kind of fascinating and terrible freak. No wonder she hated the thought of him constantly at her side day after day.

He narrowed his eyes and let the full force of his determination flow between them. "Think about it, Your Honor. You're about to preside over the most publicized trial we've had in New Mexico in twenty years. Two highly visible members of the press are dead. It makes perfect sense for you to have personal protection. In fact, it's the rational thing to do. Otherwise, the press might wonder why you feel so damned confident."

He punctuated his words with a curt nod of his head. End of discussion. Period. Amanda read his body language with rising anger and began to seethe. He didn't have to be so damned arrogant, even if he was right.

But that wasn't all that was bothering her. The man was slouched in her hand-carved chair like he owned it, his eyes cool and calculating and unmoving. It was unnerving, the way he was taking over her house and her life, and she didn't like it.

"What about Santalucci?" she challenged. "What's he going to think?"

"That you're not as helpless as he thought." He played with his knife, drawing sharp slashing lines across the linen place mat. "If he asks, tell him you're taking normal precautions, to cover yourself and him. He'll understand."

"Easy for you to say. It's not your daughter who's in danger."

His brow lifted at the sarcasm coloring her voice, and one side of his mouth twitched. "No, just my neck."

He grinned suddenly, and Amanda had to school herself not to stare. His face had come alive, his eyes sparkled and his lean cheeks creased into the sexiest male dimples she'd ever seen.

If he could bottle that sex appeal and sell it for a dollar a pint, he'd make enough to buy every house in La Placita.

"Saint George was at my funeral, did Cy tell you? Came to pay his respects, he said. Seemed really disappointed that the casket had to remain closed."

His grin faded as he glanced down at his belly, and Amanda felt a chill, as though the sun had suddenly gone behind a cloud. "Someday I hope to attend *his* funeral."

His hatred radiated across the table, smothering her with its power. It was a living entity, forming a barrier between them, a virulent, bubbling caldron of violent emotion, the kind that was invariably destructive.

She toyed with her spoon. Suddenly she was very glad that she was not on the receiving end of that kind of enmity.

"You faked the accident because of the bounty on your head, didn't you?"

In the turmoil surrounding their arrival, she'd forgotten for a moment the very real risk he was taking just being here with her, and she was suddenly ashamed of herself for resenting his presence in her home.

He nodded. "I really did hit that bridge abutment, but I had my seat belt on, and all I got was a busted ankle and cuts from flying glass." He fingered the scar on his temple. "The car was a wreck, though, and there was a lot of blood on the windshield and the seats. Cy was the one who came up with the idea of my death." He shrugged. "Seemed like a good idea, since I'd planned to disappear anyway. My life in this town wasn't worth very much. Still isn't."

Buchanan didn't seem to be aware of the effect he was having on her as he tipped his chair backward, reaching behind him for the coffeepot at the same time. "Another cup?" he asked politely.

She shook her head. She was jittery enough as it was.

He shrugged, then poured a full measure for himself before replacing the pot on the warming tray. His large hands cradled the steaming cup in front of him as he leaned forward. "Now, about Jessica—"

Amanda sat up abruptly. "What about her?"

"What kind of story did you put out to explain her absence?"

"I didn't say anything, really. Most people think we're in Las Cruces for the long weekend, visiting my brother-in-law and his family. When I decided to drive into Mexico, I called John and told him we weren't going to be able to visit this weekend after all because Jessie had a touch of the flu."

He nodded, approving. "We got a break because of the holiday. Most people are too busy to notice who's doing what."

He frowned, deep in thought. "That takes care of the weekend, but what about this sitter you told me about? The one who thought you picked up Jessie at the stables."

"I'll tell Elena that Jessie's staying with her uncle for a while."

"Huh uh. No good. That's too easily checked in case the press gets snoopy." His eyes narrowed. "Tell the sitter, and everyone else who asks, that she's away for a month or so visiting her grandparents, someplace in the East, I would guess." He cocked a questioning brow in her direction.

"My father lives in Boston," she said with a faint smile. "My mother's dead."

His lips slanted in satisfaction. "I thought I recognized a few hard Yankee consonants under that perfect diction."

Amanda was impressed. Most people, if they said anything at all, thought she was originally British.

"You have a good ear."

"One of the tricks of my trade," he said in a perfect imitation of her measured speech. In rapid succession he gave her a Texas drawl, a cracker twang and a soft Mexican-American accent.

Her jaw dropped. "Amazing," she said softly, her hands pressed to her cheeks. "Where'd you learn to do all those?"

He took a sip of coffee. "My father was a master sergeant in the army. I was born at Fort Benning, so technically I guess I'm a Southerner, but I can't really claim any place as home. Except a whole bunch of army bases." His grin was fleeting. "I counted it up once and figured that we moved thirty-two times before I left home at eighteen.''

"How sad," she said before thinking, and immediately regretted her words as his face closed up.

"Not at all," he said without inflection. "Moving around so much forced me to learn how to take care of myself."

He stood up and stretched, his muscles flexing in a powerful rhythm. "Right now I'm going to unpack and grab a quick nap." He glanced at the large black watch on his wrist. "If I'm not up in two hours, come bang on the door. Okay?"

Amanda gave him a startled look. His words sounded almost intimate, the kind of request a husband made of his wife on a lazy Saturday morning. "Two hours." She glanced at the antique kitchen clock on a shelf behind him. It was nearly nine.

He gave her a curt nod and left the breakfast room. She watched him go with tired eyes. The man was an iceberg, dangerous enough on the surface, but with most of his destructive power carefully hidden. Suddenly she was extremely frightened.

It was very possible that in trying to defeat one dangerous, unpredictable man, she'd invited an even more dangerous and unpredictable one into her life.

The guest room was sandwiched between the master suite and Jessica's room. It was small, but looked comfortable enough, even if the pale peach bedspread was a bit too feminine for Devlin's taste.

The furnishings were sparse, consisting of a brass bed, a couple of dressers that were obviously antique, and one oak rocking chair that looked too frail to accommodate his weight.

He unpacked swiftly, not bothering with any kind of order as he stuffed his underwear and shirts into the empty drawers.

He felt like an intruder, tromping through Amanda's home with dusty boots, a fully loaded Beretta in his belt. He could never feel comfortable in this place.

This was a rich woman's house, the kind of place where Amanda Wainwright belonged. It went with her expensive finishing school accent and her Back Bay lineage.

The lady was a thoroughbred, used to careful handling, while he was more like a scrub mule, sired, he'd always suspected, during one of his father's drunken binges.

She was used to the best. No doubt she'd attended the best schools, been recruited by the most prestigious law firms, been appointed judge with the approval of the state's elite. Class, all the way.

He caught a glimpse of himself in the bowed mirror of the oak dresser. Classy was not a word he'd used to describe the face that stared back at him. It was battered and scarred and nothing matched.

His nose had been broken twice and was still crooked in spite of the surgery designed to let him breathe again. His jaw was too square, his mouth too big, and one front tooth was chipped on the edge, giving him the unfriendly look of an old-time outlaw, even when he smiled, which wasn't all that often. No one, not even his mother, had ever called him good-looking.

Scowling, he remembered the portrait of Amanda's husband in the den. Justin Wainwright had come from old money with impeccable family connections and the best of reputations, while Sergeant Buchanan's son had gone to college on a wrestling scholarship, served in Vietnam as an infantryman and gone to law school at night on the GI Bill. As a junior FBI agent he'd settled on undercover work and never looked back.

No, Devlin thought, he sure as hell wasn't the type of man she was used to seeing in her house.

He finished unpacking and threw his empty duffel bag onto the floor of the closet. He tugged the gun from his belt, jerked back the spread, and slipped the Beretta under the pillow.

Yawning, he sat down heavily on the edge of the bed and pulled off his boots. The mattress was hard, too hard. He was used to a few lumps and sags. He flopped on his back and stared at the ceiling.

He'd never lived with a woman before. Never really wanted to. Correction, he told himself with a grim smile. He was living in the woman's house, that's all, and even that was on sufferance.

He bit back a groan as he remembered the big bed that dominated her bedroom. It wasn't meant to be the pallet of a nun.

For an instant, he allowed his mind to probe the possibilities. He'd heard the stories about the Judges Wainwright, a May-September marriage of two brilliant legal minds. And yet, under Amanda's sleek facade was a strong current of passion flowing just beneath the surface, a kettle of sensuous response just waiting to be stirred. He'd sensed it when he'd kissed her.

He sighed and punched the pillow under his head, trying to find a comfortable spot. His body was exhausted, but his mind wouldn't shut down. The woman had him remembering things he'd forgotten long ago.

Like the time he was nineteen and in love with a colonel's daughter. He'd taught himself to fit into her upper-class world of gracious surroundings and party manners, but he'd always felt uncomfortable in a starched collar and tie. So when his debutante girlfriend dropped him for the son of a general, he'd been secretly relieved. Polite conversation over martinis had bored the hell out of him, just as living Amanda's conventional life would bore him now.

He was only here because her house was an ideal base of operations for him, a place to sleep and eat and shower before he had to pound the streets again. And, he realized, the best place to keep his eye on her.

Somewhere nearby a door closed, followed by the sound of movement in the next room. Buchanan sighed and flopped onto his side, his eyes staring at the wall between his room and hers. Listening to her move around in her bedroom was oddly intimate, even provocative, and Devlin closed his eyes, trying without success to block out thoughts of that seductive little body next door.

Was she undressing? Maybe exchanging his shirt and shorts for something more feminine? He stopped breathing, listening for a clue, but the muted sounds of movement had ceased. He exhaled slowly and forced his tense muscles to relax. He took a deep breath, which caught suddenly as the sound of running water broke the silence. She was taking a shower.

Devlin's face burned with a flush of instant response. She was only a few feet away, her perfect tawny skin covered only in warm water and soapsuds. His hands clenched as he thought about massaging sweet-smelling suds into all the soft, secret places his clothes had covered.

Good thing she hadn't known what kind of thoughts had tormented him during those long uncomfortable hours driving north, he thought without humor, or she never would have let him into her house, no matter how hard he'd insisted.

His body stirred as he remembered the torture she'd put him through—without even knowing it. Every bump in the road, every bounce of the springs had jostled her head against his body until he'd been so turned on he could scarcely drive. Kissing her at the door had been only partially for show. He'd wanted her so badly he hadn't been able to help himself.

He groaned and buried his hot face in the feather pillow. He was here for one reason only—to get Santalucci. Nothing more. And he'd damn well better remember that.

Chapter 6

"Buchanan, it's after eleven."

Amanda hated to wake him. He looked so tired, with fatigue etched on his face like a harsh mask.

His lean body lay faceup, sprawled diagonally across the mattress, his long legs stretching to the corner of the double bed. One huge, half-closed fist lay by his cheek, the other hand hidden under the pillow.

His face was turned toward her, his thick, straight lashes resting on his bronzed cheeks, his jaw relaxed, his lips slightly parted. His breathing was barely audible and regular, like a small child's. Except that this was no little boy lying here in her grandmother's brass bed. This was one very adult, very lethal male who'd overslept by fifteen minutes and showed no sign of awakening on his own.

Amanda sighed and reached out to shake his shoulder. "Buchanan, wake—"

He moved fast, uncoiling from the mattress so quickly that she scarcely had time to gasp. His fist crushed her fingers as he rolled onto her and forced her arm above her head. Then something hard and cold jammed into the skin under her ear.

His face, stiff and angry and pale beneath the tan, was only inches from hers. His lips were drawn back, his teeth bared, his breath hissing in anger. "Don't *ever* do that again," he ordered in a frigid voice that was only one tone above a growl. He moved the gun barrel away from her neck and slid the Beretta under the pillow, his expression still dark.

"You *said* to wake you up," she shot back, her heart racing, her mouth dry. His crushing weight made it difficult to breathe.

"I *said* to bang on the door." His fingers eased the pressure on her wrist, but he retained his hold. Amanda struggled to move away, but she was trapped beneath him.

"Oh, for heaven's sake!" she exclaimed impatiently. "What difference does it make? You said to wake you up. I woke you up. Now, get off of me. I can't breathe." She squirmed beneath him, struggling to escape. Her breasts brushed his rib cage, and the sudden intake of his breath rasped between them.

Her face flamed as her nipples puckered, pushing noticeably against the soft knitted cotton of her dress. Awareness, turbulent and intense, flared in his gray eyes, and her breath faltered in her chest.

"If it'd been pitch black in here, you might be having permanent trouble breathing, Your Honor." He glowered down at her, his thigh pressing her hips to the mattress.

Defiantly she met his icy gaze without blinking. "Thanks for the warning," she said tartly. "I'll make a note of it for the future. Never do Buchanan a favor; you might get shot for your trouble."

His scowl deepened. "What favor?" He moved slightly, bracing his body on his left hand.

"You looked exhausted. I didn't want to startle you, so I thought I'd sort of nudge you awake. Silly of me, wasn't it?" She felt like a fool—a helpless, soft-hearted fool.

He looked disgusted. "Not silly. Stupid. Never sneak up on a man with a price on his head."

"I'll remember that."

"You do that."

His body blanketed her with warmth, sending little surges of tingling energy through her dress to spread along her skin. She moved slightly, and the muscles of his chest contracted involuntarily; she could feel it through the double layer of thin cotton separating them.

Buchanan relaxed until his forehead was resting on hers. He closed his eyes and tightened his lips. Sighing suddenly, he raised his head and looked down at her. "Let's make a deal," he muttered. "You stay out of my room, unless invited of course—" his grin flashed "—and I'll stay out of yours."

"Thanks a lot."

"You're welcome." His grin widened, tilting upward on one side, and downward on the other.

Amanda blinked, caught up for an endless moment in that endearingly imperfect smile. Dangerous and sexy, wrapped up in one incredibly hard body, she thought breathlessly, that was Buchanan. Suddenly she felt as though she'd just decompressed and was fighting for oxygen. Her mouth opened as she struggled to drag more air into her lungs.

His grin slowly faded as he gazed down at her. His deep-set eyes, so still and watchful, held her captive, mesmerizing her, tantalizing her, seizing her. What was he thinking, this strangely compelling, quixotic man who'd taken over her life? His eyes were so gray, so alive, so...so what?

The room was unnaturally quiet. Even the noise from the street was muffled and indistinct. The air had a heavy quality to it, reminding Amanda of the electrically charged moments before a thunderstorm.

Trapped beneath him, she could feel every inch of his body where it rested on hers. His muscles were smooth granite and just as unyielding, forcing her softer body to accept the imprint of his.

His thumb moved almost imperceptibly over the thin skin of her wrist. It was a tiny movement and exquisitely gentle, but she had to force herself not to jerk her hand away. The sensation was delightful, provocative, sweetly entrancing, and she didn't want to enjoy it. Heat rose in her body.

"It's been a long time since I've been this close to a woman," he said indistinctly, his voice a male purr. "I've forgotten how good it feels."

She heard the words, even understood them, but she couldn't seem to drag her eyes away from his mouth. He had a quick way of speaking, his lips forming each syllable stiffly, his teeth chopping off words at the end with arrogant authority. And yet his lips looked too soft for such hard-bitten speech. They looked more suited for kissing.

They *were* suited for kissing, she admitted silently. She could still feel his lips caressing hers, could still remember the jolt of pleasure she'd felt when his tongue had brushed hers.

"Don't look at me like that," he muttered harshly, his brows drawn. "I'm not made of stone."

Amanda stared at his mouth, her tongue moistening her bottom lip. She couldn't seem to move. "Let me up, Buchanan," she whispered softly, her free hand pushing at his shoulder.

"Not yet. Show me how you were going to nudge me awake."

His eyes shone with sudden humor, seductive and playful, with an added element of challenge.

"I wouldn't dare."

"Yes, you would. You'd dare anything, if it really mattered to you." His mouth hovered over hers. "Kiss me, Amanda. I want to taste you again."

Kiss him. Lord yes, she wanted to kiss him. She wanted to feel that wild, soaring exhilaration she'd felt on the porch. She wanted to feel his muscles tighten under her hand. She wanted to hear that low growling purr he'd made deep in his throat.

But that had been pretense. All of it.

Her temperature plunged, as though she'd been tossed into an icy bath. She had to put distance between them. Right now.

"Let me up," she ordered again, this time in the firm, authoritative voice she used on the bench.

Buchanan's head snapped up as though he'd been hit from behind. The air crackled between them as he stiffened.

"Yes, *ma'am*." The chill in his voice lowered her temperature even further. He rolled off her and stood up in one fluid movement. His expression showed very little, but every rigid line of his body radiated anger.

Amanda sat up and rubbed her wrist where his fingers had shackled her. His eyes darkened as he noticed the movement.

"Sorry if I hurt you," he said in a neutral tone. "I'm not used to handling someone as...small as you are."

The man was also not used to apologizing, that was obvious, but she could feel he was telling her the truth.

"I'm sorry, too, for not following your instructions. Next time I'll know better."

Amanda scrambled off the bed and turned to go. She'd reached the door when a sudden thought occurred to her, and she turned around, catching him looking at her with the strangest expression. As though he'd just lost something very valuable.

"Buchanan—"

His face changed instantly as though fog had suddenly come between them.

"What now, Judge?"

"Uh, I just remembered about Rosalie's truck. Should I take it back to her?"

"I'll do it. I want to see her anyway." He picked up his boots and sat down on the edge of the bed. "Give me your spare keys, in case she's not home."

"What if the Volvo isn't there?"

"I'll figure out something." He sounded impatient, as though he couldn't wait for her to get out of his room.

"That's what I'm counting on," she said tersely. Before he could answer, she turned and left the room.

Devlin pulled the brass butterfly knife from the pocket of his black leather jacket and practiced flipping it open and closed with his right hand.

He was rusty, too rusty. He had to be careful, or his cover would be blown before he'd even asked a question.

He felt self-conscious, standing on Rosalie's porch with his hair greased down and his tight black jeans cutting into his circulation, but he wanted to see her before he drove downtown to the bikers' bar he used to frequent.

His phone call had caught her just as she was leaving for an appointment, but she'd told him to come anyway.

He rang the bell, his hooded gaze surveying the area. He'd lost the Chrysler easily, but Santalucci was no fool. He could have planted more than one spy near Amanda's place.

Rosalie threw open the door and stared up at him, her big blue eyes filled with questions he didn't want to answer. He hadn't seen Tony's wife in two years, since the day of his acquittal, in fact. She'd been cold and distant, wrapped up in her own anger—at him and at fate. He hadn't pushed her.

But now there was no sign of that anger as she hung on to the edge of the door and stared at him.

"I can't believe you're really here. Alive." Her eyes glittered accusingly. "I could kill you for letting me think you were dead."

Guilt tightened his face. "I had no choice, Rosa. Besides, it was better that way. I'm not much for goodbyes."

She blinked up at him. "You've decided to help her, that nice lady judge?"

He nodded. "I guess I'm just a sucker for a pretty face."

Rosalie laughed. "Don't try to con me, Dev. You're not a sucker for any woman. You never will be. You're too much of a loner."

"Yeah, I guess I am at that." His grin flashed. "Besides, what woman would have me? I'm not rich, I hate kids, and I snore."

She giggled. "You're right. You'd better stay a bachelor." She pulled on his arm. "C'mon, let's sit out back. I want to hear all about your new life."

"You look terrific, honey," he said as they walked down the short hall.

Amanda was right. Rosa was definitely thinner. And a lot sexier than he remembered, even in the tailored blue suit that looked expensive.

"Place looks nice," he said as she led him into the kitchen. "Fancy." He glanced around the remodeled area curiously. The house looked different, smelled different, even felt different.

When Tony had been alive, it had been filled with the mingled scents of his cigarette smoke and the spicy food he loved. The old-fashioned kitchen always had a pot of chili on the stove, a bowl of limes on the counter, and a bottle of tequila in the cupboard.

His gaze rested on the gleaming new cabinets. "Got any Cuervo in there?"

Rosalie's smile slipped. "No. Just some Scotch."

"Since when did you change from white wine?"

"A while ago. There've been a lot of changes in my life, Dev."

"So I see."

"You think it's wrong, me making a new life for myself with...with other men, don't you?" He could feel her resentment and guilt. It was as though she felt she had to make excuses.

A deep sadness settled over him. Life was so damned complicated sometimes.

"Rosa, I'm the last guy to pass judgment on anyone, especially you. Life's too short to worry about what other people think."

He knew it hadn't been easy for her, married at nineteen to an undercover cop, trying to manage on an agent's pay, never knowing when her husband was coming home. Or if he was coming home.

Devlin was suddenly glad he'd never been tempted to marry. He could never put a woman through the hell Rosa had endured.

"How about a beer?" she asked in a tone he didn't recognize.

"Sure. Corona, if you have it."

Rosalie handed him a bottle from the refrigerator and poured herself a short measure of Scotch. They took their drinks to the covered patio.

It was nearly noon, and the sun was blazing hot overhead. The backyard had been newly landscaped, with a free-form, black-bottomed pool replacing the scraggly patch of grass Tony had struggled to keep green every summer.

"Looks like you're doing well," he said, gesturing with the sweat-beaded bottle.

"I have to admit I am. I found out I have a knack for selling houses." She giggled and flipped the ruffled collar of her blouse with her fingers. "Imagine me, a successful career woman. A few years ago when Tony took me out of that hash joint where I was waitressing, I thought that would be as impossible as you wearing three-piece suits every day." She glanced at his tight clothes and smiled.

"That'll be the day," he muttered, his rueful grin answering hers. "It's those damn guys in suits that made me decide to pull the plug and get out while I still could. They nearly drove me crazy with their don'ts and shall nots. They were so busy worrying about the Bureau's image, they forgot what the job was supposed to be about."

He sighed impatiently. "There's got to be a compromise someplace between the guys in the trenches and the guys behind the desks, but I sure as hell don't think it'll ever happen."

"Tony said you were an idealist—only you didn't know it."

Devlin stared at her. "Tony said that?"

"A lot of times. He said you wanted things too much for your own good. That it would destroy you because your standards were so high, especially for yourself."

Devlin laughed. "Tony was wrong. I'm just a guy trying to get along the best way I know how."

Rosalie's lashes dipped. "I know what you mean. Life can be the pits sometimes."

As they sipped their drinks, she told him about her job as a real estate saleswoman. The company for which she worked was new, she explained with a proud smile. The owner was from the East and relied heavily on her advice. She expected to be made manager within the year.

By the time Rosalie ran out of words, Devlin was ready to leave. He had things to do, and so did she. Besides, the longer he stayed, the more he felt like a stranger.

Maybe it was her fault, maybe it was his, but he no longer felt the closeness they'd shared when Tony had been alive. He finished the beer and gave her a regretful smile.

"I doubt I'll see you again for a while," he told her as he stood. "The trial starts Monday, and I'm going to be pretty busy."

Rosalie seemed sorry to see him go. She walked him to the door, her arm linked through his. For the first time he noticed her perfume. It was heavy, almost too heavy, like incense, and not at all the kind of scent he would have chosen for her. But then he was hardly an expert on women's perfume.

He'd only bought the stuff once, and that was when he was ten. He'd bought it for his mother's birthday, using every cent of the money he'd made mowing lawns on the base. She'd loved it, but his father had ripped into him for wasting his money on foolishness. His mother had never worn it, and he'd stopped buying presents.

Rosalie had left Amanda's keys in the mailbox, and she retrieved them with a strained smile. "Take care of yourself, Dev." Her voice took on a brittle edge. "I mean that."

"You, too," he said gently, leaning down to kiss her forehead. He left her standing there, watching him, her eyes cool and very remote.

And suddenly, without really knowing why, he was certain that she still blamed him for Tony's death.

The water was warmer than she liked. Amanda sat on the edge of the pool and kicked her feet. The splashing drops of water caught the sun and shimmered with rainbow brilliance, the bright colors competing with the fuchsia polish on her toes.

Where is he? she thought, kicking harder. She wasn't worried, not really. Except that Buchanan had been gone for hours. She'd just heard the grandfather clock in the hall strike five.

She'd had lunch, sorted through her mail, done a little house-cleaning, anything to keep from dwelling on Jessie's empty room down the hall, and still he hadn't come home.

Swimming laps had helped, but she'd run out of steam. She glanced at the French doors leading to the family room. She'd given him a key, and he'd tucked it into those awful black jeans without a word.

Amanda leaned back and studied her bright toes, thinking about the man she'd once called dangerously irresponsible.

Whether he believed her or not, the faults and loopholes in the legal system got to her sometimes, too, but she had too much respect for the law to break it, no matter what the provocation.

Still, it was frustrating, and she'd vented a lot of that frustration against him that day in her courtroom.

Buchanan had stood stiffly behind the defendant's table, his fists clenched, his brows pulled into a thunderous frown. "You're wrong, Your Honor," he'd said coldly when she'd finished. "Sometimes what's right is more important than what's written in a book on a shelf someplace." His voice had been as condemning as hers and filled with that same frustration she'd felt. Opposing poles, she thought. Positive and negative. But which was which?

A shiver ran up her back, and Amanda looked up. He was standing in the doorway looking at her. His mirrored sunglasses hid his eyes, but she could see the fatigue in the deepened lines of his face. And yet there was something different about him, something vital in his posture that suggested tremendous energy in spite of his tiredness.

"I was worried," she said softly as he walked toward her. His heavy biker's boots thudded dully against the patio tile as he approached.

"Were you? Why?" He stood looking down at her, forcing her to shield her eyes as she glanced up at him. He smelled of beer and stale cigarette smoke, and she tried not to wrinkle her nose.

"Because you were gone so long," she said, her anxiety turning to annoyance. The fact that she'd been worried about him obviously didn't concern him one bit. "And because I didn't know what was going on."

Instead of replying, he walked over to the patio table and sat down. His face was grimy with sweat, and his hair had curled into greasy ringlets against his forehead. As she watched, he tugged off the soiled kerchief tied above his heavy brows and wiped his face. It didn't help much.

"Did you find out anything?" Her voice caught nervously, and she winced, hating her lack of control.

"A few things," he replied, watching the play of the sunlight in her hair. It had a sheen of reddish gold, and her eyes were the color of rare jade.

The conservative, shiny black swimsuit she wore showed every alluring curve of her body in ways that made his back teeth grind together.

Devlin caught a whiff of his own clothes and frowned. He was a mess. No wonder she was looking at him as though she'd like to have him arrested.

Without looking at her, he removed his glasses, stripped off his T-shirt and jacket and tugged off his boots and socks. He stood up and, on a dead run, dived into the deep end.

Amanda watched as he swam laps, head down, breathing every third stroke, his long powerful arms cutting the water cleanly. He was a good swimmer, better than she was. His jeans slowed him down, but he was making very good time across her small pool and showing no sign of stopping.

Amanda tucked her feet close to her thighs and wrapped her arms around her knees. The sun was still hot overhead, and the glare from the pool was giving her a headache. She should have put on her sunglasses when she'd climbed out of the water.

She sat in silence, watching him. He seemed tireless. His back rippled in easy rhythm and his tanned skin glistened as he swam, his eyes closed, his expression taut. He looked as though he were trying to wear himself out.

Finally, after nearly twenty minutes, he stopped. He stood in the shallow end a few feet away, his back to her, the water lapping at his trim waist. His jeans rode low on his hips, revealing an intriguing inch of white skin below the tan line.

He turned around suddenly, and Amanda gasped. His torso was a mess, puckered with rough scars and deeply cratered where the bullet from D'Amato's gun had slammed into his midsection. In the bright light, the scar tissue seemed obscenely white against his bronzed skin.

According to the testimony at the trial he'd been saved by a heavy brass buckle in the shape of a death's-head that had deflected some of the bullet's impact. But obviously not all of it.

"What's wrong?" he said, scowling as he noticed the frozen look of horror on her face.

"Your stomach. I didn't realize..."

He glanced down. "Ugly, isn't it? I've gotten used to it." His face closed up completely, freezing her out.

"No, I mean I hadn't realized how badly you'd been hurt. It must have been awful."

"I survived." He sounded angry—at her.

Amanda bit her lip. Nothing she said seemed right, not from the moment they'd walked into her house.

He tossed his head, sending droplets of water flying in all directions. The water had cleansed the grime from his skin and the grease from his hair. He ran an impatient hand through the thick locks, flattening the blond thatch into tousled waves against his head.

"I needed to wash away the street dirt," he said as he strode toward her, his powerful thighs pushing aside the water easily.

"Is it that easy?" she asked before she thought. The silver flash in his eyes told her that she'd made a mistake.

"No, it's not easy," he said evenly, his voice cool. "Some might say it's impossible."

He hefted himself to the lip of the pool next to her. His wet jeans clung to his thighs, molding the heavy muscles clearly. In the heat, the tight denim began to steam. Several feet separated them, and yet Amanda felt the heat flow over her. She averted her eyes.

"I was being flip; I'm sorry," she said, studying a yellow rose petal floating in the water. "I guess I'm just scared." She forced herself to meet his eyes.

His face changed. "I'd worry about you if you weren't," he said with surprising gentleness, a look of sympathy in his eyes. For a moment she thought he was going to touch her, and her smile faltered. Instantly the sympathy faded from his expression.

"Things haven't changed much at the places I went today," he said, wiping his lean cheeks with his palms. "Same old creeps, same old scams. Some new faces, some not." His husky voice was tight.

"Did you find out anything pertinent?"

He hesitated. "You're not going to like it."

Amanda froze, her hands tightening around her knees until her joints hurt, and her heart began racing. "What is it?"

"Word is, Santalucci is full of himself these days. Making plans to expand his drug operations after his trial is over. Recruiting pushers with claims of big bucks down the road a few months from now."

Amanda bristled, her breath quickening in anger. "Sounds like he's pretty sure he's going to win."

Buchanan dipped his head. Without his sunglasses, his eyes were narrowed against the glare, fanning deep lines into the corners. The tips of his lashes were pure gold.

"He's claiming he has a lock on the verdict." His lips drew down at the corners. "People on the street believe him, he sounds that cocky."

Amanda stared at Devlin. "What does that mean?"

He lowered his eyes. He didn't want her to see the truth there. It meant that the Saint was feeling pretty damned confident that he had the girl hidden in a place no one would ever find. It meant that the bastard held all the cards, and he knew it. It meant that they'd be damn lucky to find Jessica Wainwright any time soon, if they found her at all.

But Amanda didn't need to know that. She was functioning on guts and nervous energy as it was. If she did have to find out the whole truth, he'd give it to her straight and hard, but until then, it was enough that he knew.

"It means he's vulnerable," he said evenly. "A man that cocky always has a blind spot—his own supreme arrogance. He feels invincible, and that makes him careless. Ultimately that's what will bring him down."

If we're damn lucky, and the guy doesn't get me first, he added silently, his face deliberately impassive. He'd told her as much of the truth as he dared.

He watched her absorb his words, analyze them for flaws, and then with a nervous, half-sobbing laugh, accept them.

"So it's good news."

"Yes, Your Honor, it's good news." As far as it went, it was good news, and if he could keep the terror out of her beautiful eyes for another few hours, he'd do it. She'd have enough to handle very soon.

Her face crumpled, and she dropped her head to her knees. She wasn't crying, not really, but he could see her shoulders heave. He raised his hand to comfort her, then dropped it to his thigh again.

In that sexy black suit she was far too tempting. Once he touched her, he wasn't sure he'd be able to restrain himself. It had been a near thing earlier in his bedroom. If she'd kissed him, he would have taken her then and there. He'd been that hot.

He'd met a lot of women, and bedded a fair number, but he'd never met one like Amanda, so cool and unapproachable on the outside, and so damned explosive on the inside.

He ached to feel her come alive under his touch, to feel her lips tremble with need under his, to feel her small hands pulling him hard against her.

But in all his years living on the edge of normal society he'd never once taken advantage of a woman in distress, and he wasn't going to start now. Especially when he wasn't as much in control of his own feelings as he wanted to be.

"Do you have any plans for dinner?" He tried for a light touch but he was out of practice, and his words came out more gruff than teasing.

Her head went up with a jerk. "I forgot. You must be starving. I defrosted steaks." She smiled. "After all, we have your...your good news to celebrate. Don't we?"

The hope in her green eyes was almost more than he could stand. He tried to rub the image from his eyes with a tired hand, but wasn't successful. He'd intended to grab a bite to eat and fall into bed, but suddenly, he changed his mind.

"Sure we do," he said. "And then I have to go out again."

Her smile faded, "Go out? Where?"

"I'm going to see a woman named Lola Grimes. Until a year ago she was Santalucci's mistress. I hear she's pretty bitter, maybe even looking to get even. And if anyone knows where Jessie might be hidden, it's Lola."

Chapter 7

"I'm going with you."

Amanda stood with her hands on her hips, blocking the door to the garage.

Buchanan continued to move toward the door. "We've already settled this, Amanda. I'm going alone."

Even in her heels she stood nearly a head shorter. Her chin was a fraction of an inch higher than the open V of his shirt, and her shoulder would fit nicely under his arm.

He braced both hands on his hips and tilted his head, angling his gaze toward those snapping green eyes that continued to fascinate him. Her face was composed, her soft lips set in a pursed expression of determination that tempted him to give her the kiss she was unwittingly inviting. But what would that get him? Another night of torture, that's what. And he was stretched thin enough already.

Wise up, Buchanan, he thought angrily, the woman is off limits, period.

"Excuse me, please," he said with what he hoped was the right amount of civility. No sense arousing the temper he could see simmering behind those tiny gold flecks. He was having enough trouble with the woman as it was.

Tension tugged at the back of Amanda's neck as she forced herself to stand her ground. She'd made a serious tactical error, she could see that now. Buchanan was not a man to take orders, especially from her.

All during dinner they'd parried. She'd been polite, he'd been blunt. She'd demanded to go, he'd refused to consider it. Amanda had pushed as hard as she could, but when his eyes had turned to flint, she'd wisely retreated.

Then, while he'd been in his room changing into clean jeans and a yellow sports shirt, she'd changed too, into tailored linen slacks and a short-sleeved silk blouse, both in a rich shade of ivory—suitable, she decided after a few minutes of frowning reflection, for visiting the former mistress of a mobster.

And right now, she told herself again as she met his annoyed gaze, she intended to do just that. If Buchanan went to see this Grimes woman, she was going with him.

"Look, Buchanan, I know you think I'm an amateur, and maybe I am, but I also know the female mind. You go barging in there, and she'll clam up. If she's furious with one man, chances are she's furious with the whole bunch of you. But with me, maybe she'll be more willing to vent her anger against Santalucci for throwing her out."

"Yeah, and what if she tells Santalucci you were with me? Then what?"

"If she tells him you were asking questions, he'll know I sent you, so I can't see what difference it would make whether I'm there or not. I know it's risky, but I'm willing to chance it."

"I'm not."

Buchanan, tired of playing her game, moved suddenly, brushing hard against her, but she stood her ground. "Stop that," she ordered, then flushed when his grin flashed.

"So get out of my way." He dropped his eyes, touching the swell of her breasts with a speculative gaze. "I don't want to fight you every step of the way, Amanda, because you'd lose." His eyes moved upward to rest on her mouth. "We'd both lose." His voice was whisper soft, reminding her of the first time he'd spoken to her in Mexico.

She lifted her chin a fraction higher, and forced a persuasive note into her voice, the same logical tone she used when addressing a jury. "Be reasonable, Buchanan. If I'm going to defy Santalucci by bringing you here, at least let me feel like I have *some* control over what you do—even if I don't."

She recognized the flash of wry humor in his eyes and told herself he was weakening. She hastened to press her advantage. "I have to do something to help, anything, even if it's simply going along for the ride. Otherwise, I'll go crazy just sitting here worrying like I did all afternoon. And after all, it's technically my problem. I should have *some* say in what's happening."

Buchanan studied her mouth. When she was wheedling him like that, her lower lip drooped into the sexiest pout. And if she licked her lips one more time, he was going to go up in smoke, right here in her shiny, custom-designed blue-and-white kitchen.

He forced his mind into safer channels. "Amanda, I don't know what I'm going to find there. I...don't want to put you in danger."

"I'm not afraid, not with you." And suddenly she knew that she'd spoken the absolute truth. With Buchanan she felt totally protected. It was an unfamiliar, but pleasing, feeling.

"C'mon, Amanda. Think what you're saying! If I couldn't save Tony, what makes you think I could save you if one of Santalucci's goons starts shooting?"

"You saved me in Mexico."

"Yeah, but we got lucky. I don't put a lot of faith in that kind of luck holding forever."

Why was he putting up with this? he asked himself in growing impatience. Why didn't he just pick her up and move her out of the way?

Sweat dampened the shallow depression between his shoulder blades at the thought of touching her again, and he swore silently.

"All the more reason I should go along," she insisted, refusing to be deterred. "You said Santalucci needs me alive. If we're together, those hit men won't dare shoot."

He shook his head and sighed heavily. "Forget it. I don't need you to be *my* bodyguard."

"I'm just being practical. You can't help Jessie if you're dead."

His lips twitched. "Well, that makes sense, anyway."

She nodded, feeling a dawning of hope. He was being protective rather than stubborn. She'd just have to convince him she didn't need his protection, just his help.

Buchanan closed his eyes, blocking out the sight of the bullheaded determination settling over her patrician features. He'd known she would be difficult to handle, no matter what she'd promised, and he'd actually looked forward to matching wills with her. He liked the idea of taking on the haughty, self-possessed Judge Wainwright and making her back down. But somewhere along the line, he'd begun fighting for his life with the woman—and losing.

Slowly, knowing that he shouldn't, he opened his eyes and lifted one hand, slipping it past her jaw to curve his fingers around the slim column of her neck.

"I thought we settled this, but if we haven't, let's do it now."

His fingers massaged the sensitive skin below her hairline, and Amanda schooled herself not to respond. She shouldn't like it. She *didn't* like it. She just couldn't seem to stop shivering.

The ball of his thumb traced the line of muscle from her ear to her throat, massaging the skin with faint pressure, and Amanda bit her lip. She should make him stop. They had things they had to do, important things, necessary...

"I'm in charge here. I make the decisions," he whispered hoarsely. "Say it, Amanda." His mouth was so close she could smell the minty freshness of his toothpaste.

Her head began to swim. She'd never willingly given over control to anyone, not even to her husband. She wouldn't give in to Buchanan. Not without a fight.

"No."

His lips softened, and his lashes lowered. "No?" His mouth took hers so suddenly she couldn't retreat. He held her head, preventing her from escaping.

She tried to kick him, but he moved his muscular thigh between hers, pinning her to the door.

"Stop fighting me," he ordered, his lips barely removed from hers. "Stop..." His voice changed, softened, drifted into silence as his lips settled over hers again, this time gently, teasing her mouth with sweet little kisses that shouldn't taste so good, shouldn't feel so good, but they did. And his lips were so soft, so tempting.

"Say it."

"You...you're in charge. You make the decisions."

Her lips surrendered to his, moving eagerly as his moved. A racing sense of urgency began building inside her, blocking out all rational thought.

Her hands clutched his shirt, pulling him closer, drawing his hard body against hers. His heart pounded under the heel of her right hand, slamming hard against her skin.

She was wrong. This *was* what she'd wanted, someone to take the control that sometimes weighed so heavily on her, to take some of the burden from her when she needed a respite. To be strong when she wasn't, to hold her when she was frightened, to make the impossible decisions when she couldn't.

Buchanan felt the difference in her immediately. Her muscles stopped bunching and became sweetly pliable, relaxing against him with a warm acceptance that was more arousing than the most ferocious struggle. And yet her kiss was wild, out of control.

He could take her now, here on the counter. She was a provocative bundle of womanly passion, sweetly alluring, wildly seductive. Everything he'd known she would be. She was his....

What was he thinking? Was he out of his mind? Buchanan tried to withdraw his mouth, but she whimpered in protest and followed his lips with hers, refusing to let him go.

He couldn't seem to think clearly, not when she was rubbing against him like that. Not when he could feel her catching fire for him. Whatever she wanted, she could have. Whatever it took, he had to have her.

If she wanted the words, the promises, the commitment—

"No," he said harshly, forcing his head up. "This is crazy." He couldn't give her any of those things, and she hadn't asked him to. He was just thinking with the wrong part of his anatomy.

He took a step backward, trying to ignore the racing of his heart. She blinked up at him, the flame in her eyes slowly dying. "Yes," she said evenly, breathing erratically. "This is...crazy."

Deep breaths, she ordered herself. Don't think about the things he'd done that had felt so good. Change the subject. Anything to keep him from seeing how close you came to making a complete idiot of yourself.

Crazy, he repeated silently. He didn't feel crazy, he felt frustrated as hell. And furious with himself for letting things get out of hand.

"Don't worry about it," he said, forcing a casual note into his voice. "You're tired and upset and mad as hell because I won't let you go with me, and I'm not real pleased about having my decisions challenged every damn time I turn around. Things just got a little hot for a while."

Heat flared inside her as he slid the tip of his tongue across his bottom lip, as though wiping the taste of her from his mouth.

"I guess that's it," she agreed hastily, slowly unclenching her fists from his shirt. As she dropped her hands to her sides, she could still feel the thudding of his heart against her palms.

But nothing terrible had happened. Nothing irreversible. She was in control now. Completely.

Devlin combed his hands through his hair, feeling like a pink-cheeked schoolboy caught necking behind the football stadium.

He hated the way she was looking at him, as though he'd suddenly slapped her hard across the face, but he didn't know what to do about it. If she expected an apology, she wasn't going to get it. Not from him.

He glanced around her neat kitchen. He had to get out of here before he really made a fool of himself. "I'd better get going."

She stopped him with a hand on his bare forearm. "I still want to go with you. If you're afraid I'll make a mistake, I won't say a word. I'll just listen. I promise."

Her voice ended on a pleading note that stabbed him hard. He'd made her beg, and he hated himself for that. She didn't deserve that, not this brave, gutsy woman.

Devlin stifled a sigh of defeat. Somehow she'd got what she'd wanted, in spite of his resolve to keep her as far away from him as possible.

"You must have been hell on wheels arguing a case in court," he said with a wry grimace. "I bet there wasn't a jury from here to El Paso that dared to find against you."

"Does that mean I can go?"

"Yes, you can go, but remember your promise. Let me do the talking." His expression was controlled, his voice neutral. It was as though the kiss they'd shared had never happened.

They were followed. Buchanan pointed out the black Chrysler as soon as they hit the interstate. In the gathering twilight, the headlights glowed like the eyes of a predator.

"Hang on," he said, gritting his teeth. He checked the rearview mirror, then spun the Volvo to the left. The gray sedan bumped over the center divider, wheels spinning wildly on the gravel, engine whining in protest.

Amanda clutched the armrest with her right hand and braced her left on the dashboard as she cast a frantic look over her shoulder. The big black Chrysler had disappeared.

The tires squealed as Buchanan accelerated, rocketing onto the pavement ahead of an eastbound truck. Amanda held her breath and stared at the speedometer. They were going ninety-five and still climbing, heading back the way they'd come.

Outside the window the distant mountains were a brown blur, whipping past them in a terrifying rush. The wind whistled over the windscreen with a shrill screaming that exhilarated her even as it shredded her nerves.

"I don't see them," she said, struggling to keep her voice steady. Her heart was pounding so ferociously the veins in her neck felt distended.

He flicked a glance into the mirror. "Best put some distance between us, just in case." He glanced in her direction, a quick grin creasing his cheek. "Let me know if you see a trooper."

The car skimmed the road, weaving in and out of traffic like a graceful dancer, responding instantly to Buchanan's adept touch. When they hit one hundred he eased off slightly, watching his mirror. At the outskirts of the city, he began to decelerate.

"Looks okay," he said, flicking on his signal and changing lanes.

Amanda's muscles were stretched like rubber bands and her stomach was quivering uncontrollably by the time he pulled up in front of an upscale apartment complex off Lomas Boulevard.

Four stories in height and stuccoed in flaming pink, the building looked out of place nestled in the brown and green foothills of the Sandias.

"What's the matter?" he said as she sat perfectly still, her hands still clutching the armrest. She wasn't sure her legs were ready to support her.

"I'm going to need a new set of shocks, and you're going to pay for it," she said in shaky annoyance.

Buchanan gave her a startled look and then burst out laughing. His face crinkled into captivating lines of amusement that took years off his age, and Amanda found herself staring.

"It's a deal," he said, opening the door and sliding out.

She'd done it again, given him one of those wide-eyed, sexy-as-hell looks that were driving him right out of his mind. Why couldn't she be like she'd been at his trial, when she'd repeatedly infuriated him, making him want to strangle her with his bare hands? Now all he wanted to do was make love with her.

Amanda waited for him to come around to open her door, but he was standing by the left fender, hands in his pockets, his eyes studying their surroundings.

Sighing, Amanda scrambled out and hurried around the car to stand at his side. "This looks expensive."

He shrugged. "Maybe Santalucci pensioned her off when he showed her the door." His voice was a cynical indictment, cold and caustic, and Amanda nodded. He was beginning to change, to pull inside himself and withdraw from her, and she suddenly felt very alone.

Side by side they walked up the cholla-lined walk to the entrance. A huge wrought-iron gate with an electronic lock barred their way.

"Now what?" she asked.

Buchanan didn't answer. Instead, he scanned the list of tenants, then punched a button.

"Yes?" The voice was distorted by metallic vibration and came from a small speaker above Amanda's head.

"Flowers for Russell, ma'am," Buchanan answered, winking at Amanda.

Mrs. Russell twittered with middle-aged pleasure. A buzzer sounded, and the gate clicked. Buchanan pulled it open. "After you," he said, standing aside. Amanda hurried through, and he followed.

"What happens when Mrs. Russell doesn't get her flowers?"

He shrugged, his narrow gaze inspecting every inch of the enclosed courtyard as he led the way to the elevator. He kept his hand under Amanda's elbow, keeping her close.

"Reminds me of L.A.," she muttered, letting her gaze rest for an instant on two plump cherubs cavorting in the center fountain.

Buchanan snorted. "Reminds me of a brothel in Saigon."

Amanda shivered as they entered the elevator and the small car moved upward. "Do you think she's alone?" she asked quietly, taking a firmer grip on her heavy purse. The garish building was making her very nervous.

"We'll soon find out, won't we?"

Lola Grimes lived in the penthouse. Her door was unmarked. No name, no number and no guard.

"Stand behind me," he ordered and waited for Amanda to comply before he rang the bell.

The door opened a crack, and she caught a whiff of jasmine-scented musk as a breathy voice asked, "Yes?"

"My name's Buchanan, Lola. Devlin Buchanan."

The woman exclaimed in alarm, and then the door opened another four or five inches, giving Amanda her first look at Santalucci's former mistress. She was tall and slender, with the pinched look of a chronic dieter. Her long straight hair was bleached platinum and was the texture of cotton candy.

She was wearing black designer jeans that had gone out of style at least two years ago and a teal-blue silk blouse that needed cleaning.

"I don't believe it." Lola's voice wavered. "You're...you're dead. I went to your funeral."

Buchanan stepped back to give her a better look. "What do you think? Do I look dead?"

"Georgie said you were."

"Georgie was wrong."

Lola opened the door wide and stared at him in mingled disbelief and anxiety. The moment her peripheral vision caught sight of Amanda, she pulled back in alarm.

"Who's that?" she asked, her face closing up as suspicion darkened her watery blue eyes. Her voice lost some of its ingenuous softness.

"A friend. Her name's Amanda." Buchanan stepped between the two women. "Are you alone?" he asked curtly, his eyes sweeping the room behind her.

"Yes, but—"

He cut her off with a jerk of his head. "Let's talk inside."

Lola clutched the lapel of her shirt. "What about?"

"Inside. We'll talk inside."

Buchanan moved forward, and Lola yielded, allowing them to enter. Amanda could sense the woman's fear, and her stomach knotted painfully. Lola was obviously terrified.

Her apartment was a study in white. White walls, white shag rug, sculptured white furniture, but like Lola there was a slightly used, even seedy air about the decor that made Amanda extremely uncomfortable.

"Sit there," Buchanan told Amanda curtly, gesturing toward a brocade divan that had a greasy spot on the arm. She obeyed with outward calm, but inside she was seething at the peremptory order.

His mouth tightened in warning before he turned and faced Lola, his arms crossed over his chest, his body between her and the door.

"I hear you and the Saint have parted company." He sounded sympathetic, and Amanda relaxed slightly. She gave Lola a forced smile that the other woman ignored.

"That's a lie," Lola said, bristling. "Georgie just wanted me to have my own place, for tax reasons, you know. Him and me—we're still like we always was...were." Two bright spots of pink dotted her cheekbones, emphasizing the pallor of her skin.

Buchanan arched a skeptical brow. "Are you? Word on the street is that he got tired of you. Found himself another lover. Young, they say, and classy. No one knows who she is. He keeps her all to himself."

Lola looked so stricken Amanda felt sorry for her. But, she reminded herself, the woman had been the willing mistress of a known criminal. Whatever had happened to her had been her own doing.

"It's not true. Georgie loves me, and I love him. He's...he's going to take me to Vegas as soon as his trial is over." Lola's chin lifted proudly, and she darted a quick look in Amanda's direction, as though to gauge her reaction. Amanda managed to let nothing show on her face.

"Is he? He must think he's going to win." Buchanan's voice was smooth, too smooth, Amanda realized. There was no reserve of friendliness in his expression, no dry humor in his voice. His body was like tempered steel, poised to move, and his narrowed gaze was focused directly on Lola's pale face, daring her to defy him.

The moment they'd stepped across the threshold, he'd become a different person, a menacing and dangerous man who frightened Amanda with his unnatural calm.

"Of course, he's going to win," Lola exclaimed shrilly, twisting her hands together. "He told me about those trumped-up charges, about how those reporters were out to get him, and how the prosecutor wanted to make a big name for himself."

"C'mon, Lola. You don't really believe that, do you? How long did you live with the man? Eight, nine years? You know what he does for a living, and it ain't managing pizza parlors."

"Georgie never talked about his work. We had other things to do when we were alone." Her blue eyes glittered frantically.

"It won't wash, doll. Santalucci's the talkative type. Bullies usually are." His lips curled. "I'll bet he talked to you a lot. A whole lot."

"What's this all about, Buchanan?" Her voice lost its breathy lightness, becoming hard and ugly. "Why the muscle?"

"I didn't tell you Amanda's full name," he answered with steely quiet. "It's Wainwright. As in *Judge* Wainwright. She's presiding over the Saint's trial."

Lola's expression reminded Amanda of a jackrabbit frozen in the glare of oncoming headlights. Her eyes darted from Buchanan's face to the door.

"No way out, Lola," he said with a chilling smile. "I'm bigger and faster and a hell of a lot more determined."

Her head swiveled toward Amanda. "I don't know nothing—anything. I swear."

Buchanan moved closer, and Lola took a step backward. His gaze shifted to a silver frame on the white mantel. The boy in the picture had flaxen hair and Lola's pale eyes.

"How's Timmy these days?" His question slipped out quietly, a rapier thrust that found its mark and drew blood before Lola could take a breath.

"He's fine," she said coldly, her face suddenly a lot less attractive.

Her bony fingers twisted and clenched each other, whitening the knuckles and pinching the skin.

''Judge Wainwright has a daughter,'' Buchanan said in a silky voice. ''She's seven.'' His eyes flicked toward Amanda. ''Isn't she?''

Amanda swallowed. ''Yes, in September.''

''Why don't you show Lola a picture of Jessica?''

Amanda reached into her purse for her wallet and extracted Jessie's latest school photo. Lola leaned forward to look, her pale face turning a sickly gray. ''She looks sweet,'' she said in a thin voice, glancing furtively at Buchanan.

Buchanan grasped the blonde's clenched hands, prying the fingers apart one by one until he held both of her hands in his. Her fingernails were long and painted crimson, and her skin looked very white next to his.

''Your good buddy Santalucci says he's going to kill that sweet little girl if Amanda doesn't see that he's acquitted.''

Lola's heavily made-up face twisted with fear, and she tried to jerk her hand out of Devlin's grasp, but his fingers tightened, trapping her wrists.

''I need to know his hiding places, the secret spots where he keeps the drugs or anyplace you can think of where he could hide a little girl without attracting attention.''

Lola shook her head, her eyes glaring, the fine lines around her mouth suddenly very pronounced. ''I don't know any places. Honest I don't.''

''I'll see that you get protection. I give you my word.'' His voice turned persuasive. ''You'd get a new identity, a new start for you and your son. And you'd save a little girl's life.''

Lola shook her head. ''No, no. He'd find me. I know he would.'' She cowered, her eyes pleading as they sought Amanda's, tears clotting the mascara on her lashes. ''Don't let him hurt me,'' she whimpered piteously, and Amanda's head jerked.

Was it an act? Or was the woman really frightened? Amanda's heart began to pound.

Buchanan shook his head. ''She won't help you, Lola. No one will. You've run out of friends.'' His slow grin was cold, a white, deadly swatch in his dark face. He took another step forward, forcing Lola against the wall.

His eyes were determined slits. His body was tense, his corded muscles hard and ready. ''You know what I do to people who cross me, don't you, Lola?'' His thumb stroked the back of her hand. ''Remember Gus D'Amato?''

Amanda stared in shock. He's going to hurt her, she realized suddenly. He's really going to hurt that poor woman if she doesn't talk.

She bit her lip. Jessie. She was doing this for Jessie. Buchanan was doing it for Jessie. And Lola could take it. Couldn't she?

Amanda's stomach began churning. Could she just sit here and let Buchanan do whatever he wanted? Even for Jessie? Was it right to allow his verbal abuse to escalate into actual physical violence?

She stared across the room, her emotions in a turmoil. She didn't want to have to choose between her daughter and her principles.

"I'm waiting, Lola." Buchanan's hand began to tighten, and the woman winced in pain.

"Please, Buchanan. I can't help you."

"Yes, you can." He towered over her, his face a thundercloud. His fingers traced the thin skin along her jaw, his touch a threat and a promise. Lola cringed.

"Don't hurt me. Please don't hurt me," she cried out, her voice shaking pathetically.

"*Stop!*" Amanda shouted, leaping to her feet.

Buchanan turned on her, his face twisted with anger. "Stay out of this." His voice throbbed with warning.

She shook her head. "I can't let you hurt her. Please, Buchanan, let her go."

He flushed darkly all the way to his hairline. His eyes frightened her, but Amanda refused to move. She swallowed hard, then directed a shaky, reassuring smile at Lola. "It's okay. No one's going to hurt you."

"Don't count on that, Lola," Buchanan said, his jaw barely moving. "I'll be back. And I'm going to expect answers. Or else." His hand cupped her jaw. "Do I have to spell it out for you, what will happen if you don't have the answers I want?"

Lola shook her head, her chest heaving. She kept darting beseeching looks in Amanda's direction.

Buchanan stared down into her faded blue eyes, his lips compressed, his anger a living force, swirling with black power around the three of them.

"Think about it," he said finally, stepping back.

Before Amanda could say anything else, Buchanan crossed the room, grabbed her arm and marched her toward the door. He moved so quickly she was forced to trot to keep up.

Outside the apartment she tried to speak. "Not one word," he said through a tight jaw as he dragged her toward the elevator. "Not one more word."

They rode in silence, neither of them looking at the other. Buchanan drove slowly, carefully, checking his mirror, but his lips were clamped together so tightly his skin was white, and his gray eyes were alive with seething anger.

Amanda braced her feet on the floorboard and pressed her rigid spine into the seat to keep from shaking. The man was two hundred pounds of gunpowder ready to ignite, and she was going to take the full force of the blast.

She took a deep breath as the remote control operated the garage door, and Buchanan brought the Volvo inside. As the heavy double door slid down behind them, she climbed from the car and went into the kitchen.

Inside, she tensed her spine, lifted her chin and turned around to face him. She had to make him understand that she couldn't condone violence in any form, no matter what she'd promised.

Before she had a chance to speak, his fist hit the wall next to her head, punching a jagged hole in the wallboard and splitting his knuckle. Amanda flinched, but held his gaze.

"You broke your word, Judge," he said in a flinty tone, tearing off each word in rapid-fire cadence.

"I couldn't stand by and let you hit that poor woman. I wouldn't have been able to live with myself."

Buchanan's head snapped back. "Poor woman? Are you *crazy*? That *poor woman* was probably an accessory in half of Santalucci's deals. Using the *legal* definition, that is, Madam Justice."

His face was dark, the flush of anger still staining his skin. Blood trickled from the cut on his hand, and Amanda's eyes flickered toward the red stream.

He caught the direction of her gaze and impatiently wiped the blood from his fist with the palm of his other hand.

"Now, let me tell you what you just did. By letting Lola know you're on her side, you very effectively cut me off at the knees and raised the odds against us. She was the fastest route to Jessica. She was *my* ace, and you, Ms. High and Mighty Principles, just trumped it." He raked a bloody hand through his hair. "I'm going to bed. Maybe if I'm lucky, I can come up with another damned lead to follow tomorrow, but don't hold your breath." He stalked off, his boots pounding angrily on the tile.

Amanda's knees began to shake and she felt sick. Creeping slowly like an old woman, she crossed the kitchen and sank into her chair in the breakfast room.

Her daughter's small face wavered in front of her eyes, accusing her. She shuddered and tried not to think about what might happen to Jessica because she'd interfered, but her thoughts tumbled and twisted, torturing her with unanswerable questions. Her head dropped to her hands and she closed her eyes. Her temples began to throb.

"Mommy, mommy. Where are you?"

Amanda sprang from her chair, her heart pounding furiously. It was Jessie.

Chapter 8

"*Jessie!* Where are you?"

Amanda raced through the house, tears streaming down her face. Jessie was safe. Her baby was safe!

Laughing and crying, Amanda ran down the hall. At the door to the den she stopped, her heart thumping, her eyes streaming, her mouth stretched into a joyous smile.

Buchanan was the only one in the room. He was standing behind her desk, his back to the door, his hands braced on either side of the leather blotter, his head down, listening. Jessie's voice was coming from the answering machine plugged into the phone.

"I want to come home, Mommy, but the man said I have to stay here because you're busy with some dumb old trial. Why can't I come home? I won't bother you, I promise." There was a humming silence, then the slick of a broken connection.

"No, dear God, no," Amanda whispered, sagging against the door frame. She began to shake violently, and her stomach twisted in a sharp spasm of fear. Her newborn joy drained from her in a shuddering rush, leaving her weak and frightened as she clutched at the cold wood for support. Gasping for air, she stared at Buchanan in a haze of disbelief. "My poor baby."

His head jerked up and he whipped around, his body moving instantly into a crouch. His hand halted halfway to his gun as his gaze locked with hers.

"Damn," he muttered and crossed the room in two strides. He caught her just as her knees buckled.

"I'm sorry," he muttered into her hair as he lifted her off her feet and into his arms. "I didn't realize you could hear the recording in the kitchen."

Amanda began to cry, harsh, racking sobs that were torn roughly from her chest. She couldn't breathe. Her arms were so empty, her heart filled with an anguish that clawed at her relentlessly. How she ached to hold her little girl, just as Buchanan was holding her.

But Jessie was all alone, God knew where, thinking her mother had sent her away. A fresh deluge of helpless sobs overtook her, flooding her eyes with hot, tortured tears. She didn't want to think, she didn't want to feel.

"It hurts," she whispered. "It hurts so much. She needs me, and I can't help her."

Buchanan sighed deeply, then pressed his cheek next to hers. Her tears wet his skin, and his lashes squeezed shut as though he were in pain. "Cry, baby," he murmured in rough comfort. "Let it all out. I'm here."

"She's a-alive," she whispered brokenly between sobs. "Jessie's alive." She clung to him, the fingers of her right hand bunching the material of his shirt over his heart.

"And she's going to stay that way. I guarantee it." Devlin said the words with a confidence he wanted to feel but couldn't. There *were* no guarantees in this life—except death.

His stomach muscles contracted painfully, reminding him of his own tenuous hold on survival. Santalucci had come close to destroying him, but Devlin had fought like hell to deny the bastard the ultimate victory. Just as he was going to fight like hell to give this woman back her daughter. If he had to die to do it, his death would at least have some meaning—which was more than he or anyone else could say about Tony's.

Amanda shivered suddenly, and her teeth began to chatter. "I'm s-so cold," she said in a trembling voice. "So c-cold." Her voice came from a great distance, and she frowned. She shouldn't be shaking like this.

"You're in shock," Buchanan muttered, moving quickly to the leather couch opposite the desk. He tried to put her down in the corner, but Amanda clung to him.

"Don't let me go," she whispered brokenly. "I feel so...so helpless. So alone.'' Her voice broke, and she shut her eyes. ''Please don't leave me.''

Buchanan muttered something under his breath, then turned around and sat down, Amanda still cradled in his arms. He adjusted his body to hers, and she found herself huddled in his lap, her breasts crushed against his chest, her knees pressed into his side.

''Here, this will help.''

Amanda felt the soft brush of wool against her bare arms as he pulled a crocheted afghan over her. It was Jessie's, the pale pink one she used when she curled up on the couch to read while Amanda was working.

Amanda buried her face in the cover and inhaled the familiar scent of licorice and mild soap that was Jessie's. A fresh deluge of tears shook her, wetting Buchanan's bronzed skin above his shirt collar.

He rocked her gently, his callused fingers massaging her temple.

''It's okay,'' he said over and over, his voice a rough satin mantra that gradually drowned out the terrifying echo of Jessie's pleading words.

''She thinks I sent her away,'' Amanda whispered through her pain-clogged throat. ''My poor little girl thinks I d-don't have time for her.''

He kissed her forehead, calming her, comforting her. His hand rubbed her back in long, soothing strokes that eased the terrible tension gripping her spine.

''Most likely the kidnappers told her what to say. Sounded to me like she was reading from a script.''

Amanda lifted her head. ''But why...?''

''Look at you,'' he said gently, wiping a tear from her cheek with his forefinger. ''You're a basket case right now. If I weren't here, would you still try to fight Santalucci?''

Amanda stared at him. ''Yes. No. I'm—I'm not sure.''

He chuckled. ''Knowing you, I think you'd take on the devil himself to save your baby. But the Saint doesn't know that. He expects you to crumble. I told you the man knows how to run a good bluff.''

Amanda could feel the tension draining from her muscles as his big hand worked its magic on her spine. ''Yes, you did. And you're right. I would have been frantic if I'd heard Jessie's voice all by myself.''

Amusement grew in his eyes. ''So maybe it's not so bad after all, having a temporary boarder?''

His gaze collided with hers, and heat pushed into the faint hollows of her cheeks. She liked the way his brows lifted at the inner corners when he started to smile. He didn't look so dangerous then. In fact, he didn't look dangerous at all.

He was so different from the hard-eyed man in Lola Grimes's ghastly white apartment, and yet, for some reason she couldn't fathom, she knew that this was the real Devlin Buchanan. This was the man behind the calculating eyes, the man no one ever saw.

"It's not so bad," she admitted, studying the crooked line of his nose. His face was actually quite handsome, in a tough sort of way.

"No, not so bad," he echoed almost absently. His smile faded as he pressed his cheek against the top of her head, and his broad palm cupped her hip, supportive, reassuring.

Warmth from his body cocooned her, giving her strength even as the adrenaline pounded through her. The last two days had been stressful enough to last her for a lifetime.

"Buchanan?"

"Hmm?" He lifted his head.

"You're really a very nice man." Weariness slurred the words, even as she tried to make them forceful and precise. He'd been uncommonly kind to her, even though he was only doing his job.

He hesitated, then said gruffly, "Just a few minutes ago you were convinced I was going to slug Lola, remember?"

"Please, let's not talk about her. I don't want to fight with you anymore. Not now. I just want to rest for a minute."

Her hands unclenched and slid up to his shoulders. He was real, solid as granite, a bulwark against the pain.

"Move forward a little," he muttered, twisting to the side. Amanda leaned away from him, and Buchanan reached behind his back for the Beretta that was digging into his spine.

He put it on the seat next to his left thigh, which moved restlessly under hers, and for the first time she realized the intimacy of their position. She struggled to sit up, her eyes darting to his. She'd imposed on him long enough.

His strained expression told her that he was as aware of the closeness of their bodies as she was. "Buchanan—"

"My name is Devlin." His voice was dipped in honey, encircling her with warmth, pulling her toward him.

"Devlin."

Buchanan could hear the question mark in her words, and he bit back the sigh that was forming in his throat. She had no idea what she was doing to him, nestled against him so trustingly, her sweetly rounded bottom pushing against his groin.

In the space of the last few hours she'd done more to upset his equilibrium than any woman he'd ever met. She'd praised him, lectured him, castigated him, infuriated him and turned him on so powerfully he was in real pain.

But she was tired and upset, and there were rules about that. He'd be a gentleman if it killed him.

There it is again, Amanda thought. That look.

For the briefest instant he'd dropped his guard, and an expression of smoldering hunger had sizzled in his dark pupils. She'd seen it before, just before he'd kissed her in the kitchen.

A heady excitement shivered through her. It was a combination of desire and fear that made her stomach flutter. She had the same feeling when she watched the big cats in the zoo and tried to imagine what it would be like to confront one in the wild.

"It's getting late, and I'm beat," he said suddenly. "If you're okay now, I think we'd better get some sleep. I plan to spend tomorrow checking out some more of my old haunts."

"You'll be careful, won't you? I mean, when you're undercover."

A trace of surprise flitted across his unsmiling face. "I'm always careful."

"Yes, I imagine you are. So am I."

The warm hand on her spine suddenly stopped moving. "I'm glad," he said softly. "I like to think you can take care of yourself."

"Yes."

His lips moved closer, and just before they met hers, opened in anticipation.

"Aren't you going to stop me, Amanda?"

She should. She really should, but somehow, she knew that she wouldn't. Her lashes drifted down as she shook her head.

"I tried," he muttered as though to himself before his mouth took hers.

His caressing, seeking tongue gently pushed apart her lips. Liquid fire passed from his mouth to hers, sending a searing sliver of flame through the skin to her bloodstream. Desire flooded through her, pumping urgently to bathe every cell of her body.

Her breath hissed through her parted lips and into his mouth. With a groan, Devlin threw off the afghan and began stroking her thigh with his right hand, his fingers trailing heat through the linen of her slacks.

His left hand cupped the rigid fingers grasping his shirt and folded over them, trapping her small hand against his warm, hard palm. His wrist rested against her breast.

"I can't seem to get enough of you," he murmured against her lips, his breath hot and sweetly moist. "I've been hungry a long time."

His loneliness was a living thing, cutting through the last of her restraint like a heated blade. She could feel his need, different but just as desperate as her own.

She offered her lips, answering the thrust of his tongue with hers. The raspy surface abraded the inner lining of her mouth, raising glorious bumps of pleasure on her skin. Their breath mingled, hot and volatile, fueling the sensation of tingling delight spreading through her.

His lips began exploring the fragile spot beneath her earlobe, moving upward, his tongue tracing the delicate whorls of her ear.

Amanda shivered and her fingers threaded through the crisp thickness of his hair, tugging in drugged pleasure as wave after wave of heated shivers ran over her skin.

Beneath her hip his body hardened and bulged insistently against her. She felt an answering response between her thighs, heightening the delectable feelings swamping her.

She was out of control, spinning in a vortex of helpless desire. Her fingers clutched his neck, and she turned her head, longing for his lips on hers.

His fingers slid between her legs, the heel of his palm moving slowly over the slight mound at the juncture of her thighs in slow, exquisite circles.

Amanda inhaled sharply as sweet spirals of purest pleasure spread through her core. She wanted him, violently, irrationally, irresistibly.

Suddenly he groaned and opened his eyes. She could see naked longing there, and something more, something unfamiliar and powerful.

"I want to make love to you," he murmured in a raspy urgency.

"I know."

He inhaled sharply. "Is that what you want too?"

"Yes. I need you," she whispered, stroking his hard cheek. "I want you. Just for now, for tonight."

"For tonight, sweetheart, I'm all yours."

He moved suddenly, getting to his feet with Amanda still held against his chest. He carried her quickly across the room, his stride confident and steady as she wound her arms around his neck and clung to him.

Her bedroom was bathed in silver light from the full moon. It shone through the loosely woven drapes, leaching the color from the sheets on the four-poster and anointing the walls with a surrealistic wash of glitter.

"This is a dream," he whispered as he let her slide down his body to stand on her feet. "In a few minutes I'm going to wake up and hurt like hell." He looked down at the bulge stretching his fly.

"No dream," she answered in a voice she knew was much too sexy to be hers. She began unbuttoning her blouse, her gaze fastened on his face.

"No dream," he echoed, peeling off his shirt.

His eyes glowed as she threw the blouse onto the end of the bed and kicked off her shoes. She slid her slacks down her legs, watching him tug off his boots and socks and shrug out of his jeans. The moonlight caught in the downy hair covering his long legs, turning the pale blond to silver.

She started to slip out of her panties when he stopped her. "Let me," he whispered, his voice catching in his throat.

His hands were shaking as his fingers slid beneath the elastic, and his palms felt rough as they pushed the lacy satin past her hips.

She moaned as the smooth material slithered down her legs and puddled at her feet.

Then he released the clasp of her bra, stripping away the wispy lace. His breath shivered audibly past his lips as she stood before him, the moonlight outlining her body in shimmering detail.

"Beautiful. So beautiful." Even the harsh note of reverence in his voice was erotic, and Amanda found it hard to breathe.

She trembled, wanting to reach for him but knowing instinctively that he needed to be the aggressor.

"You're shaking, sweetheart. Am I going too fast for you?" He stroked her arm with his left hand.

"No, no."

"Not fast enough?" His whispery voice carried a current of humor, and Amanda realized he was trying to relax her. Or maybe he was asking for direction. Or reassurance. She wasn't sure.

"Just right," she told him with a trembling smile.

"Good. I want to be right for you."

Suddenly he removed his briefs and reached for her. Before she could move, Amanda found herself on the bed, sprawled on top of him, her breasts crushed against the hard plane of his chest, her chin hovering over his sternum. His face was shadowed by the moon-beams falling across his shoulder, and his eyes were silver slits that mesmerized her with the raw hunger gleaming there.

Amanda inched upward, eager to bring her lips close to his. Her thighs brushed his, and her abdomen pressed against the hard bulge of his arousal. She froze, and Buchanan groaned.

"Careful, sweet, or this will be over before we start." His moist breath bathed her face with heat. She placed her palms on his shoulders, feeling the latent power beneath his skin, and then tilted her head, a slow, sensuous smile curving her parted lips.

His breath was coming in short bursts and his face was tight, his brows drawn. "Don't tease me, Mandy. I've been thinking about this since the moment I watched you walk into court the first day of my trial."

Amanda felt a thrill shiver through her as she let her lips settle slowly on his. She loved to hear him say her name so intimately.

His hand burrowed under the thick fall of her hair and curled around her neck, his thumb massaging the throbbing pulse under her jaw. The tiny movement sent waves of scorching signals straight to her brain, turning up the heat.

"Mm," she moaned, as he suddenly rolled over, trapping her beneath him. He straddled her hips, his knees pressing against her thighs, the thrust of his arousal pushing against the gentle swell below her navel.

He looked down at her with glittering eyes, the raspy sound of his breathing filling the room. She could feel his need, his naked desire pulsating between them like a crackling current.

First one warm hand, then the other began to caress her breasts. At the first touch her nipples hardened into throbbing peaks, causing the sensitive dark skin surrounding them to tingle.

His thumbs rotated slowly, teasing, tantalizing, sending little bursts of excitement spurting through her. She closed her eyes, magnifying the delectable sensations a hundredfold.

Then she gasped, and her eyes flew open in shock as his thumbs met in the hollow between her breasts and began trailing down over her ribs, creating rivulets of pulsing heat that flowed through her body.

His fingers traced the hollow of her navel, massaging, kneading, pleasuring, before moving lower until his fingers pressed against the tightly curled thatch of hair at the apex of her thighs.

His lips followed his hand, exciting her beyond bearing, and she began to writhe helplessly. She kicked her heels against the hand-embroidered coverlet, trying to push her body upward to rub against his lips and his hands.

"Easy," he whispered, his tongue teasing her with exquisite skill.

She moaned, and he backed to one side, his bent knee pushing her thighs apart.

"Devlin, oh, Devlin." It was a moan, a plea, a tortured whisper of sound. His body jerked, then stiffened.

"Say it again," he demanded in a scorching whisper. "Say my name like you really know who I am."

Amanda lifted passion-heavy lids and looked at him. His hard features looked strained in the shadowed light. "Devlin," she whispered, capturing his face with her hands. His whiskers were rough against her palms, but instead of causing her pain, the raspiness only added to the need consuming her.

She was a flaming pyre, kindled into a frenzy of need. Inside her center, a throbbing heat was building.

His voice came from a distance, velvet soft and tinged with pain. "I can't wait any longer, sweetheart."

Amanda closed her eyes and waited, her body twitching and ready. She moved her thighs restlessly, trying to ease the hot ache deep inside her.

He entered her slowly, pushing with gentle insistence against her tight muscles. She could feel herself opening, swallowing him inch by hot inch, until he filled her completely.

She moaned and moved against him, seeking relief. She could hear the intake of his breath as she arched frantically toward him, urging him to go faster, harder.

The ache was an unbearable pleasure, driving her, torturing her.

"Now," she sobbed. "Oh, Devlin, *now!*" She reached for him, raking her nails along his sides as she tried to absorb him fully.

Devlin gasped, his muscles straining as he thrust into her over and over, his breath shuddering in a litany of ecstasy.

Her release came in wave after wave of purest joy, bathing her with dazzling golden light. She was spinning, soaring, her legs and arms quivering with the most delicious tingling she'd ever felt.

Heat bloomed between her breasts and spread upward to bathe her neck and face with color.

Devlin stilled, his body still throbbing in hers. He touched her lips with a shaking hand, then lowered his body until she could feel her nipples rubbing his chest.

With one final thrust, he exploded inside her, filling her in hot celebration.

He groaned against her breast and lay still, his fists clenched, his breathing rapid. His skin was covered with a fine layer of musky sweat and his hair was a tangle of damp, disheveled curls that clung to his bronzed forehead in a boyish cap.

Amanda lay beneath him, her breathing mingling with his. She'd never felt such supreme relaxation, such contentment. She was at peace, her body fully sated, the terrible tension of the last few days gone.

She sighed and nuzzled her nose against his neck.

"Mandy," he murmured, turning his head to kiss her gently on her passion-swollen lips. "It was never this good before, never." He smiled against her cheek. "My special lady."

He shifted to her side and pressed his face into the hollow of her shoulder. He was asleep in less than a minute.

Amanda smiled dreamily and let her lashes drift down. You're special too, my Devlin, she told him silently. More special than you know.

Devlin came awake with a jerk, his hand dipping under his pillow for the Beretta. But his fingers only felt cool cotton. Someone had taken his weapon while he slept.

Adrenaline surged through him, and his leg muscles tensed, ready to propel him from the bed as his narrowed gaze searched the room. He inhaled sharply as his gaze collided with the gleaming tangle of silky brown hair resting on his shoulder.

Amanda was here, curled up next to him, her face turned toward the window, her warm, rounded bottom teasing him into an abrupt arousal that refused to be ignored.

He inched back slowly, trying to find a more comfortable position, but his body throbbed insistently. Just seeing her creamy body, naked and bathed in the predawn light, was enough to keep him hard for a lifetime.

He felt his breath catch as his gaze followed the graceful swell of her shoulder, the gentle indentation of her waist, the enticing curve of her hip.

His heart hammered so furiously he was afraid he was going to pass out, and the inside of his mouth turned to sand. It hadn't been a dream.

Devlin swallowed a groan and ran a hand down his rough cheek. He'd really done it this time, and he hadn't even been drunk.

He opened his mouth and exhaled slowly. His lips felt bruised and swollen. Hell, he felt bruised and swollen all the way to the bone, he thought wryly, and it wasn't only physical.

She whimpered softly, stirring as though she were caught in the throes of a disturbing dream, and he pulled her toward him, wincing as her buttocks slid against him. She sighed in her sleep and relaxed against him, as trustingly as a much-loved wife.

Devlin dropped his forehead to the nape of her neck, inhaling sharply as the delicate floral scent of her shampoo filled his nostrils.

Wife. His wife. His mind toyed with the word—and the thought.

He'd never let himself think about marriage and a family during his years on the street. Sooner or later his job would have destroyed any kind of permanent relationship, even if he'd wanted one. And now that he no longer had the job, he was too burned out to give commitment a try.

The taste of regret stung his throat. If he were younger and less cynical, if he had a profession that brought him the same kind of respect that she commanded, maybe—

Devlin stopped cold. He was a fool, thinking about building a future with a woman who could never really forget his past. She might find him sexually stimulating, an acceptable one-night stand, but Amanda would never love him. Hell, she didn't even trust him. Not really. And she'd wanted to. He'd seen her trying.

But only a person who had experienced evil firsthand could understand the demons that drove him. Evil was a newborn baby screaming in pain because his heroin-addicted mother had passed on her addiction. Evil was a rum-soaked teenager with the face of an old man, sitting in the gutter, his strong, young heart pumping out his blood through a knife cut in his belly. Evil was men like George Santalucci who sold death on the installment plan.

Devlin felt his soul reach out to the sleeping woman nestled against him. *Make me forget, Mandy. Take away the memories, give me a new life.*

Even as he breathed the silent plea, he felt the familiar black fog begin to crowd into his head. It was too late for him, too damn late. His rage was so much a part of him it didn't allow room for any other emotion.

A laser-bright shaft of sunshine thrust through the opening between the curtains and fell on the bed. Devlin could feel the warming ray caress his shoulder.

Last night he'd had the best sleep he'd had in a long time, and now unexpectedly, he found himself looking forward to the day. This morning seemed somehow brighter than yesterday, as though it were brand-new and fresh.

Devlin inhaled slowly. He'd stopped looking for the good in his fellow man a long time ago. He thought he'd lost hope of ever finding it. But now, suddenly, here was a woman who was kind and decent and intensely loving. He knew without question that she would die for the little girl he'd only seen in a photograph. No doubt she would even risk her life for him if it became necessary.

He glanced around the pretty, subtly sensuous room. He'd never before slept in a bed with ruffled pillowcases and monogrammed sheets, but God help him, he felt at home there. At peace.

The bitter sadness that had been with him so long didn't throb quite so much when he was with Amanda. He felt…hopeful, renewed, as though he really could start over again. Maybe that job the governor had offered him was still open, he thought suddenly. It wouldn't hurt to check, would it?

Amanda moaned softly, bringing him back to reality with a jerk. He was only kidding himself, thinking he could fight his way past the memories and the anger to try again. He simply didn't have the heart for it. He was too old and too burned out.

He sighed heavily. Beside him Amanda stirred and stretched, her foot sliding against his shin and her bottom twisting with satin softness against his tensed thighs.

Devlin froze, waiting. It took her less than two seconds to realize that she wasn't alone. Her body stopped moving, and her muscles went completely rigid.

He squinted against the shaft of brilliant sunlight shining over her shoulder and took a deep breath as she scooted away and turned to face him, pulling the sheet over her nude body at the same time.

"Buchanan?" Her voice was pinched with guilt.

"Good morning." He waited, watching her face closely. Her hair was in wild disarray around her face and her lips were pink and slightly fuller, swollen by his kisses.

The arousal that he told himself he shouldn't have prodded him as she licked her lips and cleared her throat. "G-good morning." Her eyes searched his face. "I…what time is it?"

Devlin glanced at the clock. "Ten past six."

Her face flamed. "I…you, I'm so ashamed."

Devlin felt as though he were strangling to death. "Damn it to hell," he muttered, throwing off the sheet draped over his thighs and jerking toward his side of the bed. His stomach protested the abrupt movement, and he halted, pushing his hand against his belly to ease the strain on the permanently weakened muscles.

"Wait! Don't go." Her voice rose in protest.

"I'm not made of stone, Amanda." His voice was a hoarse growl. "When a lady tells me she's ashamed to have slept with me, I figure the game's over and I lost. No sense sticking around to hear the formal announcement.''

"Not you, Devlin. Me. I'm ashamed of myself.'' Her voice broke, and she bit her lip. "How could I have forgotten about Jessie? How could I have...'' Her voice trailed off, and she sat in silence, the yellow sheet bunched against her throat.

"Enjoyed yourself so much?'' he finished very softly, holding his breath.

She nodded, her eyes downcast, her breathing shallow and irregular. "I was only thinking of myself last night. And...and what you were making me feel. How could I have been so selfish?''

A wave of tenderness cascaded over Devlin, easing some of the tension imprisoning his spine.

She watched him with guilty eyes as he arranged the ruffled pillows against the massive headboard, then leaned back and pulled her into his arms. She stiffened, then settled back against him, her head resting in the hollow of his shoulder.

"You're not the least bit selfish,'' he whispered into the silken tumble of her hair. "You're warm and loving and most of all, human. We're both human.'' He paused, searching for the right words.

There was so much he *could* tell her, about the emptiness inside him that she'd filled with her light, about the lonely childhood that had taught him more about discipline than about love, about the weary sorrow that followed him wherever he went, but he'd never shared his innermost feelings with anyone before, and he was afraid to try.

He took a deep breath. "Last night you needed to feel alive, and so did I. We needed each other.''

She tossed her head from side to side in agitation, and Devlin tightened his grip.

"But I was out of control,'' she whispered, twisting the sheet. "I ignored everything but myself. Everything. My daughter, my responsibilities to the public, my reputation.''

"So?''

"So I've never done that before. I feel...guilty.''

"Hm, so because you feel guilty you're going to spoil the comfort we gave each other. Is that it?'' His voice was gentle. "Would it make you feel better if I felt guilty too?'' He stroked her arm with his palm.

Amanda inhaled sharply. "No, of course not.'' Her voice had lost some of its desolation, and he pressed his point.

"What we created together was beautiful, Mandy. It was...a kind of affirmation, a testament of faith that we haven't lost the ability to feel, to reach out to another human being. That the future is still there for you—and for Jessie."

"What about your future?"

His lids dipped. "In my business you learn to take things a day at a time. I've gotten out of the habit of thinking about more than that."

My poor Devlin, Amanda thought, dropping her gaze. How terribly unhappy he must be, not allowing himself to think beyond the present.

"Don't look so sad, sweetheart," he said gently, crooking a finger under her chin and lifting her face to his. "Santalucci can't spoil the magic we made last night, not unless you let him. He's not all powerful. And we can beat him. We can get Jessie back." He brushed his lips over her furrowed brow.

She looked so lovely, her face still slack from sleep and yet so fragile and vulnerable. He wanted her so much his bones hurt, but he wasn't kidding himself. A physical relationship would only lead to problems. Serious, dangerous problems for both of them. What had happened last night must be the end of his obsession, not the beginning. It wasn't going to happen again. He wouldn't let it happen.

He threw back the sheet and stood up. "Stay in bed as long as you like. I'm going to go for a run." He bent down and brushed a kiss across her lips.

Amanda smiled and closed her eyes. She had to admit she was still exhausted. As she drifted off to sleep, she thought about his words. He was right. They'd helped each other last night, giving and receiving out of caring. How could that be wrong?

Buchanan was standing at the kitchen counter when she wandered in at a few minutes past eight. He was dressed in white denim cutoffs and a skimpy tank top bearing the logo of a famous Ensenada cantina. On his feet he wore an expensive pair of running shoes and white socks with mismatched stripes.

A damp, ragged V trailed down the back of the orange shirt and disappeared beneath the handle of his gun, which was tucked snugly into the waistband.

"Don't tell me you run with that gun stuffed into your shorts?" she said in amazement, forgetting the sudden embarrassment she'd felt the moment she saw him.

"It goes where I go. I'd feel naked without it."

Just the smell of her hair was exciting him, bringing up memories of burying his hot face in that seductive mane.

Amanda turned away and busied herself pouring a cup of coffee.

Skittish, he thought. Like she wasn't used to handling the morning after. But then, inexplicably, neither was he.

She brushed by him, her body moving with dainty grace, and he felt a hot surge of blood to his loins. Damn, he thought in silent chagrin. He was supposed to be over this type of adolescent infatuation.

He wiped his brow with a paper towel and leaned against the tiled counter, his arms and ankles crossed.

"Feeling better?"

She gave him a startled look. "Actually, I feel wonderful." She blushed. "Thanks to you."

A balloon of happiness inflated in his chest before he ruthlessly burst it. "It was my pleasure." Oh great, he thought. Double entendre in the morning.

Her jaw dropped, and then she giggled. The balloon swelled again, and he inhaled deeply. He didn't want to feel like this. He couldn't risk this kind of lightheartedness. It would hurt too much when he had to leave her.

Turning away, he poured himself some coffee, holding the ceramic cup between his palms. Silence lengthened between them as he stared down at the sparkling counter.

Less than seventy-two hours ago he had had no responsibilities, no obligations, nothing to tie him down. He thought that he'd been content enough, but now he realized he'd simply been hiding. From Santalucci, from the life he'd come to hate, from himself.

Standing here with Amanda, he was suddenly face-to-face with all the things he'd tried so hard to forget. He sighed and took a deep swallow of coffee, letting the caffeine stir his blood.

"I listened to the tape again," Amanda said suddenly, her face somber. "I tried to imagine what Jessie must be feeling, but...I had to stop." She squared her shoulders. "Once, when I was about three or four, I got lost in the crowd at the beach. All I could see were people's knees, and everyone looked alike." She stared into her cup. "I was so scared I couldn't even cry."

He turned around to face her, his face impassive. "What did you do?"

"I found a little clump of grass and sat down on it. My mama had told me not to get my new playsuit dirty." A self-conscious smile curved her mouth. "All I could think about was doing what my mama told me."

Devlin wanted to touch her, to kiss away the poignant wisps of memory lining her brow. But he didn't dare. "You were being a good girl," he said, leaning back against the counter. "Following the rules."

"Yes. Always." She picked a dead leaf from the geranium on the shelf over the sink and threw it into the trash. She smiled wistfully. "My father found me finally. He said I was very smart to wait for him in a safe place. He said I'd make a good attorney someday because I understood logic." Her smile faded. "At the time I didn't know what logic was."

"My pop believed in a good left hook." Devlin flexed the fingers of one hand. The knuckle was purple, and there was a black scab sealing the split skin. His hand slowly closed into a fist. "Tony's the one who believed in logic. He had a golden tongue. He could talk a lion into baby-sitting a lamb."

He turned his head and stared through the window at the brilliant red rosebuds waving in the morning breeze. The velvet pedals reminded him of blood.

"He was forty years old when he died, an idealist who believed in the system—like you. He felt sorry for that damned Montez. Used to give him money. Thought he could trust the kid." He hung his head, his big shoulders heaving. "I told him, Amanda, never trust anyone but your partner, but he wouldn't listen. Montez tipped Santalucci about the buy we'd set up."

Amanda hesitated, then put a hand on his shoulder. He jerked and spun around to face her. His eyes were empty, as though he'd gone far away.

"Devlin, Tony made the mistake, not you. Stop trying to take the blame. Stop beating up on yourself."

He touched her hair, letting the dark, sweet-smelling tendrils sift through his fingers. "I don't have a lot of friends, Mandy. Working undercover, it's damn near impossible to have a private life. I guess I just...miss him."

His slanted smile was self-conscious, and Amanda's heart filled with pain for him. She covered his hand with her own, and he threaded his fingers between hers. His palm felt warm and dry.

"I understand. It's a little like being a judge. I never see my attorney friends anymore. On the bench I have to be completely impartial, and it's hard if I'm close to one of the lawyers arguing before me."

His eyes kindled into a warmth that enthralled her. He was not a man for sentiment, but somehow she'd touched him.

He lifted their entwined hands to his lips and kissed the back of hers. "I wish I'd met you a long time ago, Mandy. Maybe...maybe it could have worked out, the two of us."

Her heart swelled with some unidentifiable emotion. It wasn't love, it couldn't be. But it hurt her to hear the unspoken message underneath his words, even though he was right. A relationship between them now was unthinkable. He opposed everything she believed in, and she would only make demands he couldn't fulfill.

Besides, he didn't love her and she didn't love him. No relationship could work for long without love sustaining it. She knew that. So why did she feel as though she were grieving?

"How about breakfast? I'll buy," he said gruffly, and Amanda knew that he was embarrassed to have shared a piece of himself with her.

She gave him a cheerful smile. "Sounds nice, but let me wake up first."

He chuckled and released her hand. She sighed and carried her mug into the breakfast room. He'd brought in the Sunday paper, and it lay on the table in front of her.

Sinking into her chair, she stared at the colorful comic section, sadness welling inside her.

"What's wrong?"

"Sunday morning is our time, Jessie's and mine. Our special time together."

His rubber soles whispered softly on the tile as he walked around the table and sat down.

"Tell me."

Amanda touched the rim of her cup. "She brings me coffee and we read the paper in bed. Then we go riding in the foothills before we have breakfast at a pancake house." Her voice trembled. "I'd better call the stable, tell them we're not coming."

She started to get up, but Buchanan reached out and stopped her with a hand on her arm. "Don't. I haven't been riding in a long time, and it'll do you good to get some exercise. Help diffuse some of the stress." He massaged the back of her hand with his thumb. "Besides, this is a chance to practice your explanation for Jessie's absence. And be sure to tell them she won't be in town for her lessons for—make it a month. Okay?"

"Okay."

It made sense. Lying was difficult for her; she could use all the practice she could get.

Buchanan stood up. "It'll take me ten minutes to shower and change, and then we can go." He hesitated, eyeing the white cotton jumpsuit and yellow huaraches she'd put on after her shower. "Unless it'll take you longer to, uh, get out of *that* thing."

An involuntary smile tugged at her lips. He sounded very appealing all of a sudden, in his masculine confusion.

"Ten minutes will be perfect."

Chapter 9

Buchanan rode Dervish, the temperamental black stallion that was part Arabian. He slouched forward in the saddle, his hat pulled low over his head, his thigh muscles tight. His style was purely Western. Hardly pretty by show standards, Amanda decided, but very sexy.

The stallion was eager to run and pranced excitedly down the rutted lane leading to the open country behind the barn. Melody, the spirited roan who was Amanda's favorite, sidestepped nervously, her eyes fixed on the larger horse next to her.

"You know the country, you lead the way," Buchanan told her, glancing around the empty mesa.

Amanda tried to ignore the long black Chrysler gliding to a stop on the weed-lined access road bordering the stable grounds, but a sudden flash of sunlight on glass sent a chill sliding down her back. Someone in the car had binoculars trained on them.

"They're watching us," she said uneasily.

"Looks like it." Buchanan shrugged and leaned the heel of his left hand on the high pommel of the Western saddle. He was wearing jeans and a faded plaid shirt under a tan leather vest. Beneath the vest was his shoulder holster. "Gonna be hot today. Serves 'em right if they're charbroiled by the time we're finished with our ride."

In spite of his unconcern, Amanda was jittery, and as soon as they were safely away from the congestion of the stable yard, she gripped the braided reins tightly and urged her mare into a gallop, eager to escape those prying eyes.

Melody snorted eagerly and surged forward, mane flying, hooves thundering over the sunbaked terrain that contained little more than piñon and juniper.

Behind her, Amanda caught sight of Buchanan's startled expression as the roan spurted ahead of the stallion, and she grinned. Now it was her turn to show him a thing or two. She'd been riding since she was five and had even won a few blue ribbons in local shows while she'd been in high school.

Putting her mouth close to the mare's dark ear, she shouted, "C'mon girl, let's fly."

The wind whipped at the long sleeves of her white silk blouse and fluttered her fawn-colored breeches. Her hat flew from her head and trailed from its chin strap behind her.

She loved the feeling of control it gave her to handle such a high-strung animal, and her spirits lifted. For the moment everything else was forgotten except the exhilaration of the ride.

Ducking her head, she risked another look back. Dervish was gaining, coming up hard on Melody's right flank. The stallion was running effortlessly, his stride smooth and graceful. Buchanan was leaning low over the horse's powerful neck, his heels tucked tight, his back straight.

Damn, she muttered to herself. There were going to catch up. She shouted encouragement to the mare and crouched lower to reduce wind resistance. Adrenaline pumped through her veins and her heart pounded. She loved a race.

The stallion would win easily over distance, but in a sprint her skill and the mare's quick start gave her an advantage, one she intended to press to the fullest.

"*Faster, Melody!*" The wind whipped the words from her mouth, and she gasped. Never before had she ridden so recklessly.

As though she could sense her rider's determination, the mare ran faster, muscles pounding, lungs straining, hooves barely touching the ground.

But the stallion was gaining. His nose was even with the mare's flying tail. With her sweat-flecked flanks. With the saddle.

Amanda's frustrated gaze locked with Buchanan's and he grinned, his gray eyes alight with the glint of battle. She ground her teeth. He intended to beat her.

Dervish pounded forward until his nose was even with Melody's.

The two horses galloped side by side, matching strides, neither pulling ahead.

The thunder of the iron shoes on packed dirt filled her ears, and the high desert wind reddened her cheeks. She yelled encouragement to the mare, but Melody was starting to tire, and Amanda knew they would have to slow down.

She turned to Buchanan, intending to concede a tie, when Melody suddenly broke stride and swerved to the right, avoiding a large cholla in her path. Dervish swerved as well, to avoid the faltering mare.

Amanda could feel the horse going down, but there wasn't anything she could do. The stallion was to her right, too close for her to jump free.

She made her body limp and ducked her head, preparing to hit the ground. She heard a hoarse shout, then hard hands snatched her from the saddle. Before she could blink, she was pulled across Buchanan's thighs, his left arm holding her against him. She hung on to his waist, feet dangling, head tucked into his side, as he fought to control the frightened stallion.

His muscles were sinewy bands beneath her as he kept Dervish from rearing in panic. Melody faltered, and then, freed of the weight of her rider, managed to right herself. She ran on, her pace slowing gradually until she finally stopped, her chest heaving.

Dervish stood panting, his head down and his tail swishing. Sweat glistened on his slick black flanks, the distinctive moist odor mingling with the pungent scent of horseflesh and leather.

Amanda's nose was buried in Buchanan's side, her rasping breath dampening the leather of his vest. Her thigh hurt where the saddle horn had bruised her flesh, and she was dizzy.

"Are you all right?" he asked urgently, his voice rough.

"Yes." Her pride was as bruised as her thigh, but other than that she was unhurt.

Buchanan grunted, then put a warm hand on her bottom. She hadn't expected the intimate touch, and surprise loosened her grip on his lean torso. She started to slide, her hip rubbing hard against his thigh.

She felt his swift intake of breath a second before his hand yanked on her belt and pulled her upright. His arm kept her from overbalancing, and she ended up sitting in his lap, her hips squeezed between the high pommel and his abdomen, her shoulder angled into his. He held her as easily as if she were a child, but the feelings he was exciting in her were not in the least childlike.

Their eyes locked. For the first time since she'd met him, he looked frightened.

"I thought I was going down." She tried to keep the quaver from her voice but failed.

"So did I." His lashes lowered, hiding his expression.

His shirt was damp, and Amanda could smell the faint spicy scent of his after-shave mingling with the musky odor of sweat and the pungent aroma of heat rising from the sandy wash bottom. Beneath the cotton shirt a strong, vibrant beat echoed in his chest.

Her hand tightened around his neck, and she dropped her head to his shoulder. A sense of peace spread through her, and she closed her eyes. The sun was warm overhead, and the mesa was blissfully quiet. She was safe here and content. Buchanan wouldn't let her get hurt. Not ever.

A shaky sigh escaped her lips, and she nuzzled her cheek against his collarbone. Nice. This is nice, she thought as the dizziness gradually faded.

"Let's go see if the mare's all right." Buchanan's voice was gruff.

Buchanan set Dervish into a walk. His arm held her like a band of iron, yet it was supple enough to cushion her against the motion of the stallion's gait.

The play of his hip muscles against hers sent prickles of pleasure shooting along the sensitive network of nerves just under her skin, and she pressed her thighs tightly together in an attempt to remain perfectly still.

When they reached Melody, Buchanan dismounted first and helped Amanda from the saddle. His hands encircled her waist with rough strength, lifting her easily and setting her down gently.

As her boots touched the hardpan she stared directly at the hollow of his throat. A heavy pulse pounded beneath his tanned skin, contradicting the impassive calmness of his shadowed features.

The mare had stopped at the edge of the dry wash, near a stand of stunted piñon. The trail had turned toward the road at this point, and there were only a few dozen yards separating Melody from the traffic.

"She looks all right," Amanda said aloud. "I was afraid she'd bolt into the road."

"She's too smart for that."

Buchanan tied Dervish to a nearby pine and began to examine the mare. His touch was light but thorough, his voice low and soothing, as he ran his hand over each of her legs in turn.

A strange feeling of emptiness came over Amanda as she held

Melody's bridle and watched Buchanan work his way around the animal's flanks.

He was such a complex man. More complex than she'd first realized. In her courtroom and again at his house she'd seen only the toughness, the leashed violence, the barely contained anger that seethed just beneath the surface. But the longer she was near him, the more she realized there was a wellspring of kindness buried deep inside him and a gentleness that he ruthlessly denied, perhaps even to himself.

Sadness filled the emptiness as she realized that he had deliberately chosen the life he'd led. He'd made the choice between violence and compassion. He was the one who scorned kindness, the one who denied the gentler side of his nature.

He'd chosen his path a long time ago, Amanda thought, sighing. Why did that realization make her so damned mad?

Buchanan stood up and patted Melody on the rump. "She's fine." He grinned. "Proud of herself, too."

The roan was breathing normally now, and her intelligent eyes were bright with curiosity as Amanda rubbed her nose. "Good girl," she murmured softly. "You won by a nose."

"Uh-uh. It was a tie." Buchanan took off his hat and wiped his brow with a blue bandanna that he took from his pocket.

"No way! The race was over once we reached that stand of junipers on the right."

Buchanan laughed, a surprisingly carefree sound that warmed her intensely. "Is that right? How come you didn't mention that before we started?" He carried his hat in his hand and moved closer.

"You can't expect a mare to run as far as a stallion," she protested as he towered over her. In the bright sunlight the thick lashes framing his silver eyes cast spiky shadows on his bronzed cheeks.

"Tsk, tsk, Amanda. That sounds like a sexist remark to me." His body shadowed hers, keeping the blazing sun from beating directly on her.

"It's not," she protested. "Besides, a gentleman would never dispute the word of a lady."

"We both know I'm not a gentleman, don't we?"

A gust of wind blew a waving tendril of hair across her lips, and before she could brush it away, Buchanan reached out and trapped the thick brown wave in his hand. He was riding without gloves and his fingers were raspy against her cheek.

"While you're undeniably a lady." His knuckles brushed the skin of her cheeks, mesmerizing her like the falling of a steady rain.

"You make that sound like some kind of...of dreaded condition."

He chuckled. "If it is, I like it." He tossed his Stetson onto the pommel of Melody's saddle, and threaded both hands through Amanda's hair, trapping her. Slowly, inexorably, he tipped her face upward until her lips were in a direct line with his.

"You make everything so special," he murmured. "You make even a hard case like me feel special. I've never felt that before."

"You *are* special. Maybe that's why you're such a complicated man."

"I'm not complicated, Mandy. I know what has to be done and I do it. I just don't spend a lot of time second-guessing myself or the world I live in."

His face filled her sight, dark and intense, his eyes lit from within. The heat radiating from his skin rivaled the sun for warmth, and there was a fine layer of moisture darkening his hairline.

"Isn't that lonely?" She swallowed the urge to trace the strong curve of his upper lip with her tongue. "Always being so sure you're right?"

"I don't know. I've always been alone."

He tilted his head, bringing him closer, and his mouth lowered until his lips were only a fraction of an inch from hers. His breath was moist and sweet. "Darling Mandy. You're making me feel things I don't want to," he breathed softly as his lips took hers possessively.

His body jerked, as though he couldn't control it, and then his arms dropped to her shoulders, his hands wrapping over her upper arms like a warm blanket. His fingers massaged her skin, pleasuring her, exciting her.

Slowly his left hand came up, tracing the gentle slant of her shoulder, the delicate curve of her throat, the sweep of her jaw. His fingers slid beneath her ear and his thumb began massaging the hollow below her hairline.

A rush of need flooded her veins, moving through her in a hot wave, gathering strength with each beat of her heart. The breeze ruffled her hair and cooled her heated cheeks.

His tongue traced the full outline of her lower lip and Amanda sighed. She slid her hands under the vest and around his rib cage to the hollow of his spine. She loved the hard, rugged lines of his back and the unyielding steel of his muscles. His raw masculinity made her feel more feminine, more seductive, than she'd ever felt before. For once she let her emotions take over, blocking out the intellect that usually ruled her.

She wanted him, here, now, with the wind caressing their skin and the scent of sage in the air. It was foolish, it was impulsive, it was real.

Last night he'd taken her beyond her carefully set boundaries, beyond the rigid control she'd kept on her mind and body. And now that the door was open, she wanted to rush through again, to immerse herself in that magnificent feeling of fulfillment he'd brought into her life.

"Devlin," she whispered, loving the sound of his name.

"Hmm?" he murmured against her lips.

"I want you."

"What?" He lifted his head and stared at her, his angular cheeks flooding with dusky color.

"Make love to me."

He inhaled swiftly. "Oh baby, don't do this to me. I'm already in over my head as it is." He raked his hand through his disheveled hair. "Mandy, I'm walking a very thin line here. I've been where you are. I know what emotional stress can do to common sense, and I—"

"Don't you want to?"

"God, yes, but I—we can't. When this is all over, I want to walk away with my pride. And if I took advantage of you now, I'd hate myself."

She felt the sting of rejection, and the warmth fled from her soul. He didn't want her. Twisting away, she tried to escape, but his hands prevented her from moving.

His sigh was ragged. "I'm trying to be noble here, but I need some help." He crushed her to his chest. "Tell me you understand."

His heart pounded in her ear, and his chest muscles were hard planes of tension. He was trying to protect her. From him or maybe from herself.

Gratitude mingled with the hurt. "Of course, you're right. We have to be realistic. I understand," she said in a muffled whisper against his vest. He didn't love her. He could never love her, and he was trying to tell her the truth without causing her more pain.

"Good. I'm glad one of us does."

He dropped his arms, and she stepped away. Above her head the sun dipped beneath a towering cloud bank, and she felt a sudden urge to laugh. Appropriate, she thought. That's just how she felt, as though a warm light inside her had suddenly been extinguished.

Nearby, Melody took a little dancing step and snorted. Dervish whinnied in response, and the mare stepped backward until the trailing rein stopped her.

Devlin lifted his head and swore.

"What's wrong?" she asked urgently, following his gaze. The black car was now parked along the narrow road, a scant fifty feet away.

"Damn Blades," he said with a cold look. "C'mon, let's go back. This wasn't such a great idea after all."

Amanda nodded, her body still alive with the urgent feelings he'd aroused in her. "I hate this."

Devlin flinched. He'd wanted to make her forget for a while, to give her a rest from the terror that must be inside her. He'd wanted to take some of the burden from her, at least for a time. Instead, all he'd done was hurt her. Just as he always seemed to hurt the ones he cared about.

He sighed and reached for the mare's reins. "That's why I'm going back to see Lola this afternoon. This time she's going to tell me what I want to know."

"No!" Amanda stared at him in disbelief. "I won't let you."

The sympathy fled from his face, and his eyes became glacial.

"You don't have any choice, Amanda. You promised to give me a free hand, remember?"

Hesitantly she touched the faint indentation in his cheek where his rare smile sometimes formed a crease. He stiffened, but he didn't move away.

"I know it's not fair, but I—I can't seem to get that poor woman's face out of my mind. She's just a victim, Devlin. As much as Jessie. And she has a child who needs her." Her voice broke. "Please try to understand."

Devlin hardened his defenses. "You're the one who needs to understand, Mandy. I wasn't going to hurt her. She just needed to think that I would."

She wanted to believe him, but she could still remember the clutch of fear in her stomach when he'd backed Lola up against the wall. She couldn't bear to think of Devlin turning into that cold frightening man again. For some inexplicable reason it would hurt her terribly.

"You can find Jessie without her help, I know you can."

His stomach tightened at the beseeching look darkening her vivid green eyes. A dozen different emotions shot through him. Not once in twelve years as a cop had he ever compromised. Not with his superiors, not with his personal code of ethics. He hated restraint of any kind. As a scruffy kid he'd fought it so ferociously his father had finally used brute force to whip him into line.

But if he refused her request he would hurt her even more than he already had. If he couldn't give her physical comfort, at least he could give her some emotional peace.

Calling himself every kind of fool, he gave in. "Okay, if that's what you want. I give you my word I won't visit Lola again." The words left a foul taste in his mouth, and he scowled.

"Thank you."

She'd certainly made a mess of a promising morning, Amanda told herself in disgust. And made an idiot of herself in the process. She'd been clinging to him like some kind of wimpy heroine in a melodrama. Where was her pride? Her vaunted self-control? Buchanan was right. Emotional stress was making her far too vulnerable.

No more, she promised herself. She'd make no more personal demands on him.

In silence, he helped her to mount, then settled himself in the saddle. The ride back to the stable was slow and easy and neither of them said a word.

When they drove past, the black car was still there, waiting to follow them home.

Buchanan dug the sharp blade of his pocketknife deep into the soft pine, removing the bark with quick, efficient strokes. A shower of rough splinters fell to his feet as he leaned forward in the tubular patio chair, his boots planted wide apart, his forearms resting on his knees.

As he worked, the knife flashed in the sun, releasing the cool scent of pine. He loved the smell of newly cut wood. It reminded him of Christmas when he was a little boy.

Christmas Eve, the night he and his sisters decorated the tree, had been one of the few times Sergeant Buchanan had relaxed the rigid rules that governed his household, one of the few times laughter had sounded in their Spartan quarters.

Devlin ran his fingers over the rough outline he'd carved, studying the grain. He'd found the log in a stack next to the garage, nicely seasoned and unknotted, the kind he liked.

He'd started carving during his trial, teaching himself as he went along. Working with his hands had kept him from drinking too much during the empty hours he'd spent alone and brooding. His first project had been a replica of the gun he'd used to kill Gus D'Amato.

This was going to be a bear, a chubby panda. He told himself it was a welcome-home present for Jessica Wainwright. He'd decided to make it for her when he'd gone looking for Amanda and found her sitting on the little girl's bed, poring over a large, leather-bound picture album.

The kid was cute, he had to admit it, with big green eyes like her mother's and long wavy hair that was a shade lighter than Amanda's but just as thick.

He'd stood in the doorway, listening as Amanda had told him story after story about her daughter, stories that gradually painted a portrait of a loving bond between the two, a bond Devlin had trouble fully understanding. He and his father had been adversaries from the day he'd taken his first steps, and his mother had never dared to interfere.

Devlin squinted past the pool and studied the brown hills beyond. He'd been uncomfortable listening to Amanda talk about her daughter. She'd been perfectly pleasant to him since they'd returned home, but he could sense a new desolation in her. It was as though she'd been trying to find some relief in her happy memories.

He'd felt the same way himself, lots of times, when a particularly grisly case had gotten to him. But he'd never had anyone to share his pain.

Devlin pushed the blade into the wood and twisted. The tendons in his wrist bulged as he gouged a ragged chunk from the pine.

Muttering a crude obscenity, Devlin threw the log onto an empty chair and shoved his knife into his pocket. He was too restless to concentrate. He needed to move, to burn off some of the tension that was tying his muscles into knots.

Moving into Amanda's house had been a bad decision, he knew now. But he was stuck. Stuck listening to the seductive cadence of her melodious voice, stuck smelling the elusive scent of her perfume, stuck wanting her more than he'd ever wanted another woman.

Devlin stood up and began pacing the patio. He'd thought the physical need would go away, once he'd made love to her. That he'd stop thinking of her in ways that made him squirm with hunger.

Always before, when he'd been with a woman, he'd called the shots. He'd offered his body and taken hers with a detached kind of passion that had satisfied his physical needs, but little else. It was the way he'd wanted it.

But Amanda had gotten inside him, to a place he'd kept private and untouched. She'd pushed aside the scar tissue and made him long for a normal life.

Devlin stood at the fence, his hands gripping the cedar as though he wanted to rip the boards from the ground. He didn't want to care about her.

Come clean, buddy, he told himself angrily. You refuse to care because you're just plain scared. And with damn good reason. It wasn't safe to care about anyone. Sooner or later they all died.

Like his mother who wore herself out trying to please that demanding bastard she was married to. And his kid sister, Angie, who'd fought so hard to live before the leukemia had finally defeated her at twenty-one. And Tony, his best friend who made him see the beauty amidst the filth.

His fist clenched, and he beat it softly against the fence post. He'd lived on the fringes of society so long he'd learned not to care about anything but the next bust. He was alone because that was the way it had to be.

Amanda and her daughter were simply another case to him, a fortuitous twist of fate that allowed him to go after Santalucci with the unofficial sanction of the law.

A hard smile froze on his lips as he thought of the symmetry of providence. He was going to kill a man he hated with every ounce of strength he possessed, and probably end up a hero in Amanda's eyes.

She'd be grateful and generous in her thanks, and maybe she'd even love him a little, but it would soon fade, once her life had returned to normal.

The truth lay there, harsh and bitter, scalding him with acid. She'd responded to him because he was a skillful lover and because she was scared and vulnerable. But in the cold morning light, he was the last guy she would ever want.

And even if she did want him, what did he have to offer her? A questionable reputation, a modest pension that barely covered his needs, a family tree that had more scoundrels than gentlemen hanging on it? In a nutshell, he was a bitter, burned-out cop without a job. He knew it, and so did she.

Devlin swore aloud and turned on his heel. He had to get out of this place for a few hours, maybe have a few beers in a bar somewhere and try to get a fix on his next move.

Amanda was still in Jessie's room. She looked up in surprise as he paused in front of the open door, her car keys jingling in his hand.

"Amanda, I'm going out for a while. Do some more scouting around." He wasn't used to explaining his movements, and it annoyed him to have to do it now. But he could sense that she was depressed and upset, and he didn't want her to do something stupid while he was gone.

"I'll go with you." She stood up, her eyes darting to the large album lying open on the frilly white coverlet. Jessica's round face laughed up at them, her eyes sparkling with childish glee. "What should I wear?"

Guilt twisted around his heart, making him angry at himself. He'd been out by the pool, thinking only of what he wanted while Amanda had been contemplating her daughter's death.

"This is a solo trip," he said, forcing himself to meet her anxious gaze.

"You said you were going to lay low until we made the announcement about your being my bodyguard. I think I should go with you, just in case."

Worry crowded the wariness from her thickly fringed eyes, and Devlin felt as though a baseball bat had just slammed into his patched-up gut.

"I changed my mind," he said brusquely. "I have something I have to do, and you can't come."

He saw the blush of anger rise past the open collar of her softly clinging shirt, and he grunted to himself in satisfaction. That anger would keep her from worrying about him.

He gave her a curt nod and walked away. For some reason he suddenly didn't feel like leaving.

On Sunday afternoon George Santalucci played golf at the Albuquerque Country Club where he was a member. It was the part of his routine that had never varied during the days when Buchanan and Tony Cruz had been trying to turn up enough incriminating evidence on the man to indict him for dealing, and Buchanan was pretty sure he hadn't changed.

A discreet phone call had confirmed the presence of Santalucci on the course, and Devlin had shown up on the eighteenth green, unannounced. He'd taken a chance, betting that the burly crime czar would feel more intrigued than threatened by his sudden appearance.

"So, *cop*, I was right all along. The fancy full-dress funeral was a fake," Santalucci said as he braked his cart to a stop next to the bench where Devlin was sitting.

His foursome consisted of his two top lieutenants, trim, sharp-faced men with razor cuts and two-hundred-dollar golf shirts, and his bodyguard, a former linebacker for the Los Angeles Raiders.

"Looks like it," Devlin drawled, raising his arms to show the bodyguard his gun.

The beefy man shot a questioning look at his employer, and Santalucci shook his head impatiently. "Look around. He's not going to shoot anyone here, in front of so many witnesses. Not even a gun-slinger like Buchanan would be that stupid.''

The bodyguard nodded and took up a position behind Buchanan, his arms folded over his massive chest, his eyes dutifully trained on his boss.

Santalucci was a big man, nearly six foot five, taller than Devlin by three or four inches. He'd worked as a stevedore in his youth, and his body still carried some of the hard muscle of heavy physical labor in spite of the sloppy paunch pushing against the custom-designed knit shirt. He was in his mid-fifties, his tanned face slickly handsome and his thick hair showing little gray.

Devlin made his amusement obvious. Santalucci was letting him know he was in charge, which was fine with him. Spreading his arms along the back of the bench, Devlin waited. Let the bastard come to you, he reminded himself calmly. Let him wonder.

"I got your message," the older man said tersely as he climbed from the cart. The two lieutenants remained seated, their cold eyes fixed on Buchanan like rifle barrels.

"Which message?" Devlin crossed one booted ankle over his knee and flicked a blade of brown grass from the toe.

"About your cozy relationship with the lady judge." The crime boss's voice sank to an oily purr. "Blades tells me you two were going at it hot and heavy this morning, out on the Turquoise Trail." Santalucci's knowing laugh sent spikes of fury digging into Buchanan's spine, but his expression remained fixed.

"I'm glad he enjoyed it."

"I shoulda known after you beat that murder rap you had a thing going with the judge. A hotshot like you always has an angle."

Buchanan shrugged. "A man's got to take care of himself."

Santalucci's full lips curled into a sneer as his reptilian gaze lingered on Buchanan's flat belly. "I heard they pumped nine pints of blood into you before they could stop the bleeding and get you sewed back together. Next time you won't be so lucky."

Buchanan could feel waves of malignant anger rolling toward him, and an instant jolt of adrenaline flooded his veins. His mind, however, remained clear. Santalucci had taken the bait. Now it was time to reel him in.

"If you hit me, you might as well kiss off an acquittal." His grin flashed, icy hard and derisive. "Like Blades says, the lady likes what I do for her. She has a vested interest in keeping me around, about as much as she has in keeping her daughter alive."

Santalucci's black brows lifted skeptically. "Too bad Gus didn't aim lower with that .357," he said in a cold, angry voice.

Buchanan let his grin widen. "Actually, he did me a favor. The lady likes my body all cut up. Think it's sexy as hell, a real turn-on. She likes her men...rough."

Inside an acid wash of revulsion stung his stomach. He was painting a picture of a woman who was as far removed from Amanda Wainwright as she could be, and he hated to give Santalucci this kind of sick gossip to spread around the city, but right now he had no choice. A bluff was his only weapon.

"If you're such a *good friend* of the lady, how come you've been out of town for two years? Seems to me it'd be pretty hard to make it with her long distance, even for you, Buchanan."

Devlin gave him a pitying look. "What makes you think I haven't been here? You have someone following me around all that time?" He forced himself to take regular breaths. The hook wasn't set, not yet.

Santalucci frowned. "All right, what's your point?" A faint red tinge mottled the tan of his bull neck as his jaw thrust forward belligerently.

"Just this. I'm willing to act as a go-between in this deal—for a price."

A gleam of interest flashed briefly in the flat, black pupils. "How much?"

"Two hundred thousand."

The red spread along Santalucci's cheek bones in an angry wave. "Very funny, *cop.*"

"Yeah, ain't it. I figured if I was worth that to you dead, I ought to be worth that alive. *If* I help you beat the rap, that is."

Santalucci glanced over Buchanan's shoulder, an ugly look of cunning masking the handsome features.

Devlin knew that he was very close to dying. One word from Santalucci and that mountain of a bodyguard would snap his neck like a twig before he had a chance to reach for the Beretta. He steeled himself to move at the flick of Santalucci's eyelid.

"How do I know you can deliver?"

Devlin felt the relief all the way to his bones. The hook was set. "Because I say I can." He waved an impatient hand. "Think about it, George. What good would it do me to con you? You know where I am, you can send your hit squad anytime you want."

Santalucci was listening, his tiny eyes narrowed with concentration. "Go on."

"The judge wants me to pretend to be her bodyguard. I'll be with her twenty-four hours. Anytime you want access, anytime you're not happy with the way things are going in court, you send me a message. I'll pass it on without anyone knowing."

A muscle jerked along Santalucci's jaw. "I'll give it some thought."

"You do that, George." Devlin dropped his leg and leaned forward, signalling that he was going to stand.

Santalucci gestured the bodyguard closer. Buchanan waited until the man was next to his boss. He didn't want to spook him; the guy looked like his shoe size was larger than his IQ.

"One more thing, George," he said as he stood up. His stomach muscles were tighter than usual, and his skin was uncomfortably sticky under the shoulder holster.

Santalucci watched him intently, his body tight and alert. "What?"

"The judge needs to know her daughter's safe. Often." He laced his words with the kind of venom Santalucci understood. "And I mean safe. You catch my meaning."

The locked glances, and the air between them seemed to ripple with shock waves. Devlin's stomach cramped painfully, but he forced his body to remain motionless. In his peripheral vision he saw the bodyguard tense, and he prepared to fight. Santalucci looked away first, shrugging dismissively as he turned his back on Buchanan and reached for his putter.

"You'll get your proof, Buchanan. Just make sure you deliver."

"I'll deliver all right. And one more thing, old buddy. No more cute messages from the kid. Spook the judge like that again, and she's liable to crack. She won't be much use to you in the nuthouse."

Devlin walked away without waiting for Santalucci's answer. He'd gotten what he wanted. Time.

Chapter 10

On Monday morning Amanda's alarm went off at six. She'd been awake for hours, sick to her stomach and so nervous her mouth was as dry as the feathers in her pillow.

The house was quiet, still wrapped in the half light of dawn. The curtains at the open window hung limp and unmoving, waiting for a breeze to stir the tepid air.

Amanda rolled onto her back, straining to hear a sound coming from the next room, but the rhythmic ticking of the grandfather clock in the hall was the only break in the silence. Apparently Buchanan was still asleep.

No wonder, Amanda thought sourly. He'd gotten in very late, sometime after midnight, and he'd been drunk, or close to it.

She remembered the relief she'd felt when he'd come through the door to the kitchen, his hat in his hand, a startled look covering his rough features when he saw her sitting at the counter, huddled over a cup of hot chocolate she hadn't really wanted.

She'd just spent the last hour imagining him bleeding in a dirty gutter somewhere, dead or dying, and his unconcerned expression was infuriating.

She'd torn into him on the spot, her voice shaking. "Are you completely crazy, making yourself a target and then getting so blind drunk you couldn't defend yourself even if you had to?"

His lips had curled into a smile that had seemed more sad than angry.

"Don't worry, Mandy. I'm not going to let you down." He'd left her sitting there and gone off to bed.

Amanda studied the elongated splash of sunlight on the Navajo rug by the bed and rubbed her calves against the smooth sheets in an effort to relieve their sudden tightness.

She was the one who'd been crazy, waiting up for him like that. He didn't want her to worry about him, to care about him. He'd only wanted her body, and maybe a little human warmth thrown in, and he didn't even want that anymore.

He'd made it all perfectly clear. And for good reason. The two of them were like oil and water, clearly never meant to mix.

Amanda yawned and tried to ignore the empty feeling of loss spreading inside her.

"Good morning."

Amanda looked up in alarm, her heart pounding, her fingers clawing the pillow next to her cheek.

Buchanan was standing in the doorway, a cup of coffee balanced on a saucer in his hand. "I thought you might need this." His voice sounded husky in the quiet room.

"Th-thank you," she managed, trying to blink the scratchiness from her tired eyes. She couldn't believe this was the same man who wore scruffy cutoffs and a ragged T-shirt, drank his liquor neat and carried a gun tucked against his butt.

He was dressed in a lightweight suit of tan gabardine, a classic in severe lines that showed off the lean length of his body. His shirt was pale blue and crisp with starch, his tie was silk, with beige and brown stripes, and his hand-sewn brown loafers gleamed. His thick hair had been blown away from his forehead and he wore it without a part. He looked so sexy that for a moment Amanda forgot why he was here filling her bedroom with his large presence and looking decidedly uncomfortable.

She sat up and slipped a pillow behind her back. "Uh, it's only six. We're not due in court until ten."

As she leaned back she was suddenly very conscious of the skimpy top of her thin cotton nightgown. She edged the sheet upward, fingering the embroidered hem with nervous fingers, knowing that she was being silly. It wasn't as though he didn't know what she looked like under her nightie.

"I've been up since four-thirty," he said, his eyes fixed on a spot over her left shoulder. "I met Cy Tanner in Old Town at five." He crossed the room in three easy strides and set the cup gently in her outstretched hand.

His hard knuckles brushed against her palm, and Amanda felt the shock wave all the way to her center. He jerked his hand back, and her cheeks burned with embarrassment. He didn't even like to touch her.

"Uh, was that wise, meeting Cy I mean?" She took a tentative sip, careful to keep her expression neutral. He was very tense. She could see it in the slope of his broad shoulders and in the tautness of the bronzed skin covering his freshly shaven jaw.

"The risk was minimal," he said carefully, and she nodded. She was beginning to feel extremely ill at ease, propped against her frilly pillows. Only a thin sheet and an even thinner scrap of cotton were between her and this big man who'd started to scowl the moment he saw her.

"Does Cy, uh, agree with your plan? About being my bodyguard, I mean?" She took another sip, grateful for the caffeine lift that was diffusing some of the fog from her brain.

"He's okay with it. He's not so okay about the publicity, but I, uh, convinced him it was necessary."

Her throat closed up, and she began to choke. The cup shook in the saucer, and droplets of coffee fell on the yellow sheet. "My God, I never thought about that," she exclaimed when she got her breath back. "It'll be a circus."

Buchanan opened his jacket and shoved his hands into the side pockets of the perfectly fitting trousers. He was wearing dark blue suspenders, a touch that seemed out of character to her. Every defense counsel under forty who'd argued a case in her court in recent months had been wearing suspenders. But few of those elegantly groomed and expensively dressed men had Buchanan's ability to appear ruggedly masculine and well dressed at the same time. Mentally Amanda shook her head. He was certainly a man of many facets, the majority of which she was sure she never wanted to see.

He glanced out the window. "I figure my best defense is high visibility," he said with studied calm. "I'll dance the media around my fake funeral for a few rounds, give them some line about burnout as the reason, and then slip in a reference to the trial." He shifted his gaze to her face, and Amanda felt as though he were touching her. "I intend to say that I'm going into the private security business, that I contacted you and offered my services for a fee." He paused, then added curtly, "Unless you have a problem with that." His voice was very dry.

Amanda considered the implied question. "No, not as long as you're careful to say that you have no comment on the trial itself." Her mind had begun to function more normally, and she frowned in thought as she ran through all the possible complications arising from such a story.

"I don't want any irregularities that could throw the case into an appeals court later, especially if I were to be indirectly involved. Santalucci's counsel is the best I've ever seen, a real pro, and I don't want to give her any ammunition."

"No scandal, no innuendo, no gossip, is that it?"

"That's it," she said firmly. "If I were to be thrown off the case for any reason, Santalucci would no longer need me. And he certainly wouldn't need Jessie." She felt a spasm in her throat, and she swallowed hard. "She could just...disappear." She looked up. "Couldn't she?"

Buchanan's expression was unreadable. "Yes," he said brusquely. "But I don't intend to let that happen."

He spun on his heel and strode toward the door. At the threshold he paused, bracing both hands against the dark wood and leaning forward, head down, his hips still.

She waited, her pulse pounding in her ears.

His sigh was audible as he turned around. "I meant to tell you," he said in a voice that was surprisingly gentle. "It'll be okay today. I'll be with you every minute. If you feel yourself losing control, just give me a look and I'll take care of it. And you."

Without giving her a chance to respond, he turned around and left the room.

Amanda stared after him. He was a man she'd never understand, never in a million tries.

"All rise"

The bailiff, a tall black man with grizzled gray hair, nodded courteously as Amanda strode through the door, her robe billowing around her legs.

Her courtroom was the largest of the six on the third floor. Recently repainted, it had ivory walls, a high ceiling and no windows.

All of the seats on both sides of the wide aisle were occupied, and members of the press had taken up standing-room positions along every inch of available wall space.

As she climbed the shallow step to the bench and sat down, Amanda looked out at a sea of faces, each one turned toward her, waiting, expectant. She pressed her fingertips against the polished walnut and waited for her nerves to settle.

The room was too warm, and the air smelled like stale cigarette smoke and lemon furniture polish. An undercurrent of tension flowed across the rail and hit her with a nearly palpable force.

Buchanan was seated directly in front of her, on the aisle, on the defendant's side of the room. She'd arranged for a special permit allowing him to bring his weapon into the courtroom. All other civilians had been searched before admittance had been granted.

He dipped his head a fraction of an inch as she looked his way, a subtle gesture that only she saw. He'd done that before, on the first day of his own trial. At the time she'd considered the gesture an insult and just another indication of the man's supreme arrogance.

Over those weeks long ago, he'd watched her constantly, a faintly sardonic smile playing across his lips whenever she'd glanced his way. He'd been thinner then, and his face had carried the pallor coming from weeks in the hospital, but his vitality had been undiminished.

The vivid memory blended with the present as their glances locked and held. He was clearly remembering too, and from his expression, his thoughts were far from pleasant.

Amanda lowered her gaze, a sudden inexplicable regret crowding out the memories. She had today to worry about.

The bailiff called the court to order, and the spectators sank into their chairs, whispering excitedly.

Inside the low walnut railing were two tables approximately ten feet apart with three chairs behind each table, all of which were occupied.

George Santalucci and his two attorneys sat on Amanda's left, the assistant district attorney and his two associates on her right. In front of the bench and slightly to the right sat the court reporter.

She took a deep breath and nodded toward each table. Pamela Devereaux, the cool blond defense counsel, was wearing outsized glasses, a tailored black dress and low-heeled pumps. She was smiling confidently, already courting the jury with subliminal signals of competence and credibility.

Arthur Francis, prosecutor, had recently undergone gall-bladder surgery, and he looked far older than his forty-five years.

Amanda felt her confidence in Francis slip. She'd been counting on him to carry the burden of the trial. Sighing inwardly she glanced toward the clock above the rear door. In ten seconds it would be 10:00 a.m., and she would officially begin the trial.

"Act naturally," Buchanan had whispered gruffly in her ear before he'd left her chambers to take up his position in the courtroom. "Try to pretend it's just another murder trial."

As promised, he'd been with her all morning, with the exception of the first twenty minutes following their arrival at the courthouse. As she'd foreseen, the press had gone for Buchanan like a school of barracuda, and she'd continued on to her chambers while he'd fielded their questions.

His rugged countenance would be on the evening news and in all the papers tomorrow, she was sure. And maybe that was a good thing. Santalucci would think twice about ordering Buchanan's death during the trial.

Amanda curled her fingers around the gavel and mentally prepared herself to look Santalucci straight in the eye. As of this moment, he was just a man, not a monster, she told herself, a defendant in her court, innocent until proven guilty.

The citizens of New Mexico had given her a sacred trust to make sure his rights were protected to the best of her ability. She had to totally divorce her personal feelings from the proceedings, to give George Santalucci the best she had to offer, no matter how bad her personal agony became—or she'd never be able to live with herself.

She raised her head and glanced at him impassively. He returned her gaze with a look of cruel satisfaction. His lips were slightly parted, and a greasy, confident smile hovered on his handsome features, displaying large white teeth that seemed to mock her with their gleaming perfection. She could almost believe he was the wealthy businessman he claimed to be. Almost, but not quite. Not with cold eyes like those.

Forcing a cool smile, she banged the gavel and signaled to the bailiff to begin the reading of the formal charge. As she listened, she leaned back in her chair, her spine pressing into the leather for support.

Steady, Amanda, she told herself forcefully, swallowing the panic that pushed at her throat. You can handle this. You can get through this. Involuntarily her eyes darted to Buchanan.

He caught her gaze and held it, his gray eyes steady and reassuring. He was there for her, just as he'd said he would be. It was as though he were wrapping her in his strong arms, sheltering her from this scalding pain with his powerful body. His strength was hers, and his courage was slicing through the panic to sustain her.

I'm here. Don't worry. She could hear the words as plainly as if he'd whispered them in her ear.

She took a deep breath and held it. Slowly the edges of hysteria receded. She exhaled slowly, feeling the last of the fear disappear. She was in charge again.

The bailiff finished reading and sat down. Amanda cleared her throat and leaned forward.

"Ms. Devereaux, are you ready?" she asked with polite briskness.

Pamela Devereaux stood respectfully. "Ready for the defense, Your Honor." She sat down with studied grace and smiled at the jury.

"Mr. Francis, are you ready?"

The district attorney rose slowly to his feet and squared his shoulders. He looked worn out. "Ready for the prosecution, Your Honor."

Amanda nodded curtly. "The State may begin, Mr. Francis."

As she sat back and focused her attention on the prosecutor's opening statement, Amanda felt Buchanan's steady gaze buoying her. He was everything Cy had claimed and more. But deep inside, she had a terrible feeling no one could really defeat George Santalucci, not even Devlin Buchanan.

Amanda called a recess for the afternoon session at a few minutes past four-thirty. She ignored the billowing burst of sound that followed her through the hall as she made her way to her chambers.

This corridor was always guarded during working hours and was off-limits to the media during a trial. She breathed a weary sigh of relief. She was exhausted and in no shape to battle a gauntlet of pushy reporters.

Juana was waiting for her. Silently she helped Amanda from her robe and handed her a glass of water. Her assistant didn't know that the letter she'd read over Amanda's shoulder only four days ago hadn't been a hoax, and Amanda had decided not to tell her. There was really no need for her to know.

"Tired?" the bubbly clerk asked as Amanda drained the glass and handed it back to her.

"Exhausted." And she was. Mentally, physically, emotionally, and every other way she could imagine.

The door opened and Buchanan came in, his eyes automatically sweeping the room before coming to rest on Amanda's face.

"Ready to go?" he asked brusquely, giving Juana a brief nod.

She looked him up and down with open curiosity. She'd been Amanda's clerk during his trial too, and Amanda remembered how taken Juana had been with the enigmatic agent, just like every other female in the courthouse—except her.

"Just let me get my purse from my desk and we can leave," she said, giving Juana a warning look. The last thing she needed was a smitten assistant.

"See you tomorrow, Your Honor," Juana said politely as Amanda returned from the inner office, her bag tucked under her arm. She was wearing her favorite linen sheath, a Paris original she'd bought herself as a present for her thirtieth birthday, and Buchanan's gaze registered approval as she walked back into the room.

Amanda double-checked her morning pretrial schedule with Juana, wished her a good evening and walked out of the office, deliberately moving a few paces ahead of Buchanan. She was halfway to the bank of elevators at the far end of the corridor when a large warm hand wrapped around her elbow.

"The press is in the lobby. We'd better use the service entrance," Buchanan explained as he guided her firmly to the stairs. His touch was reassuring as they walked down the three flights and out the rear entrance to the parking lot.

As Buchanan drove home, Amanda eased her head against the backrest and let relief flow over her tired body.

The opening day of the trial was over, and she'd survived. In fact, after her first-minute jitters, she'd done remarkably well. Somehow she'd drawn on reserves she'd never known were there.

But the trial could go on for weeks or even months. How would she be able to sustain her detachment for all those days? How could she remain impartial and objective?

The questions wavered in her mind, bleak and unanswerable. She didn't know how she would do it. She only knew that she had to try. Jessie was depending on her.

Amanda woke up with a start, her heart pounding. She was in bed, alone. Something had awakened her.

The hall light she'd left on for Buchanan still burned. He wasn't home yet.

"Where *is* he?" she muttered, wetting her dry lips.

He'd left shortly after dinner. Dressed in faded jeans and a worn Western shirt, he'd planned to visit a former informant of his in an attempt to scare up a lead.

The clock in the hall struck three. Somewhere in the distance a siren wailed for a heartbeat, then faded into a wavering thread of sound before disappearing altogether.

Amanda shuddered as the silence closed around her. What if he didn't come home at all? What would she do then? She couldn't go looking for him. Not alone. But if she asked Cy for his help, Santalucci might find out. Perhaps he'd accepted Devlin, but the note he had sent had specifically warned her against the FBI.

"Damn you, Buchanan!" she whispered into the shadows. "Don't *do* this to me."

The rapid beating of her heart was the only answer she could hear. It pumped relentlessly, mocking her with her own mortality until she couldn't stand it another minute.

Throwing off the sheet, she reached for her light wrap, which she let hang open over the short cotton nightshirt. She'd make some hot chocolate and drink it out by the pool. Maybe under the stars she'd be able to ignore the anxious whispers in her brain.

She snapped on her bedside lamp, wincing as the harsh light seared her tired eyes. Blinking against the sting, she left her bedroom and made her way to the main part of the house.

The air was still warm from the sweltering midsummer heat, and the moon shining through the large arched window in the oblong living room cast grotesque shadows on the tile beneath her bare feet.

A car was driving slowly past, its rumbling engine shattering the quiet. Suddenly the car stopped and began backing up. Before she could take another breath, the engine roared with thunderous power, and a brilliant white light splayed against the front window, blinding her. She threw up her hand to protect her face, then whirled as a sound behind her sent her pulse rate soaring.

"Get down!"

She recognized Buchanan's voice a split second before she was caught from behind and pulled to the floor, his hard arms squeezing the breath from her. She landed on top of him, her hip gouging his thigh and her legs tangling with his.

He cried something unintelligible and rolled over, pinning her face-down beneath the full length of his body, his arms covering her head. Her face was pressed into the coarse wool nap of the rug and his cheek lay next to hers, his stubble biting into her skin. His breath was coming in short bursts, and his muscles were hard and tense against her spine.

Amanda was terrified. Santalucci had sent his goons after all. This time there was no escape. This time she was going to die. And so was Buchanan.

In the next second the large window exploded inward, sending splinters of thick plate glass showering down on them. An oblong metal box landed within a few inches of Buchanan's head and skidded across the rug to thud against the leg of the coffee table.

Amanda twisted in his arms, struggling to get a closer look. "Is it a bomb?" she cried urgently, his mouth inadvertently brushing the corner of his.

Her words were swallowed by a hot moist kiss that lasted only a heartbeat before he pushed her face into the hollow of his throat and covered her head with his hands. "I sure as hell hope not," he bit out in helpless frustration.

He let out a string of vicious curses into the din, and she huddled close to him as his body fitted around hers protectively.

His chest and arms were bare and hot where they touched her, and his muscles formed a flesh-and-blood barrier against the spray of bullets she knew was coming.

The thunder of a powerful engine racing outside pounded against her eardrums, before abruptly changing pitch as the car backed down the drive. The blinding glare of the headlights wavered, then was gone as the car sped down the street, tires squealing.

Silence settled around them, leaving her limp with relief. She could scarcely believe it. The killers were gone, and she and Buchanan were still alive. She began to shake.

Buchanan held her close for several seconds, then rolled away from her. "It's okay," he whispered, turning her trembling body into his arms.

He held her tightly, his fingers moving restlessly up and down her back. Amanda clung to him, her cheek rubbing against his shoulder.

His hand was gentle as his fingers brushed back the thick dark hair obscuring her cheek. "This is the second time we've found ourselves in the middle of a mess like this. I don't know about you, but I'm getting tired of it." His voice was warmly soothing and lashed with humor.

She hiccuped and laughed at the same time. "Me, too," she said forcefully.

His face was in shadow, but she felt the power of his smile as his broad, square thumb brushed across her bottom lip. "Will you be okay while I see what the box is?"

"Oh my lord, I wasn't thinking!" she said with a sudden frown. "What if it *is* a bomb?"

"Then we're in trouble, because I don't know a damn thing about explosives."

Buchanan twisted around and reached for the box. "Turn on the lamp. It's safe enough now."

Amanda scrambled to her feet and switched on the light, squinting in the sudden glare. She could see him clearly now. He was wearing a black, low-cut swimsuit—and nothing else. His skin and his trunks were still dry. He must have been on his way to the pool when the car arrived.

Thank God, she thought, exhaling very slowly. If he hadn't been there, she would have been slivered to pieces by flying glass.

"Too light for a bomb," he said as though to himself, fingering the simple lock. "No booby traps." He raised the bulky box to his ear and shook it. "Sounds like paper."

Amanda picked her way through the glass and sat down facing him. "You think it might be a message?"

"Something like that, yes." His gaze flickered toward her face, then dropped to the small pink toes peeping out from under the edge of her robe. "Maybe you'd better go put on some shoes. This glass is going to shred your feet. I'll...wait until you get back to open this."

She knew better. If the box contained something monstrous, he would never let her see it. "Go ahead, open it. I—I have to know sometime what's inside."

"Suit yourself." His hand was steady as he opened the simple lock and lifted the lid. His expression lightened as he reached inside and pulled out a long white envelope.

"I doubt there are any prints on this," he muttered, ripping open the flap. In the envelope was a Polaroid photograph.

"Jessie?" she whispered.

Silently he nodded and handed her the picture.

Amanda fought back the tears. Still dressed in the pink ruffled shirt and jeans she'd put on Thursday morning, Jessie looked bewildered and unhappy as she stared into the camera, the front page of yesterday's *Sun* held against her chest. The background was a solid wall of gray. There was absolutely no clues to her whereabouts.

"I told Santalucci you wanted periodic proof that your daughter is still alive," Buchanan said quietly, watching her with fathomless eyes. He picked up a triangular shard of glass and with a flick of his corded wrist skimmed it through the gaping hole in the window.

She ran the index finger of her right hand over the image of her daughter's skinny body, trying to send the little girl a silent message of love.

"You talked to Santalucci? When? Where?"

"Yesterday. At the golf course. I wanted him to know I was taking care of your interests."

She managed a grateful smile. "I suppose that's why you didn't want me to go with you."

"Something like that."

Her hand shook violently as she turned over the picture and scanned the large rounded scrawl on the back. "I miss you, Mommy," she read slowly, her composure slipping as a dry sob shook her.

"I miss you too, sweetie," she whispered. She pressed the precious square of shiny pasteboard to her breast and began to cry in earnest. She couldn't seem to stop, and her slim body shook uncontrollably, her breath coming in painful gasps.

"Don't, Mandy," Buchanan whispered hoarsely, shifting position so that he could pull her into his arms. "You'll make yourself sick."

Amanda pressed her cheek against his shoulder and wrapped her arms around his waist. Her breasts were crushed against his rib cage, the nipples flattened into tiny hard buttons against the silken pelt covering his hard chest. The tender underside of her thighs pressed against his.

"I hate to cry," she said between sobs. "And that's all I've been doing l-lately."

His laugh rumbled against her ear, and a warm wave of relief rolled through her. She'd missed him. During the last few hours, she'd felt more alone than she'd ever felt in her life.

"I'm so glad you're here," she whispered. "I feel so much safer when you're in the next room."

She felt his muscles contract, and a sigh whispered past her cheek. "I wish I could always keep you safe, but it's not possible. You— need to know that."

She nodded. "I know." He was warning her not to get too dependent on him. She tightened her grip on his back, then uttered a cry of confusion when her fingers encountered a sticky wetness.

She pulled away and stared down at the smear of blood on her fingers. "You're bleeding!"

Ignoring his grunt of dismissal, she scrambled off his lap and crawled around to inspect his broad back. The cut was superficial, a shallow scratch near the bony ridge of his spine. A dark clot had stopped the bleeding, but his skin was still wet where the blood had oozed downward.

"It's not too bad." Her voice was hollow with relief. "I don't think you'll need sutures."

"Good. I hate needles."

He crossed his legs Indian fashion and inspected the box. It offered no clues. None at all, but he hadn't expected the Saint to be careless.

Amanda sank to her knees next to him, her stomach muscles shaking uncontrollably. It was just a scratch, nothing to make her feel so weak and faint. She pressed her palms together between her thighs to stop her hands from shaking.

"I was going to make hot chocolate." She couldn't think of anything else to say.

"Sounds good to me." An intensely provocative grin slanted over his lips. Amanda forgot what she was going to say as she lost herself in the warmth of that sweet, lopsided smile. Involuntarily her lips parted as she ran the tip of her tongue over the back of her teeth and stared at his mouth.

Buchanan's teeth were large and white and imperfectly aligned, and the triangular chip in the front incisor had scraped against her lower lip when he'd kissed her. Her tongue darted forward, touching the spot that was still slightly tender, then pulled back quickly as she caught him watching her.

She should get off the floor and go into the kitchen—as soon as her legs stopped feeling like a rag doll's.

Before she could move, Buchanan stood up, and the light from the lamp on the low table caught in the shiny black latex of his trunks. Abruptly the memory of that hard lean body pressed intimately against hers hit her, and a flood of hot blood rushed to her cheeks.

"You're exhausted. Let's skip the chocolate and get you back into bed." He leaned forward and extended his big hand.

She rested her hand in his like a trusting child, and he pulled her to her feet. Her legs were slightly numb but able to support her.

A faint smile brushed his lips as he dropped his gaze to inspect the small palm that lay nestled in his larger one. A dark sliver of his blood trapped in her lifeline stood out starkly against the pale ivory skin. Slowly he dipped his head and touched his lips to that vivid line.

"I can't believe you're worried about a little cut after all that's happened in the last few days." His breath misted her skin, sending an intoxicating rush straight to her brain.

"I hate blood."

His face tightened. "Me, too."

He ran his large hands up and down her arms, ruffling the thin nylon of her robe.

His eyes closed convulsively, and he crushed her to him. "Invite me into your bed, Mandy," he murmured in a strained whisper. "I don't want to sleep alone tonight."

Chapter 11

He swung her into his arms so easily Amanda scarcely knew when her feet left the ground.

Her bed was rumpled, the sheets cool against her skin as he laid her gently on the mattress and looked down at her.

Amanda knew instinctively that it was more than sexual relief he was craving, and she was willing to give him whatever he needed. For tonight she wanted to be there for him, just as he'd been there for her. All of her, body and soul. And heart. Slowly, without saying a word, he reached over and turned off the lamp.

"You look very handsome in the moonlight," she whispered, drawing him down to sit on the edge of the big bed. Gently she touched the shallow cleft in his chin with her fingertip, a butterfly caress that tightened his face as though he were in pain.

"Hides the scars," he whispered roughly.

"What about the scars inside?"

"No one sees those."

Amanda leaned forward to kiss his shoulder. "I do," she murmured.

"Yes, I think you do. Maybe that's why I can't believe you really want me."

"I want you."

He inhaled slowly, then released the trapped air in a steady stream. "My Mandy," he whispered, sliding his hands over her shoulders.

Amanda remained silent as his big hands fumbled with the tiny buttons linking the nightgown over her breasts. She shifted her weight to one arm, then the other as he slipped the gown and robe from her shoulder.

Buchanan didn't take his eyes off her as he flicked his wrist and sent the bundle of clothes skittering across the room to puddle against the hand-carved wardrobe. He seemed to be waiting, looking for something from her.

Amanda whimpered with impatience and lowered her hands to the slight indentation of his hips where the trunks clung tightly. He tensed as she slid her fingers under the satiny material. He stood, allowing her to push the trunks lower until he could kick them away.

She moved over, making room for him, and he lay beside her, his hand resting on the curve of her hip.

In the shadowed light she could see the soft pelt of hair covering his wide chest. It was more than half gray and trailed in a thin line downward until it met the puckered skin of his belly.

Amanda nuzzled her face against that downy thatch, loving the faint scent of musk that rose from his body. Her feathery lashes brushed his skin, exciting visible waves of reaction in the tiny nerve endings under the deep tan.

He ran his hands over her shoulders and down her arms, needing to brand every enticing inch of her with his touch. He felt her shake, small involuntary ripples that shivered under his palms, nearly driving him over the edge into explosive release.

He forced himself to go more slowly, letting her take the lead, something he'd never before done with a woman. He was a decent enough lover, as thoughtful as the next man, but suddenly, with Mandy, he wanted to be perfect.

She seemed fascinated by his body, touching him as ardently and intimately as he touched her. Devlin groaned, feeling his skin tighten under her lips. Her breath bathed his body in moist warmth, and he felt himself drowning in the delicate scent of her. She moved over him, caressing him, kissing him, her soft skin like the most delicate silk brocade against his.

He was ready, more than ready. He could feel his control slipping. With his other lovers he'd been as detached in the bedroom as he was on the streets, unusually alert and in control at all times, but with Amanda that control was marginal at best.

He'd never felt such pleasure, such shivering need. He gritted his teeth against the shuddering ache, harsh, driving breaths shaking his chest. His fists clenched around the sheet as she bathed him with her tongue, stroking him so exquisitely he gasped hoarsely.

Amanda's body responded to the explosive sound of his need, blazing into an inferno of white-hot flame as she slid her lips lower to kiss his puckered flesh.

His scars felt rough against her lips, and she tentatively brushed her tongue against the jagged line that sliced crazily across his belly.

The ribbed muscle beneath the skin contracted into a hard slab, and Devlin groaned. "God, that feels good," he whispered in raspy gasps. "So damned good."

He arched his back, his concentration intense. He struggled for control as her lips moved over him, her fingers so sweetly awkward and so intensely provocative he writhed against her, needing her, wanting her.

Amanda felt a primitive, savage tug deep inside her. She was out of control, lost in a wild and turbulent landscape of desperate need.

"Mandy," he whispered, loving the feel of her name on his tongue. He couldn't believe the wonder of her. He'd waited so long for her, so very long. She made him feel happy to be alive. One smile from her soft and pouting lips made him forget the long years he'd spent alone and empty.

He caught her face between his palms. "I can't wait, Mandy. I need you now." Her eyes entranced him, beautiful gold lights that heated his blood. He moved, sliding her beneath him.

Amanda moaned, her body in torment. Her thighs ached to part for him, her stomach longed to feel the hair-roughened friction of his body against hers, her breasts longed to thrust upward, seeking his hard chest.

She uttered tiny, impatient cries as he parted her thighs with his hand and caressed her lovingly.

His body shuddered, his control gone, as he plunged deeply into her, filling her, possessing her, silently offering the only thing he knew how to give.

She whimpered helplessly, her hands reaching for him, her neck arched, her face intense and wildly beautiful, her hair spread over the pillow in a dark cloud.

"Now, sweetheart, now. With me. Together. Now." He couldn't wait much longer. And then she cried out, her body shuddering, and Devlin surrendered, totally, completely, holding nothing back.

For the first time in his life.

Amanda awakened slowly, feeling a delicious soreness deep inside her body. It was a few minutes before dawn, and the morning light was filtering through the curtains to pattern the floor.

She was lying on her back, her head turned toward Devlin, her cheek resting on his pillow. He was lying on his side, his hand warm and possessive on her thigh. He was sleeping deeply, his face relaxed, his mouth slightly open.

She blinked away the drowsiness and studied the hard face so close to hers.

A few days ago this man had been only a disturbing memory, and now he was her lover. She was a little confused and more than a little frightened. What scared her was the power he seemed to have over her. He'd broken through the wall of reserve that had always protected her as though it had been nothing more than a flimsy web.

In her bed he'd been giving and gentle and patient, making her feel cherished and dear, as though she were the most important woman in the world.

With him she'd kept nothing back. And that made her a woman without secrets, a woman who'd opened herself wide to terrible hurt.

Devlin sighed, and his brows drew together as though he were in distress. His head moved restlessly on the pillow, and his tongue slid along his lower lip.

In the harsh morning light he looked older than his years, his face almost gaunt, his brow lined even in repose. His bronzed skin was a map of a life that had been lived on the edge, a tough, merciless road that had taken his youth and his strength from him and given very little in return.

"Oh, Devlin," she whispered. She wanted to touch him, to smooth the lines from his face, but she didn't dare. She remembered the last time she'd attempted to waken him.

As though reading her mind, Devlin sighed again, then opened his eyes. He was wide awake in an instant. "Good morning." His voice was pitched low and carried a sensuous vibration that burrowed straight through her.

"We have an hour before we have to get up, darling Devlin." She leaned over and kissed him. Never in her life had she been so bold, yet never had it felt so right.

His lips firmed under hers, then slanted into a rueful grin as she drew back and looked at him. "I wish you hadn't done that." His gaze held hers, hypnotic, imperious, hungry. One move and he would pounce.

"Why?" she asked in a breathless rush, a thrill of anticipation darting through her body.

Only the corners of his mouth turned upward. "You're wearing me out. I'm not used to all this...activity."

His expression was tortured.

"Don't you dare smile, you little tease." His voice caught her laughter and deepened it, bathing her with seductive promise.

"Sorry."

The drowsy light of humor in his eyes slowly faded. "Mandy, I'm not a very nice guy. Not the kind you deserve. Never forget that." He took her right hand and began playing with the emerald ring on her third finger. "I couldn't afford to give you a rock like this."

She slid onto her back and inched closer. He hesitated, then slid his arm under her neck, letting her rest her head on his shoulder. "I'm not asking you to."

He sighed. "I know." He lifted her hand to his lips and kissed her palm. She slid her hand along his jaw, liking the feel of the stiff whiskers.

His hand smoothed the sheet away from her breasts, his palms sliding with tortuous slowness over first one nipple, then the other.

Amanda's heart began hammering in her chest, and her body contracted in vibrant hunger.

She looked up at him, drinking in the molten silver of his thickly lashed eyes. In the early morning light the rugged male strength in his face was even more pronounced. He was hard angles and blunt edges, cast in bronze and just as impervious to destruction.

"Sweetheart," he murmured, dipping his head to sear her lips. His mouth pressed his brand into her, claiming her as his own. She parted her lips, eager to draw him closer. His tongue caressed hers, hot and moist and insistent, and Amanda sighed with deep pleasure.

His breathing became ragged, and his hands clenched around her bare shoulders, imprinting the tawny skin with the square tips of his fingers.

"I used to think that you were cold and sexless, in spite of that gorgeous face. But I was wrong. You're sexy—" he began punctuating each word with kisses, his lips moving lower with each word "—and exciting...and exasperating...and beautiful...and damn near...irresistible." He buried his face in the shallow cleft between her breasts, his possessive hands moving lower, closer.

Desire shook her more strongly with each inch his fingers explored, and she moaned, tossing her head on the pillow.

Devlin moved even lower, pressing suckling kisses along the thin line trailing through her navel, his lips tugging erotically on her creamy skin, exciting heated impulses of pleasure with each moist kiss.

He moved lower still, his forearms burrowing under her thighs and lifting them to give him access. Amanda gasped, unable to cry out, unable to breathe. She was awash, drowning in the things he was doing to her.

"Do you want me, Mandy?" His voice was rough, urgent, hungry, nearly out of control.

"Yes." Her whisper was more a gasp. "Oh yes, hurry, Devlin. Hurry. Make me forget. I want you."

In the master bathroom the shower massaged Amanda's spine, sending pulsing needles of hot water into her deliciously relaxed muscles.

Her body was sated, but her mind was in turmoil.

Their lovemaking had become more than an affirmation, more than a respite from the terrible fact of Jessie's precarious situation.

For the first time in her life she knew what it was like to feel totally uninhibited and free, to soar on a wing of purest delight.

Devlin made her feel young and eager. His kisses were a drug, a powerful stimulant that made her lose all control. Under his tender touch she came alive, her soul reaching for the unknown, ready to experience all that life could offer.

But that kind of unfettered freedom was impossible, Amanda told herself with a sad sigh. An illusion, just as her feelings were transitory. She turned off the spray and reached for the peach bath sheet draped over the brass rod.

And yet...

She huddled inside the stall, wrapping the terry cloth around her as the truth hit her with the force of a runaway stallion.

This was love she was feeling, the wild, out-of-control kind of love she thought only existed in books and on the screen. *She was in love with Devlin Buchanan.*

Nothing else explained the way she responded to him whenever he touched her. Nothing else explained the volatile combustion between them whenever they were in the same room. Nothing else explained the deep desire she felt to bring some lightness into his life.

She gripped the shower door with both hands and stared at the ceramic tile lining the large enclosure.

It couldn't be. It wasn't possible. The man was all wrong for her. Loving him would only bring her pain. Terrible, heart-wrenching pain.

Amanda took a deep breath. She had no choice. She was deeply in love, and there was nothing she could do about it. But right now, Jessie needed her more than Devlin ever could. And she needed Jessie. They were a family.

Maybe when Jessie was home, maybe then she and Devlin could find a way to make a life together. Maybe he could learn to love her as much as she loved him. Maybe...

Amanda forced the thought of the future from her mind and climbed out of the shower. Court was due to convene in three hours. Judge Amanda Wainwright had to be ready to preside.

"If maintenance doesn't do something about the so-called air-conditioning system in this place, I swear I'm going to convene court in the parking lot."

Amanda glowered at the ceiling vent and fanned her hot face with her napkin. It was Friday noon, and she and Buchanan were having lunch in her chambers.

Devlin listened without comment as he tugged on the knot of his tie. He'd unbuttoned his starched collar the moment they'd walked into her private office.

"Cy was in the court this morning for a while and so was Rosalie Cruz. Did you see them?"

Amanda looked up from her salad and shook her head. "I try not to pick out faces when I'm on the bench. It can be distracting." She poked at a radish. "Did she and Cy come together?"

"No, I don't think so. He was way in the back and she was close to the front, a few rows behind me."

"It must be hard on her, sitting through another trial. It hasn't been that long since her husband's death."

Devlin nodded and pushed away his plate. Juana had ordered lunch from the restaurant across the street. As a presiding judge Amanda had to be ultracareful not to be seen in a place where any of the jurors or other participants might frequent, and so she usually ate in her chambers.

"Apparently she looks at it as a kind of catharsis. Or so she said. I didn't get a chance to talk with her very long."

Buchanan sat in the chair across from her desk. He was wearing a dark blue blazer and a light blue shirt over beige slacks, which made him look more like a corporate executive than a bodyguard, Amanda thought with a thrill of pride that she couldn't squash.

Since they had started sleeping together, his face appeared relaxed, and he seemed to smile more, even in his guise as her protector. She sighed, pushing the personal thoughts from her mind. "I like Rosalie. She's a strong lady."

"Rosa reminds me of you."

"She does?" Her fork stopped halfway to her mouth as she waited for him to explain.

"She does. Except I think you're even stronger than she is." He gave her a lazy look of admiration that underlined his words.

She flushed. "Don't pin any medals on me yet. I have to grit my teeth just to be able to look toward the defendant's table." She frowned. "If I knew for certain he'd harmed Jessie I'm not sure what I'd do."

"You're doing fine, Amanda." The look of admiration intensified. "It's not easy, I know. Especially when he's out there doing one-liners for the press every chance he gets."

Amanda took a bite of her salad and tried to swallow the limp lettuce without tasting the oily dressing. "If only he didn't look so damned smug," she said, her jaw tight. "To everyone else he looks like he's being affable, smiling up at me the way he does every time I open my mouth. But I know what he's really thinking."

Her voice shook, and she pressed her paper napkin to her lips. "God, I know I have to be impartial, but it's...not easy." Her voice hardened. "I've never hated another human being in my life, I don't believe in it, but..." Her voice trailed off and she looked up, suddenly feeling very self-conscious.

Buchanan returned her gaze impassively, his big hands wrapped firmly around a large plastic cup. His eyes were nearly opaque, and his lips were slightly parted and still, as though his thoughts had turned inward.

Amanda sighed. "I guess this sounds pretty awful to you, doesn't it? I mean, I was the one who was so sure the law had a solution for every problem."

"Doesn't it?" His voice was the same silken drawl that had so unnerved her in court the first time she'd heard it.

She lifted her shoulders in a jerky shrug. She'd gone this far, she might as well tell him all of it. "That's just it, Devlin. If I let the law work the way it's supposed to, my daughter will die. What kind of justice is that?" Her voice throbbed with anger. "He has to pay. Somehow that man has to pay for the evil he's done. I don't know how, I don't know when, but—'' She stopped suddenly and took a strangled breath. "Listen to me. I sound like—like..."

"Like me."

"Yes." Color heated her cheeks.

He crossed one ankle over his knee and contemplated his blue and beige socks. "Hating is easy, Mandy," he said slowly, wanting to make his words count. "Anyone can hate, even you, if you're hurt badly enough." He rubbed a smudge from his gleaming loafer with his thumb. "Only once you've hated, you're never the same. It makes you cold and empty inside. And if you hate long and hard enough, it changes the way you see the world. Makes you cynical, afraid to trust anything or anyone but yourself. It's like a poisonous toxin, once it's inside, you can't get rid of it, no matter how hard you try." He buttoned his collar and straightened his tie, then stood up. "Time's up."

Amanda threw the remnants of her lunch into the trash. He'd been talking about himself, about his life, and the bleak look in his eye had nearly undone her. He didn't like the way he was, she could feel it. But he didn't believe he could change things either.

"God, I wish I'd never been assigned this case," she muttered vehemently, wadding her napkin into a ball and throwing it in the garbage.

"You'll be fine."

He helped her slip on her robe, his fingers lightly brushing the back of her neck as he straightened her collar, and she shivered.

"Later, my Mandy," he whispered against her ear, and she fought down her emotions. They had only stolen time.

She wanted to cry.

Amanda was exhausted by the afternoon recess. The prosecution had begun to present its case, and Santalucci's attorney pounced on so many obscure points of law that Amanda began to get suspicious. It was almost as though Pamela Devereaux knew about the pressure on Amanda to act in her client's favor.

Fortunately Amanda had been able to sidestep most of the rulings thanks to Arthur Francis, who'd withdrawn several of his statements before she'd had to intervene.

She and Devlin left by the stairs again. On the ground floor he paused, his fingers tightening on her arm in silent warning. He unbuttoned his jacket and opened the door a crack. Through the opening Amanda could hear a cacophony of sound coming from the direction of the lobby, a jumbled mix of voices rising and falling as the reporters shouted shrill questions.

"He loves it," Buchanan muttered, then opened the door wider and stepped out into the corridor. He beckoned for Amanda to follow, and she hurried across the threshold, her pumps clicking loudly on the terrazzo. Beyond the barricade screening the corridor from the lobby George Santalucci stood in the center of a mob of reporters, a charming smile plastered on his face.

"Forget him," Buchanan said brusquely, turning her into the corridor leading to the service exit.

Just as they left the back entrance and started toward the Volvo a silky voice hailed Amanda from behind. It was Santalucci, flanked by his attorney and her associate and a phalanx of four large, unsmiling men in dark suits.

Beside Amanda, Buchanan stiffened and his fingers bit into her arm. His face was shuttered, his body braced. He was ready for anything.

"Judge Wainwright, I just wanted to compliment you on the expert way you handled the prosecutor's ineptitude," Santalucci said softly as he overtook them, a smugly arrogant smile spreading over his fleshy lips.

It took every scrap of strength she possessed to keep from clawing that smile from his face. Instead, Amanda forced her features into a sternly judicial look directed toward Ms. Devereaux.

"Counselor, please instruct your client not to make any statements to me outside the courtroom." Her heart thudded against her rib cage, and her palms began to sweat.

"Of course, Your Honor." The attractive attorney frowned and touched Santalucci's sleeve. "The car is waiting, George." The words of warning had no effect on her client. His eyes remained fixed on Amanda's face.

"I have to admit, though, that I'm disappointed in your taste in men." His yellow eyes flicked toward Buchanan. "The cop here claims you take your loving on the rough side, but I can't believe you'd be turned on by a beat-up has-been who can't cut it on the streets anymore." One eyebrow rose suggestively as he slid his gaze toward Buchanan. "How about it, cop? You like being a kept man?"

Buchanan formed his left hand into a fist. A murderous rage built quickly inside him, tensing the long muscles of his legs. He could drop the bigger man with one punch, but then what? Who would pay for that one moment of supreme pleasure? Jessica Wainwright?

He forced his fingers to relax. He could take the insults, but what about Amanda? He held his breath. C'mon, Mandy. Stand up to him. Don't let him shake you.

Amanda felt Buchanan's arm clench and then almost immediately relax. He had his temper under control. She took a deep breath.

"One more word, Mr. Santalucci," she enunciated coldly and distinctly, "and I'll cite you for contempt. You'll spend the rest of your trial in custody, I promise you." Her eyes pinned Pamela Devereaux who nodded slightly and stepped between Amanda and her client.

"Let's go, George. Now."

Santalucci's face twisted with hatred as his eyes locked with Devlin's. Amanda could almost smell the loathing sizzling between the two hard-faced men.

Buchanan didn't move, but his body seemed larger somehow, stronger than his opponent's. She couldn't pinpoint why exactly, but she knew that the two men had been testing each other, and that in spite of the Saint's insults, Buchanan had won.

"Later, cop," Santalucci growled and turned on his heel, stalking to his car ahead of his retinue. As soon as they were all inside, the black stretch limousine roared to life and pulled quickly out of the lot, a faint white trail of exhaust marking its route.

Amanda forced herself to ignore the icy hand squeezing her throat. She was in control, composed, in spite of the pain flooding through her.

Noise from the crowded thoroughfare beyond the parking lot swirled around her, but she heard only the appalled pounding of her heart. Slowly the cars around her faded from her view until just she and Buchanan remained.

His skin was suffused with dusky color and his eyes were lit with silver fury. A tiny muscle jumped beneath the skin covering his jaw as he clenched his teeth.

"You talked to him about us—about me, didn't you?" she said calmly. Too calmly.

Devlin tried to read her thoughts in her eyes, but they were shuttered, closed to him. It wasn't a good sign. "Yes, I talked to him. I told you that I did."

"You *told* me you discussed Jessica."

A savage frown flashed across his face. "This isn't the place to talk about it."

"Tell me." Amanda wasn't sure she could move without shattering.

Buchanan watched her. She wasn't going to give up. He was trapped.

He stared into her stormy, troubled eyes, those beautiful eyes he was powerless to resist, and tried to make himself lie to her. But, for some reason, he just couldn't do it. Not to her. His heart began thundering, preparing him for battle, and his body tensed. He took a quick look over his shoulder and Amanda's gaze followed his. They were alone.

"It's simple, Amanda," he said slowly and distinctly, biting off each syllable. "When I moved into your house, I told Santalucci that you and I have been lovers since my trial. I told him I seduced you into seeing that I got acquitted. And I told him that I'd see that you did the same for him because you like what I do to you in bed."

She gaped at him. The shock started in her stomach, deadening the nerves, then shot up to her throat. She felt the pain, sharp and punishing. She'd been a fool to trust him. A fool to open herself up for this kind of betrayal. A stupid, weak fool.

"That's why you were so eager to get me into bed, to give...to give credence to your story. Very clever, Buchanan."

His face twisted and a mocking gleam replaced the chill in his eyes. "You really trust me a lot, don't you?"

"I was beginning to. Until now." She refused to feel guilty. "What about me? How do you think I feel, knowing that a man like Santalucci thinks I'm no better than...than a whore?"

Devlin flinched at the brutal description. He wanted to grab her, to kiss away the hurt on her beautiful face, to make her understand that he'd had no choice.

"Does it really make a difference what he thinks?"

"Of course it does," she declared forcefully. "The man would love to slobber all over my reputation."

"I see. Your reputation is more important than your daughter's life. Is that how it is, Amanda?"

The blood drained from her face. "Of course not! How can you even think that?" Her voice was horrified.

Devlin steeled himself against the shock spreading over her features. He'd made her ashamed of herself when he'd only wanted to jolt her into understanding. But she was clearly in no mood to listen, not now. "I told you this wasn't going to be a picnic. Obviously you weren't paying attention."

He took her elbow and marched her toward the car. "Now let's get the hell out of here." His eyes were wintry, his lips compressed.

Amanda was pulled hard against his side, her elbow digging into his ribs, his heavy thigh jolting against her with every step they took.

Restrained violence radiated from every cell of his body, the same kind of leashed menace she'd felt from Santalucci.

Amanda waited until they were inside the Volvo before she turned on him. "You're fired," she said in a cold voice. "I want you out of my house immediately." And out of my bed, she added silently, feeling as though she were bleeding inside.

"No." He started the engine and rested both hands on the wheel, watching her closely out of steady eyes.

"Yes," she shot back, breathing more quickly with each second that passed.

He shook his head. "I told you in La Placita I was buying into your trouble, and I meant it. What you want or don't want doesn't have a damn thing to do with it."

His steely determination split the superheated air between them. "I'm sorry you're offended that Santalucci believes we're lovers, especially since it happens to be true," he went on with stiff harshness, "but right now that particular reality is all that's keeping me alive."

He backed quickly from the space and spun the wheel. The tires screeched smoke as he peeled out of the lot and headed north.

Chapter 12

The dinner dishes were in the dishwasher, her clothes were laid out for tomorrow, and Amanda had changed the sheets on her bed. She couldn't think of another chore that needed doing. Except one. Apologizing to Buchanan.

She'd been miserable from the moment they'd returned home. She'd given him her word not to interfere, to trust him. And she'd broken it—again. No wonder he was so angry with her. How could she blame him?

She sighed and slipped into her black maillot. He was out by the pool, watching the twilight colors spread across the sky.

As soon as they'd gotten home, he'd changed and gone out again to investigate another lead.

She'd waited dinner for him until the roast had been dry and the potatoes overcooked. She'd been about to throw it away when he'd returned a few minutes before seven.

They'd been stiffly polite during their mostly silent meal, speaking only when necessary. His expression had been thunderous, but his voice had been even softer than usual.

Sighing, she grabbed two beers from the fridge and padded out to the patio. The air was warm and still, and the water would be nicely refreshing after the steamy day she'd spent trapped in that smothering black robe.

Buchanan looked up quickly as she opened the French doors, his brows drawing together into an ominous frown as his gray gaze raked over her black suit.

He was wearing white shorts and a soft yellow T-shirt that showed every ridge and bulge of his powerful torso. He'd showered after dinner, and his hair had dried in a sexy tangle that made her want to run her fingers through it.

"How about a beer?" she asked.

"Thanks." He accepted the bottle without a smile. His cold, distant attitude was far worse than the blazing anger she'd expected.

Amanda swallowed the butterflies in her throat and tried to ignore the sexy way he was sprawling in the chair. His legs, one tucked under the seat, the other extended, looked longer in shorts and his shoulders broader in the tight T-shirt.

She sat down in the chair next to him and tucked her feet under her. Behind the screen of his lashes, his eyes followed her every move, exciting her even as it unnerved her.

"It's a beautiful night." Inside the fenced yard their isolation was complete. Not even the nearest neighbors could spy on them, and she felt safe for the first time in days.

"Yes." He tilted his head back and took a long, thirsty swallow.

She wrenched her eyes away from his strong brown neck and took a tentative sip. The beer stung her throat as it went down, leaving a bitter aftertaste. She took a deep breath.

"Devlin, I'm sorry."

He nodded, hoping like hell she'd drop the subject.

"I overreacted," she said quietly. "I was wrong to...to fire you."

His mouth quirked with brief amusement. "More like unwise," he said tersely. "I don't like unequivocal terms like right and wrong. Life just isn't like that." And life didn't give second chances.

Her reaction this afternoon had simply confirmed what he already knew. His past would always be there, like an unexploded bomb between them, waiting for a chance remark or a misunderstood action to set it off.

Amanda shifted to a more comfortable position. The air was cooling off, and the plastic of the chair was uncomfortable against her bare thighs. No, she was just plain uncomfortable, she admitted silently. She wasn't used to being on the defensive like this. She wasn't used to making mistakes.

Her discomfort gave her voice a strident edge. "I don't want you dead, Buchanan."

His grin slanted sardonically across his face. "That's comforting to know."

She fought down a burst of anger. He was deliberately making this difficult for her. "Why couldn't you have warned me? Why couldn't you have trusted me enough to explain what you were going to do? I would have understood, and...and I would have agreed with you."

He shook his head. "Maybe. More than likely though, you would have given me a hell of an argument, just like you have on just about everything since we left Mexico."

He was right, but she wasn't going to give up. She'd never given up, even when the odds of winning a case were clearly against her. "I'm not like that guy who sold you out, Devlin. Don't close up on me. Don't make me feel cold inside."

He gnawed on the corner of his mouth, his eyes fixed on the fat body of the half-finished panda on the table. "Mandy, you don't want to know what's inside me. A lot of it isn't very nice. You wouldn't like me very much if you knew who I really was."

"Give me a chance to find out, Devlin. Let me decide."

"Why?"

She wet her lips. "Because I...care about you. Very much. In the short time we've been together I've come to have enormous respect for you. You're very special to me." Tension hovered, knotting the back of her neck.

He finished the beer and set it carefully beside the rough carving. "I've given you more of myself than any other woman I've ever known, but—" He looked almost angry as he dropped his gaze to the black Beretta on the table. She could feel the tension tugging at her. She was losing him before she ever really had him.

"But you don't love me." A desperate longing rose in her before she squashed it. Don't expect anything more than he can give, she told herself sternly.

"No, I don't love you. Not the way you deserve to be loved." His words were spoken with ruthless honesty and deep sadness. Her respect for him rose another notch even as she fought the disappointment shuddering through her.

"So where do we go from here?" she asked.

"I still want you. I think I'll always want you."

Amanda could hear the longing in his quiet voice, and it gave her hope. Because she loved him, she had to try. "After Jessie is home, maybe then..."

"Don't, Mandy. I've already given you all the love that's in me."

He inhaled slowly, trying to ease the tightness in his chest. "I just don't have any more to give."

He hated the wounded look in her eyes. And the tremor in her voice. He hated himself for putting it there. But he couldn't let her think there was more inside him than there was.

He shifted his gaze to the shimmering surface of the pool. In the fading light the water looked like a golden lake. Everything in Amanda's life was golden. He couldn't spoil it for her with his bitterness and his rage that could spill out without notice. He cared too much for her to risk it.

She studied his profile warily. She'd seen that slight narrowing at the corner of his eyes before. But where?

She dropped her gaze as the answer came to her suddenly. His harsh features had worn the same expression when he'd first looked down at Pepe's unconscious body.

Stunned, she struggled to sort through the emotions tumbling around in her head. Was he hiding his true feelings from her? Did he really feel more for her than he would admit? Or maybe he didn't know what he felt?

She had to give him a chance to find out. To give them both a chance. "We have tonight, Devlin. One more night." Her soft entreaty fell between them like the quiet murmur of a summer rain.

Devlin turned his head to look at her. She was breathtakingly beautiful, and so very dear. He should leave her now, this minute. A gentleman would know how to make a graceful exit, saving face for both of them. But he didn't want to leave. He wanted her. God, how he wanted her. He couldn't bear to deny himself the warmth she was offering. Not yet.

"First I need a kiss to make it better," he said, fighting the urge to tell her how much he needed her. Keep it light, he told himself. Keep it fair. Don't ask for more than you can give.

Amanda pretended suspicion, her spirits rising. He was teasing her again. Star bursts of relief erupted inside her, and a smile waited behind her pursed lips. She could make him want to stay with her after Jessie came home, she knew she could. And she could make him fall in love with her, too, given enough time.

"To make what better?" she asked pertly, loving the way his head tilted provocatively whenever he intended to kiss her.

"My battered ego."

"Aha. And just where does this battered ego of yours reside?"

A seductive grin broke across his features. "Come here, and I'll show you."

She placed her beer on the table and stood up. He opened his legs and drew her between his thighs. His hands curved around her waist, pulling her close until only a whisper of warm summer air separated them.

"Now what was that about a kiss?" His husky voice was like an aphrodisiac, exciting her in a primitive, elemental way that was beyond her control.

She let her lashes swoop lower until her gaze was fixed on his lips. "Here?" she whispered, brushing his mouth with hers. "Or here?" She trailed moist kisses along the firm line of his jaw. She twined her arms around his neck and played with his hair.

Devlin groaned and pulled her into his lap, her tantalizing bottom pressing warmly against his thigh as her lips nipped at his earlobe. Heat shot through his legs and into his groin as her sharp little teeth raked the sensitive skin in seductive bites while her breasts thrust against his chest.

Her nipples were hard pebbles that rubbed delicious erotic circles against his chest, making him want to purr inside.

His fingers dug into her spine as desire erupted inside him, sending bursts of need to every cell of his body. He was being assaulted, conquered with hot, torturing impulses that made him want to take her right there on the rough pavement.

Her tongue darted forward, rasping a trail of moist heat down the sculptured column of his neck. He shivered, unable to stand it much longer. His breath began to come harder as his concentration splintered.

Devlin groaned and buried his face in the hollow of her shoulder. Her skin smelled like soap, clean and invigorating and so damned sexy he was ready to explode.

"Let's take a swim," he said in a tortured voice, glancing toward the glassy surface of the pool.

Without waiting for her answer, he swung her into his arms and walked rapidly toward the stairs.

The water was warm on her skin as he sat down on the middle step and let her bottom sink to his knees. The wavy surface lapped against her breasts, wetting his chest and turning the yellow of his shirt to gold. His nipples were clearly outlined against the cotton, and she leaned down to nip each one through the material.

Devlin groaned and unbuttoned the waistband of his shorts. The sound of the zipper was muffled by the water and Amanda giggled. Her giggles turned to a gasp as his arousal, freed from the shorts, pressed against the thin material of her suit.

It was more erotic, somehow, to feel his hot hardness through the satiny latex. She groaned and arched against him, eager to feel the fullness of him inside her.

"Don't move," he grated against her lips, his body throbbing insistently.

The water slapped against the tile in a hypnotic refrain, and the smell of chlorine brushed Amanda's nostrils as she lay against him, her body aching for him.

Slowly he eased away from her, his face shadowed and intense in the gathering darkness. His fingertips slid inside her suit, and she gasped.

A honeyed wetness spilled onto his fingers as he stroked her, sending spurts of sizzling pleasure deep inside her. The pressure built, growing, spreading, engorging her with need.

Devlin groaned, then pushed aside the material to thrust into her. Amanda gasped and locked her ankles behind his back. She leaned forward, clutching his shoulders for support, her fingers digging into his hard muscles as the ache built, growing hotter, more dazzling, more compelling. She couldn't breathe, couldn't think, couldn't feel anything but the glorious pulsating spiral that was sending her higher and higher.

Suddenly she couldn't stand it another second. The ecstasy was too powerful, too consuming, and then there was one cataclysmic explosion, a white-hot burst of light and energy that blanked her mind and shivered her body.

Devlin groaned and with one final thrust found his own release, his arms wrapped tightly around her slim back, his cheek pressed tightly against hers. He was breathing loudly, his lips slightly parted as though he'd run a punishing marathon, and his face gleamed with sweat.

They rested quietly, their breathing slowing to normal. Buchanan stroked her back, and she lay against his chest, listening to the thudding of his heart.

Darkness was stretching across the patio when he raised his head and looked up at the stars. In the thin air, the sparkling constellations were almost iridescent.

His voice was quiet but persuasive. "Mandy, about the story I told Santalucci, he has to believe it's true. He was just testing this afternoon, trying to find a weak spot. He's got to know by now I've been asking questions around town." His jaw clenched. "I wish we had more time. Sooner or later someone will say something they shouldn't, I can feel it. If I ask enough questions of the right people, sooner or later I'll get the lead I need.'' He sighed. ''There's something I'm forgetting, something that keeps nagging at me. It's some kind of a key, a trigger, but it just keeps hovering out of reach.'' His shoulders bunched. ''I'm damned rusty.''

Her heart filled with pain. He wanted to find Jessie as much as she did. And he was angry with himself because he'd failed so far.

''It's only been a week, Devlin. You've been out every night, asking questions. I don't know what else you can do.''

''I can talk to Lola.''

''No!''

''Damn it, Mandy! She's the only lead we have.''

''You promised!''

His impatient sigh shattered the connection between them. ''Some promises are made to be broken.''

''Not this one. I know you'll keep it. I trust you.''

''The State rests, Your Honor.''

Amanda nodded at Arthur Francis and glanced at the clock. It was nearly four o'clock on the second Friday of the trial.

Because the majority of the evidence against Santalucci was circumstantial, it had had to be presented in meticulous detail. Most of the prosecution's witnesses were forensic experts, called to reconstruct the crime in such a way as to link the killings through a circuitous route back to the suave crime boss.

Amanda redirected her gaze to the defendant's table. As always when she had to look toward Santalucci, she had to force herself to show no emotion whatsoever. After ten full days of graphic testimony, she was finding it increasingly hard to remain detached.

''Ms. Devereaux, if you have no objections, I intend to recess for the weekend.''

The chic attorney stood and smiled. ''No objection, Your Honor. I'm sure we could all use the rest.'' She smiled winningly at the jurors, and several of the men smiled back.

''Court is adjourned until Monday morning at ten o'clock.''

Amanda kicked a clod of dirt out of her way with the gleaming toe of her boot and squinted toward the mountains. A fluffy white jet trail curled lazily over the Sandia Crest to the west, heading toward Arizona or maybe California.

It was a beautiful morning, the kind she liked best. The scent of piñon and juniper filled the air, and the wind stung her cheeks. The air was crisp and clear and carried the promise of another sizzling summer day.

They'd gotten a late start on their Sunday ride, mainly because Devlin had kept her in bed and very busy for a long time.

They'd ridden out toward Golden in a slow easy canter, the kind of ride she enjoyed most, and now they were on foot, leading the horses in a cooling walk behind them.

She was enjoying the exercise. She'd been cooped up too much the past two weeks.

On the weekdays their routine never varied. After court they'd have an early dinner, usually something from her freezer cooked in the microwave, and then Devlin would hit the streets, prowling his old haunts, listening to the rambling gossip of drunks, prodding strung-out addicts for names, trying unsuccessfully to scare up a clue to Jessie's whereabouts. But Santalucci had put out the word. No one was talking.

Night after night Devlin would come home, shower away the stench of the bars, and slip between the sheets to make love to her. Their lovemaking was the only joy in Amanda's life, the only spot of sanity in an increasingly insane environment.

Day after day she had to force herself to listen attentively and dispassionately to the testimony, her disgust for Santalucci growing as the evidence mounted. The man was guilty, she was sure of it.

Fortunately, after a shaky start, Arthur Francis had proved surprisingly competent, and she'd had to make very few rulings.

But, on Monday, all of that would change. Pamela Devereaux would be the one asking the questions, and if Amanda's hunch was correct, the shrewd attorney would expect Amanda to grant her wide latitude in that questioning. She would go after the prosecution witnesses with a stiletto, and Amanda would be forced to make a decision. To exercise fairness, or prejudice in favor of Santalucci.

"I can't do it, Devlin. I can't let Pamela Devereaux do whatever she wants tomorrow."

Devlin's eyes were shadowed under the brim of his hat. "You'll have to be clever about it, Mandy. Very subtle. Otherwise, it won't take Santalucci long to figure out that you intend to cross him."

"I know," she said dejectedly. "And I know what he could do to Jessie. But what if...what if I helped get him off and then he killed someone else's child? Or someone's father or brother? Or mother?" She played with the end of the braided rein, her fingers stiff with tension.

"You'd hurt like hell." Buchanan's voice was matter-of-fact. "But your daughter would be alive. Is that a fair trade-off?" He shrugged. "You have to answer that one."

Dervish pawed the ground impatiently, and Buchanan rubbed the stallion's nose, calming him.

She sighed. "There's more to it than that." She gritted her teeth against the caustic taste of self-disgust. "He'd own me. For the rest of my life he'd be able to blackmail me into doing whatever nasty little chore he needed a judge for." Her face contorted into a grimace of pain. "It would be a betrayal of everything I hold dear. I can't do it."

Devlin pulled her into his arms, and the strong hand that had gentled the powerful horse began to work the same magic on her. She sighed and let herself relax against him.

"I didn't want to tell you this before I checked it out," he said against her hair, "but last night I got a line on one of Santalucci's goons who's been shooting off his mouth, complaining about black lung disease."

She stared up at him. "Black lung disease? What's that got to do with Jessie?"

"Maybe nothing, but Tully, my bartender friend, tells me that this guy Keller hasn't been around for a while, since the Fourth of July, in fact. Tully noticed because Keller is one of his regulars, a really heavy hitter, and his bar receipts took a nosedive when the guy suddenly up and disappeared."

He shoved the Stetson to the back of his head and rested his chin on Amanda's head, his eyes searching the lonely terrain.

"Night before last Keller suddenly shows up at Tully's, trying to drink up all his best bourbon. The more he drank, the more he talked. Claims he's being poisoned by coal dust. He was spouting off to Tully about this big bonus he was going to get and how it wasn't enough for the kind of risk he was taking."

Amanda grabbed his arm. "You think this...this Keller has something to do with Jessie's abduction?"

He covered her hand with his. "Yes, I think he's one of her guards."

She felt like glittering sparklers were clustering in front of her eyes. Devlin had a clue, a real lead. She took a deep breath, trying to clear her head. "Can you find him? Does Tully know where this...this Keller is? What do we do next?" In her escalating anxiety her fingernails raked his bare skin, leaving tiny white tracks in his tan.

"I've told you all Tully knows, and I had to call in every marker I could dredge from my memory to get that. The guy owed me for a few favors I've done him over the years.'' He smiled at her startled look. "Don't ask. I won't tell you.

"As soon as we get back I'm going to call Rosa, ask to see her some time after dark tonight. She grew up in this area. Maybe she can give me the locations of some abandoned coal mines."

"I'm going with you."

He shook his head. "No way. This is my job."

"But—"

"No, Amanda. I can't do my job right when you're around."

Her face flamed. "It looks like you didn't need Lola after all."

Buchanan frowned. "Don't get your hopes up. We haven't found Keller yet."

"No, but you will. I know you will."

He brushed his lips against hers and helped her into the saddle.

Frustration burned inside him. He wanted to find Jessie more than anything he'd ever wanted in his life, and yet he wasn't much closer to doing that than he was two weeks ago. He clenched his big fist around the stallion's coarse mane.

"I'm going to get that bastard, Mandy, if it's the last thing I ever do. I swear it."

Suddenly the hatred was back in his eyes, and Amanda shivered. She was very frightened—for both of them.

Buchanan returned after midnight. His left cheek was scratched and bleeding, and the knuckles on both hands were swollen and red.

He sat down on the side of the bed and pulled off his boots.

"You've been in a fight," Amanda exclaimed, touching her fingertip gently to his raw face.

"You might say that." He shrugged out of his vest and threw it in the corner.

"Two guys jumped me as soon as I got out of the car. Real sweethearts. They must have been driving without lights. I never saw them."

"You mean they followed you to Rosalie's? From here?"

He flexed his left hand, his breath whistling shrilly through his parted lips as the bruised tissue protested.

"Must have. They were on me as soon as I started to walk up the driveway. If the guy next door hadn't turned on his porch light and threatened to call the police, I'd probably be at the bottom of the Rio Grande now."

Amanda sent a silent message of thanks to that unknown Samaritan for saving Buchanan's life. "You need ice for those bruises," she said softly, wincing at the angry swelling puffing around the knuckles.

"Among other things." He grinned suggestively as his gaze dipped to the see-through top of her frilly black nightgown. It was the same one he'd stripped from her that morning with such artistry.

"Devlin, be serious. You're in pain."

"I'm always in pain when I'm around you, Mandy. I think you've cast some kind of damned spell on me. My only regret when I thought I'd bought it was that I wouldn't be able to make love to you one more time." He dipped his head and nuzzled her breast.

She caressed his strong neck, her heart pounding with relief, her throat tight. *My only regret...*

A sudden image of Devlin, battered and bloody, lying in the matted reeds by the river's edge rose in her mind, and she shuddered. "I don't know what I would have done if you'd been k-killed," she whispered, clutching him tightly.

He sighed against her breast. "Hey, I'm not dead yet. I just need a hot bath, and a stiff drink." He kissed the creamy skin above the black lace and lifted his head. He winced as his hand brushed against her thigh. "On second thought, make that a double."

She punched his shoulder and scrambled off the bed. "Take off your clothes. I'll fill the tub and get your drink."

She hurried into the bathroom, breathing a quick prayer of thanks for the Jacuzzi jets that would take some of the soreness from Buchanan's battered muscles.

Setting the water temperature to as hot as she could stand it, she searched through the cabinet under the sink until she found a box of Epsom salts.

"Wait until I get back before you get in the tub," she called over her shoulder.

"Dare I hope you want to undress me yourself?" he said in a wickedly seductive voice as she passed him on the way to the kitchen.

"Absolutely," she bantered, careful to keep the love she was feeling from her voice. She didn't want to put more of a burden on him than he was already carrying.

She returned minutes later with a glass, a full bottle of tequila she'd found in the back of her liquor cabinet and a bucket of ice on a silver butler's tray. She set the tray on the dresser and hurried to turn off the water.

The tub was nearly full and steaming hot.

"Forget the ice," he mumbled when she returned. His brooding gaze studied her face as she splashed the fiery tequila into a glass.

"The ice is for your knuckles," she shot back, handing him the tumbler.

A spark of humor glimmered through the pain as he saluted her with his eyes before downing the drink in two long swallows. He held the glass out silently.

"You want more."

"Damn straight. I intend to get blind drunk tonight." He set his teeth against a sudden spasm of pain. "I wouldn't mind smashing up my hands if the lead had panned out, but it didn't."

Amanda's hand jerked, and the bottle clinked against the rim of the glass. "It didn't? You didn't see Rosalie?"

"I saw her. She arrived home while I was trying to pull my wits together. She was so upset, wanting to call Cy and the police and everyone else she could think of, that I couldn't get a whole lot out of her. But I did find out that all the mines in the area had been sealed by the state sometime in the seventies after a little boy wandered into one and fell through a rotten timber." Abruptly he wiped the blood from his cheek. "I'm sorry, Mandy. I really thought I had something."

His voice was beginning to slur from weariness, and she felt a surge of love. He took the glass she held out and drank, this time more slowly. He scowled as the liquor slid past his throat.

"The next time I see those two stooges I'll be ready." Amanda could feel his ruthless resolve, and she went cold inside.

"The next time they could kill you," she said caustically. "And then what? Am I supposed to take out a contract on them for killing someone I...for killing a friend?" Her voice rose shrilly. "Tell me, what's the procedure?"

Devlin's brows slid into a puzzled frown. "Hey, what did I say to bring this on?"

She ignored the question. "I've never plotted revenge," she said heatedly. "Just how does one go about it?"

Buchanan's eyes lost their sleepy cast. "I wouldn't know, Amanda. I've never done it, either." He tossed down the drink and set the empty glass on the nightstand with a sharp thunk.

His movements were jerky, clearly the result of his anger, as he removed the holster and shirt. He started to tuck the gun under the pillow, then changed his mind and left it in the holster, which he tossed onto the mattress behind him.

Peeling out of his shirt was more difficult. His bruised hands were stiff, and he had trouble with the buttons.

Amanda took an anxious step forward. "Here, let me—"

"No, thanks." His curt words put a screen between them, and she dug her nails into her palms.

"You're angry with me."

"You got that right." He swore as the middle button slipped between his thumb and fingers and tried again.

"I didn't mean what I said—about revenge, I mean."

"Yes, you did. You can't believe I didn't go looking for Gus D'Amato with my gun already drawn." He raised his head and pinned her with a look. "You can't forget it, can you?"

She bit her lip. She couldn't lie to him. "No."

"If I gave you my word I don't intend to kill Santalucci unless I have to, would you believe me?"

I want to, she answered silently. Oh, how I want to. She studied his face as he waited, his cheeks suddenly one shade paler than they'd been when he returned. His left hand was clenched against his belly, the other open and vulnerable on the coverlet by his thigh.

There was strength in the firm set of his wide lips, endurance in the square jaw, tenacity in the set of his brows. And honesty etched in every line and angle of his hard, unsmiling face. She loved him so much.

"You don't have to give me your word. I believe you."

Chapter 13

Amanda had a headache, making it hard to concentrate. The overhead lights in the courtroom were too bright, and the amplification system on the witness microphone periodically emitted a high-pitched shriek that assaulted her eardrums.

She glanced toward the clock. The morning session had run over by nearly thirty minutes, and the jurors were getting restive. If defense counsel didn't wind up her questioning soon, she would have to interrupt. Hungry jurors found it difficult to pay attention.

As though on cue, Pamela Devereaux suddenly beamed at the man on the stand, her smile triumphant. "No further questions, Mr. Mileski."

The witness, a slick, well-spoken handwriting expert from New York, glanced questioningly toward the bench as though waiting for further instructions.

"The witness will please make himself available for cross-examination when we resume court at two o'clock," Amanda said, nodding toward the bailiff who made a note of her words.

Mileski had been articulate and precise, but his loud, abrasive manner had grated on her thinly stretched nerves.

"Yes, Your Honor," the witness boomed, nodding amiably toward the prosecution table. He'd sworn emphatically and with heavy-handed vehemence that the wobbly signature on the deathbed confession of Santalucci's chief enforcer was a forgery.

"Court stands adjourned until two." Amanda banged the gavel and stood up, leaving quickly, her head throbbing.

Juana was waiting for her, the usual glass of water in her hand.

"I need aspirin, too, please. My head feels like it's about to explode." She shrugged out of her robe and handed it to the clerk, who put down the glass and draped the garment over her arm, smoothing the fabric absently with a nervous hand.

"There's a man named Tanner in your office, Your Honor. He showed a badge and refused to leave. I was about to check with security when you came in."

"Cyrus Tanner?"

"Yes, that's his name. He says he's with the FBI, but he flashed that darn ID so fast it could have been from the Boy Scouts for all I know." She scowled and carefully hung the robe on the brass clothes tree.

Amanda's heart started to pound. Surely Cy would have called first before he risked being seen in her chambers, especially since he'd been so paranoid about leaks. She bit her lip and glanced toward the frosted glass pane bearing her name in gold letters.

"Where's Mr. Buchanan?" Juana asked anxiously as she removed a large bottle of extra-strength aspirin from her desk drawer and shook two white tablets into her palm.

"Right here. What's wrong?"

Buchanan glanced over his shoulder at the empty corridor behind him, then closed the door quietly and crossed immediately to Amanda's side.

His swollen fingers fumbled with the button to his jacket, giving him access to his pistol, and he swore under his breath as he flexed the bruised hand. If he had to get to his gun quickly, he was in trouble.

"There's a man in my chambers. He told Juana he was Cyrus Tanner." She took the aspirin Juana held out to her and picked up the glass of water with shaking fingers.

"Cy? What the hell is he doing here?"

Amanda swallowed the aspirin and shook her head, gulping down the rest of the water. Her throat felt better, still constricted from tension, but not as dry.

"You stay here. I'll find out."

Amanda and Juana exchanged looks. "Should I get security?" Juana asked in a strained voice.

Buchanan gave her an impatient look. "No, just stand back out of the way, both of you. Cy isn't prone to stupid acts, so he's here for a reason. I'll find out what it is."

He glanced pointedly at the two lunch containers on Juana's square desk. "Eat," he said gruffly, frowning at Amanda's wan expression. "You look pale." His gaze softened for an instant, sending a flood of warm feeling into her aching head and she nodded, trying to force a smile. It was a failure. She was too frightened.

He waited until Amanda and Juana were behind the desk, out of the line of fire from the door. He stood to the right of the walnut frame and turned the doorknob with his left hand. The door creaked in protest as he pushed it open with his foot, his hand inside his jacket.

"Hello, Cy."

The station chief was standing by the window, looking down at the midday traffic snarl. He was wearing a lightweight blue suit, and his bald head gleamed with a fine sheen of sweat. His jacket hung open, his gun clearly visible in a belt holster. He didn't smile as he turned and watched Devlin walk into the room.

"Hello, Buchanan."

Devlin felt a chill rush through him. This wasn't the greeting of an old friend, or even a colleague. His guard raised instantly. Something was wrong.

Tanner's brown gaze flickered from the angry red scratch on Buchanan's cheek to his bruised hand. "You been in a fight of some kind?"

"Two guys jumped me last night. Right outside Rosalie Cruz's place, as a matter of fact. But something tells me you already know that."

Tanner shook his head. "I know what really happened, if that's what you mean." His cold, unfriendly gaze measured Buchanan's face.

"What *really* happened is what I just told you. Two of Santalucci's goons followed me from the judge's house, and as soon as I got out of the car, they were on me."

"I suppose Rosalie will back up that story."

"Not exactly." He went absolutely still, waiting. He didn't like the cynical look in Cy's eyes.

"Care to explain that?"

"Rosa didn't arrive until after the guys had left. I was sitting on her porch trying to catch my breath when she got there."

He heard a noise behind him, then Amanda was in the room, her face pinched with strain. "Hello, Cy."

Devlin hated the desperate note in her soft voice. She was expecting bad news, and he couldn't blame her. *He* certainly hadn't been much help to her so far.

Tanner looked distinctly uncomfortable as he hunched his shoulder and returned Amanda's greeting.

"Your Honor. I'm sorry to barge into your office without being invited, but it was...necessary."

"It's Jessie, isn't it? You know something." She prepared her mind for the worst. Whatever happened she would handle it—somehow. "Tell me, Cy. Is she...is she dead?"

"No! God, no that's not it," Tanner rushed to explain, his brow furrowed in apology. "I should have made it plainer. I'm here to arrest Buchanan."

"What?" Amanda's voice was a croak of relief and shock. "A-arrest him for what?"

"For putting Lola Grimes into Southwest Memorial with a concussion, broken jaw and internal injuries." Tanner trained his gaze on Buchanan like twin barrels of a shotgun. Devlin flinched but met his accusing stare stoically.

"You're crazy," he said calmly. "I saw her once, and that was two weeks ago. Amanda was with me. Lola was fine when we left."

"That's right," Amanda said evenly. "Do you have a reason for this accusation?" There had to be a logical explanation for Tanner's words, a plausible, but mistaken reason for thinking that Devlin was implicated.

Cy shoved his hands into his pockets and leaned back against the windowsill. He looked angry and distressed at the same time.

"According to Lola," he began brusquely, "Buchanan here came to her place around eight." He raised his brows. "I presume he'd left your house by then."

Amanda sucked in her breath and glanced up at Devlin. "Yes," she said reluctantly. "He left around seven-fifteen, seven-twenty."

Tanner nodded tersely and began speaking directly to Buchanan. "Lola didn't want to let you in, but you forced her. You had a plan, you told her. If she would swear to the DA that she'd overhead Santalucci plotting to kill those two reporters, just as he'd plotted to kill Tony, you'd see that she and her son got new IDs and a new life. When she refused, you started slapping her around. When she begged you to stop, you started hitting her." His eyes zeroed in on

Devlin's cheek. "She fought back as much as she could, but you were too strong for her. She was unconscious when you left."

Devlin tightened his body, muscle by muscle, his face showing nothing but denial. He glanced at Amanda. She looked shocked and disbelieving, but when her eyes met his they were full of unspoken support. Warmth flooded his system. At least she was on his side.

"Lola's lying," he said coldly, redirecting his attention to his former superior. "Why would I do something so stupid?"

Tanner made an impatient gesture. "Revenge. If Santalucci suddenly turned up with a bullet in his head, you'd be the prime suspect. But this way, with a witness like Lola, he'd get life in prison without parole, no doubt about it."

Devlin took a steadying breath. He didn't like the way Amanda was suddenly standing so still and quiet next to him. "And the first thing Santalucci would do is kill Amanda's daughter. Uh-uh. It doesn't wash."

Tanner looked almost sad. "You had that covered too, Dev. You planned to tell Santalucci the judge would put in a good word for him with the DA if he released the girl. You shouldn't have been so talkative; Lola has a good memory."

Devlin uttered a rank obscenity that made Amanda jump. "This is a setup, Cy, to get me out of the way. Can't you see that?" He jerked his shoulders impatiently. "Santalucci planned to rough me up, but not enough to make it look like I was attacked. One of those guys deliberately scratched my cheek, and they left before I was badly hurt. It all fits. And I fell for it like a damned rookie." He was looking at Amanda, speaking directly to her.

She wet her lips and swallowed. The paneled walls of her office seemed to close in on her as she wrenched her gaze away from Devlin's face and regarded Tanner with forced assurance. "He told me about those men when he came home," she said calmly. She felt removed from Buchanan, from Cy, from everything.

"Yes, ma'am," Tanner said almost gently, "but that's hearsay, isn't it?"

She was beginning to hurt very badly, somewhere deep inside, but she ruthlessly ignored the feeling. Buchanan couldn't have done what that woman claimed. Not Devlin. Not the man she loved.

But inside her head a nagging voice kept reminding her of that night in Lola's apartment when she'd been absolutely convinced that he intended to do something violent.

"Maybe Santalucci threatened Lola if she didn't lie. Maybe he had some of his goons beat her up to make it look like D—Buchanan did it," she suggested, looking quickly up at Devlin, offering her support. His eyes flared, drawing her to him like a powerful electromagnet, ordering her to believe him.

"There's a witness."

"*Like hell there is!*" Buchanan all but shouted, and pain shot up his wrists as he involuntarily clenched his hands. "Whoever he is, he's lying."

"Guy's the night security guard, an ex-cop named Robbins. He identified your picture as the visitor who went up to Lola's apartment that night about quarter till eight." He sighed heavily and stood up. "We've got you cold this time, Dev. Don't make it any worse than it is."

A witness, Amanda thought, her mind screaming in disbelief. They had a witness, a man who'd seen Devlin go up to Lola's apartment. How could that be?

The overhead lights hissed loudly in the tense silence, startling her. Her body felt unnaturally cold, as though her blood had stopped circulating, and her throat felt pinched.

Ignoring Tanner and Juana, who was staring, open-mouthed and wide-eyed, from the doorway, Devlin placed his bruised hands on Amanda's shoulders and shook her slightly. "I didn't do it, Amanda. You have to believe me. The man's lying. Lola's lying."

Amanda slowly raised her head, her eyes open and vulnerable. "I know. I trust you, Devlin, in spite of the evidence. I do."

"Thank you," he said in a barely audible voice, pulling her against his chest for an instant before firmly setting her away.

Amanda swallowed. "We'll fight this. We'll prove that they're lying. I know you don't believe in the system, but we can make it work."

Devlin felt a heavy weariness fill his body. He was tired of fighting, tired of explaining, tired of being out there all alone, tired of trying to make sense of the whole rotten mess.

Sighing, he forced himself to speak softly, without the frustrated anger that was shaking him. "Don't count on it, Mandy. There are a lot of innocent guys behind those walls up in Santa Fe. Guys who thought justice was more than just a word." His lips quirked mockingly. "Funny, isn't it? For the first time in my life, I was trying to play by someone else's rules. Your rules." His eyes filled with scorn for himself. "Too bad you couldn't convince the Saint to do the same."

He stepped away from her and carefully opened his jacket, exposing his weapon, making himself completely vulnerable. Tanner crossed the room quickly to remove the Beretta from the holster, deftly unloading the gun before he shoved it and the bullets into his jacket pocket.

"This is really the police department's jurisdiction, but Captain Fleming called me first as a courtesy, and I told him I'd bring you in." He hesitated. "He thought you might prefer it that way."

"What's the difference?" Buchanan didn't care who arrested him. His mind had gone numb. Like an animal caught in a trap, he was concentrating on conserving his energy.

Tanner avoided Buchanan's gaze as he nodded to two short-haired men in dark summer suits and sunglasses who'd suddenly materialized as he'd been talking.

One of the men came forward, a pair of steel handcuffs in his hand, and Amanda gasped, her eyes filled with horror. Oh, Devlin, she moaned silently, hating the look that came over his face at the sight of the shackles.

Buchanan fought down the humiliation and held out his wrists, his chin tilted defiantly, his eyes proud. The agent snapped on the cuffs, and the men turned to go.

Amanda stood frozen, her veins carrying blood, her lungs expanding and contracting, her eyes blinking, and yet she felt as though she were dying.

A part of her *was* dying, she realized as she slowly turned to watch him being led from her office. The part of her that loved Devlin Buchanan was screaming in mortal pain.

At the door he stopped and looked back, his expression remote. "I'm sorry, Mandy. I did the best I could."

Before she could answer, he was gone.

Amanda stood in the hall of her big empty house, listening to the silence. Cloying and heavy, the stillness mocked her. *He's not here. He'll never be here again. In her house. In her bed. In her life.*

Before she'd left her chambers for the evening, she'd called the Chief Marshal to find out where they'd taken him. Devlin was in the county jail, locked in a crowded holding cell like a common criminal, and she was alone.

And yet his presence was everywhere. In the living room, where the new pane in the arched window winked brightly in the glow from the dying sun. In the kitchen, where the outsized coffee mug she'd bought him sat by the sink. Even in the hall, where he'd once told her that her rules didn't count with a man like Santalucci.

Like a woman walking in her sleep, Amanda made her way slowly down the hall toward his room. His things were still there, hanging in the closet and shoved into drawers. She'd have to see about packing them up for him. But where should she send them? Back to Mexico? Or to the jail?

"Oh, Devlin," she whispered into the emptiness. "I love you so much. What am I going to do?"

This time she couldn't stop the tears. They flooded her eyes in hot, painful waves and coursed, unchecked, down her cheeks. Her body shook with sobs of pain and anger.

Through her tears she saw, amidst the masculine clutter on the dresser, the fat panda that he was carving for Jessie. It was unfinished.

Amanda had just gotten into bed when the phone rang. It was only a little past nine, but she was exhausted.

"Judge Wainwright, I'm calling to offer my condolences on the unfortunate arrest of your...bodyguard. I hope you're not too upset to continue the trial." It was Santalucci's voice, silky smooth and triumphant and tinged with menace.

She froze, her breath trapped in her lungs. She exhaled slowly, gathering her wits, praying for the right words. "Mr. Santalucci, this is highly improper." She made her voice severely disapproving in case he was taping the conversation.

"Sure, sure, I know. I just wanted you to know I have your little...package safe and sound. Buchanan's bumbling won't have to cause either of us any trouble unless one of us overreacts."

She drew in her breath sharply and gripped the receiver so tightly one of her nails snapped, tearing her skin to the quick.

"And do you intend to overreact, Mr. Santalucci?" Her voice was cold and without inflection, but inside she was shaking so badly it was difficult to keep her teeth from chattering audibly.

His unctuous laugh assaulted her ear. "Not unless you do. And I have every confidence in you, Judge. Every confidence."

He hung up without saying goodbye.

Amanda slowly dropped the phone into the cradle. A murderous rage swept through her, shaking her to the marrow. She hated George Santalucci, hated him as she'd never hated anyone or anything in her life.

He was evil, a vicious, amoral killer who deserved to die in the same way his victims had, violently and painfully. No law was written to protect a man like that, it couldn't have been.

She sucked on her bleeding finger and sank back against the pillow. "Bastard," she said with angry vehemence into the darkened room. "I'll get you if it's the last thing I do."

The words hung in the air, familiar and taunting. Her stomach jerked painfully, and her head was swimming. Her hands and feet felt heavy and hot, as though her blood was pooling in her extremities. Every muscle in her body screamed in protest as she realized what she'd just said.

Revenge. She was plotting revenge. Just as she'd once accused Devlin of doing.

"Oh God," she whispered, her throat aching. How could she have considered such a thing for even a moment? A second? Her belief in the law was unshakable, her conviction an intrinsic part of her.

And yet the feelings were there and growing stronger. Every day as she watched Santalucci pose for pictures and quip with the press, she longed to wipe that smirk off his face with a prejudicial ruling. Every day she was tempted to let the jury see her true feelings. Every day she hated more.

But that would make her no better than him. And that was something she could never live with.

As she buried her face in the pillow and shut her eyes, she heard her daughter's voice, sounding softly inside her head. "What about me, Mommy? How will you feel if I die?"

For the first time she understood Devlin, how angry and frustrated and alone he felt. And how terribly hard it was to play by the rules.

She was dreaming. The phone was ringing, and it was Santalucci, telling her where to find Jessica. But she was trapped in Devlin's arms, unable to move, unable to reach the receiver.

She thrashed against the mattress in protest, but the phone kept on ringing.

Suddenly she awakened. It wasn't a dream.

Her hand groped toward the receiver as she struggled to rid herself of the nightmare. Devlin's arms had felt so real, so strong.

"This is Judge Wainwright." She blinked against the darkness, making out familiar shadows as her eyes adjusted to the limited light.

"Judge, this is Cy Tanner. Buchanan has escaped."

"But...but how?" An adrenaline rush shot through her body, prodding her into a heightened alertness.

"One of his guards in the interrogation room was a woman, and Dev talked her into letting him go to the bathroom. Regulations demand that she go with him, and when they were alone, he overpowered her and took her weapon. He was long gone before we found her in one of the stalls, strapped onto the seat with her belt, one of her socks shoved in her mouth.''

"Was...was she hurt?"

"Just her dignity." Anger thickened his drawl. "He's really done it this time. The police have an all points out on him. He'll never plea-bargain out of this one."

Amanda bit her lip, her breathing loud and irregular, her hands perspiring. "They won't shoot him, will they?" Her mind shied away from the image of Devlin's strong body riddled with more bullet holes, his beautiful eyes staring sightlessly at the sky.

"Not unless he draws that gun he took from the guard."

"I see." She didn't know what to say. She was glad he was free, and yet how could she be? He was an accused felon who'd escaped custody. Her mind whirled, her thoughts contradictory and disturbing.

Tanner spoke again. "I doubt that he'll come back to your house, Your Honor, but in case he does, let me know as soon as you can." He gave her a number where he could be reached at any hour.

"Uh, wait, Cy. Let me...let me get a pencil." She sat up and snapped on the light, squinting painfully against the glare. There was a pencil and a pad in the drawer on the nightstand and she fumbled to find them.

Finally she did. "Go ahead," she muttered, balancing the pad on her knee. He repeated the number, and she dutifully wrote it down.

"Uh, Your Honor. Amanda, I'm...sorry this didn't work out. With Buchanan I mean. If you still want me to...to help you, I could take a chance, maybe take some vacation time and—"

"I'll call you," she said, knowing that she wouldn't. If Devlin, with all his contacts, hadn't been able to find Jessie, Cy Tanner never could. She knew that now. Devlin knew his job inside and out. He was the best—strong, courageous and dedicated.

Amanda hung up, her heart heavy. How could she sleep when her bed seemed so empty without Devlin's big, warm body cradling hers, without his regular breathing lulling her to sleep, without his stubbled cheek nuzzling her shoulder? How could she rest, knowing he was on the streets, armed, maybe bleeding from a policeman's bullet?

She turned out the light and turned onto her side, away from the pillow he'd used. She'd never felt so lost and alone in her life.

Chapter 14

"Mr. Tanner called again while you were in court." Juana gave Amanda a veiled look. "He wanted you to know that a man answering Buchanan's description was seen crossing the border sometime early this morning."

Amanda nodded. She was bone-tired and not in the best of moods. It was the third Friday of the trial, the noon recess, and she wasn't looking forward to the afternoon session. "I imagine he's deep in the interior by now."

She'd expected Devlin to make directly for the border, she admitted silently as she handed her robe to Juana. It was the smart thing to do. So why did the knowledge that he was out of her life for good hurt so desperately?

"Do you have another headache, Your Honor? Can I get you a couple of aspirin or something?"

How about a new heart?

Great, Amanda, she thought wearily. Now you're really losing it. What happened to the cool and unflappable Judge Wainwright who handled everything, even her husband's unexpected death, with rock-hard Yankee control?

She gave Juana a soothing smile. "Thanks, but I'm fine. Just feeling the stress of the trial and everything. After I have my salad, I think I'll rest a few minutes. That should help." If anything could.

Juana carried the lunch carton into the inner office, and Amanda followed. Wearily she sat down behind the large walnut desk and tried to relax. The morning session had seemed interminable.

"Our illustrious defendant was certainly in good form before the session," Juana said disapprovingly as she set out Amanda's salad and unwrapped the plastic utensils. "He told the press his attorney was going to file for mistrial because of Mr. Buchanan's 'close association' with the trial judge."

"Really? I come in the back way, so I miss his daily performance." Amanda found it hard to discuss the man while hatred still burned inside her. "I did notice, though, that his group of 'personal assistants' had grown considerably overnight."

"Yeah, real intellectual types, with cauliflower ears and racing forms for brains." Juana wrinkled her nose in disgust and flopped into the chair across from the desk. "Santalucci wasn't so confident when Mr. Buchanan was around." She slipped her foot from her low-heeled pump and let the shoe hang from her toes, her expression thoughtful.

Amanda unfolded her napkin and picked up her fork. She wasn't hungry, but she had to eat to keep up her strength.

From the moment she'd convened court, she'd been on edge, her composure ragged, her nerves ready to unravel, and it had taken all of her skill to maintain her concentration.

Pamela Devereaux was painting a masterful picture of a man harassed and falsely accused, an innocent framed for a crime he didn't commit because one of his employees had once made the mistake of shooting an undercover FBI agent.

As an advocate, the woman was brilliant. Amanda hated every word, every clever piece of innuendo and misdirection the tough-minded attorney managed to plant in the record. She longed to intercept every slanted statement, sustain every objection made by the prosecutor, direct the jurors to ignore the lies.

But she'd remained judicially aloof, impassively making decisions on each objection by the rules of procedure only, keeping Ms. Devereaux on track without arousing Santalucci's suspicions.

Under her silk blouse, however, her skin felt hot and irritated, and her hands had been so numb it had been hard to hold the gavel.

The defense would rest in one more day, two at the most. Final summations would take another day, and then Amanda would be required to charge the jury.

After that it would all be over. And Santalucci would know that she had double-crossed him.

Forcing her mind away from the terrible thoughts that tormented her, Amanda finished her salad and shoved it aside. She was reaching for her iced tea when the phone rang. Juana answered immediately.

"Judge Wainwright's chambers." Juana's neutral expression darkened into a disapproving frown. "The judge never comments on a trial in process.... No, I will not. Goodbye."

She slammed the receiver into the cradle and rested her hands on her hips, irritation shining from her eyes. "Another reporter. The fifth this week." Her scowl deepened. "They all want to know your reaction to Mr. Buchanan's escape. They're trying to make him sound like public enemy number one or something, the way they keep bringing up that old case."

Every morning the paper carried an update on Devlin. The facts of his previous arrest and trial were dredged up, and the obvious comparisons made. Amanda had read them all before dumping the newspaper into the garbage.

"I don't give a damn what they want!" she told Juana with a glower toward the silent phone. "Pack of jackals."

The shocked expression darkening her assistant's face brought a rush of heat to Amanda's cheeks, but she didn't care. For once she was speaking from the heart, not the intellect, and it felt surprisingly good. If anything could feel good right now.

"Thanks for the lunch, Juana," she said, and the petite clerk shot to her feet.

"You bet. I'll just get this stuff out of your way." She bustled around the desk.

She started to leave, then turned back, her dark brows pulled into a hesitant frown. "For what it's worth, I don't think Mr. Buchanan is guilty. He's not the type to hurt a woman."

Amanda gaped at her. "What makes you think that?" she asked warily. Juana was an unusually good judge of character, when her libido didn't get in the way.

"I can see it in his eyes."

At the judge's skeptical look, Juana smiled, a sad, poignant expression that Amanda had never seen before. "He has eyes like a man I wanted to marry once. He was my childhood sweetheart, a great guy with a big heart."

"He was always helping people out, you know. If a buddy needed a loan or the answers to a quiz or even a shoulder to cry on, Tom was there. He was going to be a doctor, and I was going to be a doctor's wife." Her lips began to tremble, and she sucked on her lower lip to stop the quivering.

"What happened?" Amanda asked gently.

"He was drafted. It was the last year of the war and I told him to go to Canada instead, but he said he was proud to do his duty." Juana's brown eyes flashed with pain. "He was a medic."

"What happened?" Amanda prodded. She'd never seen the other woman so somber.

"He survived, but when he came home he was different. He kept to himself a lot, took long walks, always keeping me at a distance. I tried to be patient, but one day I'd had it, and I made him tell me what was wrong."

"Flashbacks?"

"No, although he had them. It was worse than that. His best buddy, another medic, had died in his arms, and Tom had freaked out. Killed four Vietcong prisoners before they stopped him."

"Was he court-martialed?"

"No. Apparently prisoners were shot 'by accident' all the time." She sighed. "Only Tom couldn't forget it. He said it made him sick inside, like a sore that wouldn't heal." She chewed her lip. "I tried, but I couldn't help him. On the day he broke our engagement he told me he couldn't stand any more pain. He didn't want to feel anything anymore. Not even love."

Amanda sat very still. "And you think Buchanan's like that?"

"Yes, I think he's exactly like that." She hesitated, then took a step closer. "I've also seen the way he looks at you, Judge. He's crazy about you."

Amanda shook her head, forgetting that she should keep her private life out of chambers. She needed a friend now, and Juana had been more than an assistant to her for a long time.

"I wish he were, Juana. But he's got this shell around him, and I can't get inside."

"Maybe you have, and don't know it."

Amanda lifted her shoulders slowly, trying to work out the kinks. "If I have, I'll never know it. He's long gone. I'll never see him again."

Juana's expression softened, and her eyes held a liquid sheen of sympathy. "I wouldn't count on it, Judge. If he loves you, he'll be back."

Amanda tried to smile but couldn't quite pull it off. "What happened to Tom? Did he ever come back?"

"Yes, two years later. I was married to someone else by then." Her mouth trembled softly. "The next day he shot himself out behind his father's barn."

Another photograph of Jessie was waiting for her when she returned home that evening. It was in the mailbox, along with her other mail, but the long white envelope contained no address and no postmark. Someone had hand-delivered it.

A clammy fear gripped her. Now she was really and truly alone, with no one to protect her. Any time Santalucci's goons wanted to get to her, they could.

A surge of rage shook her. How could Buchanan have left her alone like this? But of course she knew her anger was irrational. He'd been framed, and he'd left town because he hadn't trusted the system he scorned to protect him from an unfair conviction.

She forced herself to remain calm, to wait until she was safely inside the house before carefully examining the glossy photo.

This time her little girl was wearing a dark blue sweatshirt that was obviously far too big for her tiny body, and her hair had been pulled back from her face, magnifying the bewilderment in her big green eyes and emphasizing the innocent lines of her small face. Once again she was holding the latest edition of the *Sun*.

Jessie's childish scrawl filled the back of the stiff pasteboard, and Amanda choked back the pain as she read the simple message. "Please, mommy. I want to come home."

"Oh, baby," she whispered. "I want you to come home, too."

But how was she ever going to make it happen? She was running out of time. If only she knew the name of that bar Buchanan had gone to out in Corales. Maybe she could convince his bartender friend to give her more information on Keller.

She'd give him money, all she had, if that's what it took. And she had a lot. Not too many people could resist that kind of money, no matter how frightened they might be.

Tomorrow was Saturday. She'd spend the day going to every bar in the area if she had to.

Clutching the precious photo tightly, she made her way to her room. She wasn't going to fall apart, she wasn't going to panic. She'd manage, somehow.

Thinking about a suitable disguise to wear, she dropped her purse onto the skinned pine chair by the wardrobe and started to unbutton her blouse.

"Very nice."

Amanda cried out, her hand clutching the silk beneath her fingertips, her breath coming in quick little spurts of alarm.

"*Devlin!* I thought you were in Mexico!"

Buchanan glanced down at his long form. He was stretched out on her bed, his head pillowed on his folded arms. He was wearing jeans and a tight black T-shirt, and his feet were bare.

"I was," he said laconically, "but I came back. Drove all night again." His slow smile lit his face. "It wasn't nearly as much fun this time."

She took an involuntary step toward him, then stopped short. His pose, so indolent and relaxed on the surface, suggested the leashed energy of a big cat lounging in the sun. His muscles were at rest, but his eyes held an alert watchfulness that set all her warning bells jangling.

"Tanner and the police have men looking for you everywhere," she said softly. "You can't stay here."

One tawny brow lifted quizzically. "Why not? I can't think of a safer place."

"That's just it. I'm obligated to turn you in," she said tonelessly, watching his eyes. There was no reaction. No anger, no hurt, nothing but wariness.

"There's the phone. Make your call if you feel you have to."

Of course she had to, and she would, but a few more minutes wouldn't make much difference, she told herself reassuringly.

"Why did you come back, Devlin? You would have been safe in Mexico."

"I came back because I know where Jessie is."

His words, unexpected and spoken so calmly in his distinctively husky voice, sent ripples of shock up her spine and into her brain. She groped for the carved post at the end of the bed, curving her chilled fingers around the smooth walnut in a desperate grip.

"Where, Devlin? Where's my baby?" She could scarcely get the words past her tight throat.

"In Madrid, out on the Turquoise Trail, in an abandoned mine shaft."

The hard ring of certainty in his voice made her want to shout with joy.

"Then that man Keller is involved, just as you thought." Excitement and relief bubbled in her throat, and she felt like laughing and crying at the same time.

Buchanan sat up and crossed his arms over his chest. "Yes, along with others. I had some time to think while I was on the run. The truth was staring me in the face all along. I just couldn't see it."

Self-contempt, anger, frustration paraded across his harsh features. "Talk about dumb. I'm the prize turkey."

Amanda moistened her lips. This was happening too fast for her to assimilate. "I don't understand. How could you have known?" Her fingers were white where they pressed against the unyielding walnut.

"Tony told me."

"What?"

Easy, Buchanan, he told himself silently. Her face was as white as the Sandia snowpack in January, and her eyes had a hard sheen that alarmed him.

He cleared his throat and tried to gentle his tone. "Come here and sit down. It's kind of complicated."

She looked ready to slug him, and he had to keep her calm so she wouldn't do something foolish, like call Cy Tanner.

Amanda hesitated, her heart beating erratically, her stomach leaping with confusion. In spite of the turmoil shaking her she was finding it hard to keep away from him. The lure of his arms was nearly irresistible, but she forced herself to remain where she was.

"I won't hurt you. I promise."

The rough pain in his voice forced her to move. She wasn't afraid of him—only of herself, and the overwhelming need for him that had only grown stronger while they'd been apart.

The mattress dipped under her weight, and his knee brushed her spine. He moved over slightly to give her room, his face impassive.

"I don't understand, Devlin. How could Tony tell you where Jessie is?"

His smile was fleeting and sad. "I remembered him telling me once about this Mexican restaurant he wanted to open up in Madrid when he retired. Most of what he said, I heard with half an ear, mostly because it was in the middle of a cold night on stakeout. But this stayed in my subconscious, nagging at me. And then I made a bad mistake, Mandy. I trusted the wrong person."

"What wrong person?" she asked anxiously.

"Rosalie Cruz."

Icy tentacles gripped her body, freezing her in a posture of disbelief. "I don't understand."

"No, I don't imagine you do. But I can explain."

He chewed on the corner of his mouth, a subtle masculine signal of distress that moved her immeasurably.

"Rosa was lost when Tony was killed. She needed someone, a man to take care of her. I don't know how it happened, maybe when she took that job with one of Santalucci's legitimate companies."

She started, and Buchanan nodded. "Yeah, I really dropped the ball on that one. I swallowed her story whole, without really paying much attention to the name of her employer. It wasn't until I started sifting through the pieces of the mess I'd made of things that I remembered. Rio Grande Properties, sole agent for that big new development east of Tramway Boulevard." His lips thinned in derision. "No wonder her new boss was from the east. He's a distant cousin of Santalucci's."

"How did you find out all of this?"

His bronzed skin suddenly darkened. "I called a girl I know who works for the Bureau in Washington. She ran a computer check for me."

Amanda could imagine the kind of relationship he'd had with the woman for her to risk her job for a man on the run. A white-hot shudder of jealousy passed through her, but he didn't notice. He was staring at his belt buckle, his face furrowed with disgust.

"Rosalie's father owned a piece of land between Golden and Madrid that contained an abandoned mine shaft on one section. In the fifties, because he was convinced that Russians were coming, he had a fully equipped bomb shelter built inside the shaft. I remember Tony telling me how he was going to include a tour of the bomb shelter as part of the price of a meal. I'd forgotten the part about the shelter until we were out riding on Sunday. And when I remembered, I called Rosa to confirm it. She insisted I come to her place to discuss it."

"But she told you the mines had all been sealed."

"Yes. After I had some time to think about it, I realized that she could have told me that on the phone."

"You think she called Santalucci and told him you were getting close?"

"Exactly. And he set me up, then sent some of his goons to do a job on Lola." His face darkened further. "Poor sad lady. He must have threatened to harm her son if she didn't go along with the plan."

Absently he flexed the fingers of his left hand. The bruises had turned yellow, but the knuckles were still swollen. "Once I figured out what must have happened, I knew that Rosa was Santalucci's mistress, the one no one had ever seen."

Amanda couldn't breathe. Rosalie Cruz, sleeping with Santalucci, letting him put his hands all over her. *Telling him things.*

"But that means he knows everything. About my coming to Mexico to find you, about your real reason for being here." Her throat felt thick with fear.

His face twisted with stormy mockery. "Yeah, I thought I was so damn smart, playing mind games with the man when he was always one step ahead of me. It was just blind luck that sent Keller into that bar, or I'd never have gotten any closer to Jessie than he wanted me to."

He looked as though he needed to lash out, to use those big fists in fury, to vent the rage she could feel simmering in his powerful body, but she wasn't frightened. Not for herself, anyway. His anger was directed toward George Santalucci. And himself.

"You're not perfect, Devlin. You couldn't have known."

"That's just it, Mandy," he said with biting frustration. "The signs were all there. I should have seen them. If I hadn't been so obsessed with making love to you, I *would* have seen them."

Amanda twisted her fingers into tense knots in her lap. The atmosphere in the room thickened, filling her with a heightened sense of danger. "You *did* see them. Don't be so hard on yourself." She touched his thigh, and he flinched as though her fingers were a scalding brand.

"Sorry," she managed with a constrained smile, pulling back her hand and clenching her fingers into a small fist in her lap. "Do you think he knows I have no intention of following his orders?"

He straightened his leg and stared at his toes. "He might be suspicious, but he's just arrogant enough to think you'll knuckle under in the end, no matter how hard you might have tried to fight him. Especially now that he's gotten rid of me."

She wanted to believe him. It was the only way she could hang on to her control. But how could she know for sure?

"I need time, Mandy. A few days at the most to get Jessie back home. After that, you can make that call if you have to." He waited, watchful and silent, his somber expression giving nothing away. Only his eyes changed, growing dark and narrowing at the corners, protecting his thoughts and feelings.

He was a man of many passions, some she understood and some, sadly, she never would. But there was a vein of iron-hard strength that ran deep and silent within him, and a kind of gallantry within that strength that had brought him back to help her, even at the risk of his own freedom, his own life.

Fleetingly she wondered if Juana had been right. Had he come back because he loved her?

No, she told herself. He'd come back to help Jessie, not because he loved Jessie's mother. He'd promised to bring her home, and he intended to keep that promise. She focused her attention on Devlin's face.

"Unless Lola tells the truth, or unless you get yourself a hell of an attorney and a sympathetic jury, you're bound to end up in prison

for assault." They both knew what kind of hell awaited a former cop
in prison, even in isolation.

"Maybe I'll get a sympathetic judge, too." His lips smiled, but
his eyes reflected the bitter truth. There was nothing she could do to
help him if the case came to trial, and they both knew it.

"Oh, Devlin, I wish—"

He pressed warm fingers against her lips, silencing her. "I know.
I'm not asking you to compromise your principles, Mandy. I know
what that would do to you. Just give me a little time, that's all." He
removed his hand from her lips and let it rest gently against the curve
of her neck.

"A few days?"

"That's all, I promise. I have a plan. It's a long shot, but I think
it'll work."

He was waiting for her decision, his gray eyes watching her face.
Fear churned in her stomach, and her chest was tight.

She glanced at the phone. She could be impeached and disbarred
for aiding and abetting a fugitive, and she would deserve the punish-
ment.

But if she turned him in now, worse things could happen—to Jessie
and to all the other victims of Santalucci's evil. If it meant putting
an end to all that horror, a few days wouldn't matter.

"I'll do whatever you say," she said quietly. "What's your plan?"

Devlin took a moment to reply. He seemed to be having trouble
with his throat, and he had to clear it several times before his expression hardened and his eyes grew cold.

"I want you to set up a meeting with Santalucci. First thing tomorrow morning."

She took a moment to absorb his words. She was still caught up
in her own internal debate. "A meeting? What kind of a meeting?"

"A meeting with me. Alone. I want to arrange a trade."

"Surely you're not thinking of an exchange? Yourself for Jessie?"
She started to shake her head even before he answered. "No, Devlin.
No. I won't let you do it."

His remote expression softened. "Why won't you let me, Mandy."

He was watching her very carefully, his eyes becoming more turbulent with each silent second that passed.

"Because I couldn't live with myself if you were killed."

"You mean it's intellectually abhorrent to you, the thought of one
death to prevent another?" The question was silky soft.

She swallowed. If only she knew what he was thinking behind that hard facade. If only he loved her. But of course he didn't. And she couldn't risk adding to his problems by blurting out her own feelings.

"Intellectually and every other way," she said truthfully. "I don't want you to die. Not for Jessie or for any other reason. It would be wrong."

"Wrong. Yeah, I guess that's as good a description as any. Of course, from my point of view, it would be stupid, wouldn't it? Dying for a kid I don't even know."

She flinched. "Yes, it would be stupid," she repeated softly, a sick feeling spreading through her as she let her gaze rest on the thunderous frown between his brows.

"Call Cy, Devlin. Tell him where she is. He can take some men, and—"

"And Jessie would be dead before they got within hailing distance. Santalucci is our only way in."

Amanda forced herself to think rationally. "This makes no sense. Why would he take you when he already has Jessie?"

"Trust me, Mandy. You set up the meeting, and I'll make sure he goes for it."

"But—"

"Yes or not? Do you let me do it my way, or not?"

Helplessly she raised her gaze to his. There was a steady, unquenchable light shining in those steely eyes. Eyes that had watched his partner die, eyes that had witnessed things she couldn't even imagine in her worst moments, eyes that had filled with tears over a small boy's suffering. How she loved those eyes! How she loved him.

"Do what you have to do," she said quietly. She smoothed the twin lines from his brow with her fingertips. "But I'll never forgive you if you get killed." She tried to smile, but her lips were trembling too badly.

His eyes flashed silver fire before his lashes lowered. His hand wasn't completely steady as he took hers and breathed a kiss into her palm.

"You deserve vintage champagne and gentle wooing and promises of love, and I can't give you any of those. I...wish I could." His voice was filled with sadness.

Is that what she really wanted? She was too upset to think clearly. She only knew she loved him. Deeply and without reservation.

"Give me what you can," she whispered, feeling her heart swell with a bittersweet acceptance. "I need you so much."

She moved, and he moved and suddenly she was in his arms. His kiss was hot and desperate with need. Crushed against him, Amanda could feel the tension trapped in the corded muscles of his arms and chest. He was holding back, tempering his desire with a gentleness that touched her.

Eagerly, willingly, she opened her mouth and touched his lips with her tongue, offering herself to him. She wanted to feel the power of his desire, ached to feel his body shudder against hers, longed to feel him fill her completely, his body becoming part of hers.

"Devlin," she whispered against his hard, sculptured mouth. "My beautiful lover."

He wasn't gentle as he stripped the clothes from her, his face dark with naked hunger.

His own clothes came off just as quickly. She was ready for him, just as he was for her. He took her swiftly, shaking her with the power of his thrust. She inhaled sharply, feeling the pleasure flood every inch of her. She'd never experienced such glorious rapture, such divine ecstasy.

A mindless, soaring sensation took over, lifting her, carrying her, pushing her upward. The deep, hot agony increased, pulsing insistently, spreading, pressuring, building. She dug her nails into his shoulders, and her head tossed from side to side as he loved her, his body unerringly finding the right rhythm.

She moaned, and then began to shudder. As she tipped over the brink into pure, blinding, maddening pleasure, she screamed. With one final thrust, he found his own release, his harsh cry slicing into hers.

Devlin brought her down gently, his body still moving slowly in hers, his hands cradling her heated face. Slowly she felt herself return to her body, and a delicious and wonderful sensation of fulfillment began cooling her heated veins.

"Wonderful," she whispered, wanting to tell him she loved him and knowing that she never could. She touched his sweat-dampened brow with her fingertips and smiled.

"I'll say," he whispered, his voice hoarse with feeling. He rolled them over until she lay on top of him, her forehead resting against his chin. "My Mandy."

His husky voice lingered over the name that only he called her, and she wanted to beg him to stay with her always. But that was impossible.

"Devlin," she whispered, her heart breaking. "My Devlin."

She let her eyes drift closed. "I love you." She'd said the words only in her mind. Hadn't she?

Within minutes she was asleep, her soft, even breathing warming the hollow at the base of his neck, a fragrant curl of sable hair trailing across his lips.

She didn't hear the savage curse that Devlin breathed into the silence.

Chapter 15

Amanda called Santalucci at seven the next morning. She'd had to weed through three lackeys before she got the man himself. His voice had been coarse, bordering on insulting, his language crude.

Buchanan had coached her to be succinct and definite. "Tell him I want a meeting, no later than noon today, and if he doesn't agree, tell him you're withdrawing from the case first thing Monday. Make him sweat a little, but let him name the place. That way he'll feel safe."

He'd made arrogant noises of refusal, but finally agreed, and just as Devlin had predicted, insisted on meeting at a spot of his choosing.

It was an abandoned shack about five miles beyond the riding stable, not too far from the spot where the men in the Chrysler had observed them on that first Sunday ride.

At the stroke of twelve Buchanan parked the Volvo on the edge of the road and set the brake. "Great place for a meet," he muttered as though to himself. "Or a hit."

His gray eyes swiftly scanned the area, noting the points of greatest danger. The Saint had chosen well. He and Amanda would be completely exposed and totally vulnerable.

Devlin left the keys in the ignition, standard procedure in case he had to make a quick exit. Although in this case he probably wouldn't have a chance in hell, he realized grimly as he stood up and flexed his shoulders. He felt naked without a weapon hugging his butt.

The gleaming black limousine was already parked on the rutted driveway, the engine idling, the tinted windows shielding the passengers from view. The black Chrysler was behind the Cadillac, turned so that the shiny hood faced the road. It, too, idled quietly as though ready to take off at the slightest suggestion of a trap.

Two burly, bareheaded men in matching blue suits stood on either side of the limousine, brawny arms crossed over their chests. Amanda could detect the telltale bulge of weapons hidden beneath the conservative clothes.

"Stay behind me as much as you can," Buchanan said in clipped tones as he helped her from the station wagon. He'd vehemently opposed her coming along, but she'd refused to make the call to Santalucci until he'd relented. Not even Devlin was going to keep her away from her daughter a second longer than was necessary.

Balancing her head stiffly on her tense shoulders, she took a deep breath and looked around her. The tumbledown shack was the only sign of human habitation within sight.

Everything else was bleak and desolate. Lonely, windswept, forsaken—it would be a terrible place to die. She shivered and forced her chin up defiantly. It was only a place.

Twenty-five feet separated them from the Cadillac, twenty-five feet of barren, open ground. Next to her Buchanan walked with a rolling swagger, his hips loose, his shoulders relaxed. The only thing tight about him was his cold smile.

Like a gunslinger walking the length of Main Street. Only this good guy was unarmed and facing impossible odds.

Beneath the brim of his battered, sweat-stained hat, his face was shadowed, his eyes unreadable. His hand rode lightly but comfortingly against her spine, connecting her to him with invisible force.

Her heart was beating like a trip-hammer as she walked beside him, skipping a little to keep up with his long strides. The sun was directly overhead, casting little shadow on the hard, pebbly surface beneath her feet, and she felt the oppressive heat settle like a smothering blanket over her shoulders and the top of her bare head. Beneath the thin soles of her sandals, the scorching sand crunched loudly, reminding her that every step was taking her deeper into desperate danger.

As they approached, Santalucci slipped out of the dim back seat like a rattler slithering from under a boulder. He was dressed in beige pleated trousers and a silk shirt, worn open to the middle of his hairy chest to display thousands of dollars' worth of glittering gold chains.

Devlin, with his well-worn Stetson and dusty boots, looked almost seedy next to him, especially in the faded jeans with the ragged cuffs. And yet he carried himself with a rangy grace that signaled the same kind of power and confidence Santalucci projected.

Paradoxically they were evenly matched, two ruthless, enigmatic men who made their own rules and fought with a fierce determination to win. Amanda could feel the sizzling hatred arcing between them, white-hot and deadly.

"Your Honor. Buchanan." Santalucci's deep voice was tinged with smug triumph, his cocky stance anticipating victory. "This is an unexpected pleasure."

Amanda stifled a gasp of surprise as two big men silently emerged from the Chrysler to stand behind Devlin, each carrying a black machine pistol in a hamlike hand. She pressed her palms against her thighs and forced herself to take even breaths.

"I assume you've come unarmed, as instructed," the crime boss continued, eyeing Buchanan's lean body with flat yellow eyes.

Buchanan looked bored as he lifted his hands up and spread his feet. His eyes were silver slits that revealed nothing as the shorter of the two bodyguards came forward quickly and patted him down, his thick hands slapping hard against Devlin's braced body.

"He's clean," the man barked with surly disappointment, his gaze sliding from Santalucci to Amanda, who was standing a few feet away.

On Devlin's orders she'd dressed in tight jeans, a short-sleeved T-shirt and sandals. He'd also instructed her to leave her purse in the car, and now she knew why. He hadn't wanted one of Santalucci's men to touch her.

"I'm sure Judge Wainwright is unarmed, Blades," the Saint said with a curt nod of dismissal.

The brutish-looking man flushed and returned to his position by the car, his attention riveted on Buchanan, his eyes hidden by mirrored glasses that reflected the bleak desert scene in distorted, curving images.

Santalucci shoved his hands into his pockets and regarded Buchanan with an unfriendly stare.

"So, you want to trade. I find that mildly amusing, since I doubt you have anything I'd want. Except yourself."

Buchanan hooked his thumbs into his belt loops and glanced up at the azure sky, his jaw jutting forward challengingly. "How about the names of every undercover agent in the Southwest? And their cover identities.''

Behind him, Amanda gasped, but Devlin ignored her. His attention was fixed on the man in front of him, every nerve in his body focused and alert. This was the most important trap he'd ever laid, and the most dangerous. He wouldn't allow himself to think about what would happen if he couldn't pull it off.

The slitted reptilian eyes began to glow from within as Santalucci studied Buchanan's face in silence. ''And your price?''

''The release of the judge's daughter and safe passage for all of us back to the city. *Plus* two hundred thousand in small bills.'' Come on, bastard, Devlin urged silently, come on, take the bait. You want those names. You want them so badly you can taste it.

''What's to keep me from snatching the kid again, later?''

Buchanan jerked his head impatiently toward the long black Cadillac. ''Why should you? Your flunky there has been taking pictures of us since the moment we arrived. All you have to do is flash an eight-by-ten glossy of the judge here standing next to you, and she's finished.''

''You're smarter than you look, cop.'' Santalucci glanced over Devlin's shoulder. ''You know what that would mean to your career, don't you, babe?'' His voice bordered on insult as he spoke to her, and Amanda stiffened.

The stinging taste of revulsion rose in her throat as she fought down the urge to wipe that sick smirk from his face with her nails.

''It would destroy it.''

''She's right,'' Buchanan said, his voice flat. A killing rage burned inside him, searing his gut, but he allowed only impatience to show on his face.

When the time was right, that slime would pay for hurting Amanda. He would pay for Tony and for all the others. Devlin would see to it.

Amanda chewed nervously on the inside of her cheek as she watched Devlin. This was the cold and calculating man who'd stalked Gus D'Amato. This was the man who followed his instincts instead of blindly adhering to someone else's rules. This was a man who was ready to kill or be killed.

But his strength wasn't in his gun or his fists. It was in Devlin himself, in the good and decent man behind the scarred facade who'd fought with every weapon he could muster, including his willingness to die.

But what choice did he have? What choice did she have? Breaking the law wasn't right, but what Santalucci and his goons were doing was far worse.

Fleetingly her eyes caressed Devlin's harsh profile. When this was over she'd tell him that she'd been so wrong. So terribly wrong.

Devlin was tired of waiting. The longer the man stalled, the more chance there was for something to go wrong. Alone, he could handle a violent confrontation. Deep in his gut he'd welcome a chance to take on this man who'd become the object of his personal crusade. But he couldn't risk Mandy's life just to satisfy his own blood lust.

"Make up your mind, George. Do we deal or not?" A trickle of sweat snaked down his spine. His veins throbbed with adrenaline, and his stomach had shut down. His eyes were focused, his muscles tensed. He was ready.

"Give me the names," Santalucci said coldly, "and I'll tell you where to pick up the kid."

Buchanan sneered. "No way. Besides, the list's in my head. You take us to the kid, and as soon as she and Amanda are safely home, and *after* I get my two hundred thousand, I'll dictate the names to your cute little private secretary there."

He jerked his thumb toward Blades, whose lips curled in a silent snarl. "Then you and I'll drive back to the city, and you can drop me off at the airport. I have a five o'clock flight to Acapulco."

"You think I'm stupid?" Santalucci barked. "No deal. I want the names up front."

"What's the matter, George. You afraid of a has-been cop?" Devlin's chilling smile was a slash of derision across the dark plane of his face.

"Not on your best day, Buchanan. Word is you lost your nerve, that's why you quit."

"Yeah, that's why your goons are packing half the National Guard Armory."

A thundercloud raged in Santalucci's eyes, but his lips curved into a cold smile. "You have a point there." He gestured toward the limousine. "You and the judge get in the Caddy. Rocco here will follow in your car. I'll take you to the kid."

"I always like to go in style."

Devlin took Amanda by the elbow and led her toward the limousine. His touch buoyed her as she walked beside him, her heart pounding furiously in her chest. Her throat was so dry she couldn't speak if she had to.

Inside the plush gray interior, the air-conditioning blasted through the vents, raising chill bumps on her bare arms. Next to her Buchanan slid his arm around her shoulders. "You sure have a lot of trouble with air-conditioning, don't you?"

She nodded and tried to stop the shivering. His gentle teasing made her happy and sad at the same time.

He seemed supremely confident, as though they were taking a leisurely ride with friends, but Amanda could feel the rigid tension in the arm resting so intimately on her shoulders.

How did he stand it all those years? she wondered. Amanda reached for his hand and held it tightly. She never wanted to let go. His hard fingers squeezed hers, and her heart filled with love. It would hurt so much when he left her.

The trip was made in silence. She watched the familiar landscape slip by, her mind a determined blank. She wouldn't think of anything but the next few minutes, the next few seconds. Otherwise, she would lose what little control she still had.

"The next left," Santalucci barked suddenly to the uniformed driver, and the man's head moved forward in a stiff nod.

"Yes, sir."

One by one the narrow, sun-weathered houses of Madrid appeared alongside the road, lined up in a tidy row. Some were in the last stages of decay, others had been newly restored. The small town was in transition.

The turn was a sharp one, rocking the limo as the driver inched forward. There was no road sign, no markers of any kind at the turnoff, only a rudely scraped dirt trail leading up toward the blank face of a jagged mountain.

Through the darkly tinted window she could see a towering pile of rocks jutting out from the face of the mountain and beyond the rocks, partially hidden by scrub junipers, a heavy metal door that was painted the same color as the earth surrounding it.

"Very ingenious," Buchanan said with a quick glance toward the man on his right.

"The crazy old guy who built it didn't want his neighbors to know where his hidey-hole was. When the bomb hit, he didn't want to share his goods." His chuckle was derisive.

The chauffeur exited quickly and jogged around the back of the limo to open the door. The Chrysler pulled up a few feet away, followed by Amanda's Volvo.

Santalucci waited until Blades and his men were in position around the limousine, then climbed out. Flexing his shoulders nervously, he glanced quickly around the area, his eyes hooded, his brows drawn.

Buchanan followed the other man, then reached back to help Amanda.

"You're doing great," he muttered in her ear as he clamped her to his side. She clung to him, her legs rubbery, her stomach fluttering with sick anticipation. In a few seconds she would know if Jessie was alive or dead.

In front of the door, Santalucci gave Buchanan a measuring look, then nodded to Blades who took the heavy knife from its scabbard under his arm and knocked three times on the heavy door with the hilt.

Inch by slow inch, the door opened until a short, wiry man with sparse blond hair and a bad complexion was clearly visible. He and Blades exchanged curt greetings, and the door was opened wide.

"Stay with the car," Santalucci told Blades, then nodded to the man inside. "It's okay, Keller. We're coming in."

Buchanan's hand tightened on Amanda's waist, and she took a deep breath. She didn't know what she was going to find. "Easy," he said gruffly. "Lean on me."

She forced herself to match his measured pace as they walked through the opening.

It was cool inside, and the air was stale and musty, reminding her of old newspapers and dust. They were in a single room, made of concrete painted a drab gray and lit by a naked overhead bulb.

Against the far wall were two tiers of bunks, bracketed by bathroom facilities in one corner, and a crude kitchen in the other. Next to the tiny refrigerator was a small door standing slightly ajar. Beyond the narrow opening was black emptiness.

Still clinging to Devlin, Amanda stepped forward, her desperate gaze frantically sweeping the bunker. Her heart leaped wildly as she spotted a small body, still dressed in the blue sweatshirt, in one of the bottom bunks.

"Jessie!"

She ran forward and gently lifted her daughter into her arms. Dear God, she prayed fervently. Please let her be alive.

Jessie moaned, and Amanda felt her heart stop momentarily, then race with relief and happiness. She was alive! Her baby was alive and safe. Or was she?

Biting her lip, she touched Jessie's face, felt her pulse, examined her limbs. She seemed fine. Perfect. The color in her chubby cheeks was good, and her breathing was regular. Beneath her shaggy bangs a faint sheen of perspiration dotted her forehead. She appeared to be asleep.

"Oh, baby. Oh, Jessie." Her trembling lips whispered her daughter's name over and over, and her voice shook with relief as she rocked her daughter's limp body back and forth, afraid to let go.

Suddenly Jessica's lashes fluttered and she opened her eyes. "Mommy? Oh, *Mommy*, I'm so glad you came," she cried in a sleep-slurred voice. "I hate this place. I want to go home."

Amanda's gaze flew to Devlin's, thanking him, celebrating with him, loving him. A bright blaze of relief shone in his eyes for an instant, before the mask of a ruthless renegade slipped back into place.

"You haven't hurt her?" he asked sharply, and Santalucci shrugged.

"We used a few tranquilizers. Keller here said the kid was a regular chatterbox, nearly drove him crazy."

Devlin swung his gaze to the hard-faced man who was standing next to the small metal table that occupied the center of the room. Keller was in sweat-stained shirtsleeves, with his shoulder holster dangling under one arm.

"Kids are like poison ivy, know what I mean?" the man complained with a sneer. "Especially this one. Gave me nothin' but trouble. I'll be glad to get back to my old lady."

Devlin grinned. "Yeah, I know what you mean." He turned to Santalucci. "Okay if I check her out? Just to make sure the goods aren't damaged."

The other man's shrug was impatient. "Hurry up. I got better things to do today than hang around this dump."

Devlin started to slide into the bed next to Amanda, then glanced up. The space between the two bunks was too narrow for such a tall man, and he was forced to take off his hat and duck his head.

"Hello, Jessie," he said in a gentle voice as he bent over the sleepy child cradled in Amanda's lap. He rested his hat on his knee, one hand pinching the crown, the other absently sliding along the brim.

"Hello. Are you one of the bad guys, too?"

His brows arched quizzically as he shifted his gaze to Amanda's flushed face. "Am I?"

She shook her head. "No." Never, my darling. You're kind and sensitive and strong and good, and I love you so much. So very much.

"Mommy?"

Amanda brushed a trembling hand across Jessie's forehead. "This is Devlin, Jessie. He's come with me to take you home."

The little girl gave him a happy grin that brought a tightness to his chest. She was a tiny copy of her mother, a delightful, adorable little girl.

Deep inside, buried in the rubble of his past, regret stirred, and a distant hope awakened, only to be smothered by the familiar desolation that had been his constant companion for so long.

Too late. It was too damned late for him.

A savage anger shook him before he managed to control it. He took a steadying breath. They weren't out of this mess yet. And it was up to him to keep this sweet child and her mother safe.

"Can we go now?" Jessie asked eagerly, peeking around her mother's arm at the two grim-faced men across the room.

Devlin's lopsided smile was strained as he glanced from Jessie to her mother. "Soon, Punkin. Just sit still for a few minutes more, and your mom can take you out of here." Gently he touched Jessie's pale cheek.

"Stay here until I tell you to go," he told Amanda curtly. "Then drive straight home and wait for my call." His voice was thick and even huskier than usual.

She nodded, her heart aching. He would never call. In his own way Devlin was saying goodbye.

"That's enough schmaltz, cop," Santalucci ordered with a sneer. "You got what you came for, now I want mine. Let's get the hell out—"

"This is the FBI. Throw down your weapons and put your hands on your head!"

There was a chorus of sharp curses and frantic shouts outside, followed by the deafening whir of helicopter rotors and the staccato sound of gunshots.

Amanda folded her body over Jessica's squirming one, her heart pounding, her ears straining. The amplified voice had sounded like Cy Tanner's, but how was that possible?

Before the sound of the shots faded, Buchanan was across the room, his back to the door. In his hand was a tiny Derringer he'd taken from his hat.

"Drop the gun where I can see it, Keller," he ordered coldly, "or you'll be the second one to die. After your boss here." His hand was rock steady, his eyes hard as flint.

"Boss? What should I do?" Keller had his gun half out of the holster.

"Do as he says," the man ordered in a low growl.

Keller dropped to his heels and slid his revolver toward the middle of the cement floor.

Watching the weapon spin out of reach, Santalucci spat out a filthy curse, his hands bunched into impotent fists at his sides.

"I'll get you for this, cop. You'll rot in prison for the rest of your life, I promise. Unless you get pigstuck first. I got friends inside that owe me."

His yellow eyes glowed with hatred, and a thin line of spittle angled from the corner of his mouth.

"Boss, the escape tunnel," Keller said hoarsely over the sound of the helicopter, his eyes going to the half-open door.

"*Shut up*, you stupid ass," the mobster shouted, his face twisting in rage.

Devlin never took his eyes from the Saint's face as he retrieved Keller's revolver. He checked the cylinder, then tucked the Derringer into his belt above his navel and transferred the .38 to his left hand.

Outside the noise of the rotors suddenly changed pitch as though the helicopter were landing, then slowed to a stop as the pilot cut the engine.

Santalucci's eyes were narrowed, the pupils slitted and empty. Amanda shivered involuntarily as his teeth bared in a calculating grin.

Buchanan didn't move, didn't react, didn't do anything but smile. It was the lazy, indolent expression of a man who knew only victory, the wide mocking grin of a killer sizing up his next victim.

Five feet away, her daughter heavy in her arms, Amanda watched in horrible fascination as his finger tightened on the trigger. The hammer moved a fraction of an inch, then stopped.

Santalucci's face was pasty white, and fat globules of sweat beaded on his forehead. His yellow eyes were wide with fear. The cocky defendant with the oily sneer who'd tormented her in the courtroom was nowhere to be seen.

Devlin was going to blow his head off. In front of Jessie, in front of her. He was going to kill another man in cold blood.

Her heart was thundering so loudly she could scarcely think. She opened her mouth to plead with him, when suddenly, his gaze flickered toward her.

"It's your call, Mandy."

She swallowed hard. He was keeping his promise to her. "Please don't do it. He's not worth your life, Devlin. Nothing is."

Devlin suddenly looked very tired. "I'm not sure I agree with you. It would almost be worth spending the rest of my days in jail, knowing that this bastard was six feet under," he said in a flat voice.

"But it's not worth it to me."

"Mandy, I—"

"This is Cy Tanner, Dev. Is everything okay in there?"

"Just fine, Cy," Devlin yelled back. "Give me a minute."

Santalucci's face was a livid pink. "You set this up! This was a damned trap."

"You got that right. How's it feel, creep?"

Shock flooded Amanda's veins. "You and Cy arranged this?"

"Yes, this morning by phone after you called Georgie here. I told him about Rosa's father, and he ran a quick check on the tax records to find out where this place was located."

He glanced toward the sliver of yellow sunlight slipping past the metal door. "I had no idea when we arrived whether or not he'd managed to set things up."

"What about you? The assault charges?"

"I promised Cy I'd give myself up as soon as this was over."

Amanda stared at him. "You could have gotten Jessie free without Cy's help. You had it all planned, didn't you?" She glanced toward the Derringer. "You would have taken Santalucci hostage, used him to get you and Jessie past his goons."

"Something like that, yes." Devlin looked distinctly uncomfortable.

"So why did you call Cy?"

He shrugged. "You wouldn't let me come alone, and I couldn't take a chance of something going wrong with you here." His grin flashed briefly. "You're one stubborn woman, Mandy."

He did it for her. Because he was afraid for her. Hugging her daughter close, Amanda fought back the tears. Devlin would die inch by inch in prison, in any kind of confinement. His fine strong body would continue to thrive, but his mind, his spirit would shrivel. She couldn't let that happen.

Buchanan gestured toward the door with the .38. "Let's go, creep," he ordered, leveling the revolver at the taller man's belt.

"Wait!"

Three faces turned toward her, each wearing a different expression. But only Devlin's mattered. And he looked stunned, as though he'd been kicked in the gut.

Whispering to her daughter to stay put, Amanda stood up and held out her hand. "Devlin, give me the gun."

"I'm not going to shoot him, Mandy. I gave you my word."

The hurt in his voice shivered through her. He still expected her to mistrust him.

"I know that. I intend to hold these two long enough for you to escape through that tunnel. In a few hours you can be back in Mexico. Safe.'' She moved closer, her hand still outstretched.

Devlin stood very still. This was an illusion, a creation of his imagination. Because life wasn't like this. Life didn't allow dreams to come true.

"Aiding and abetting is a felony, Mandy," he said carefully. "Punished by fine and imprisonment."

A steady, sure calmness came over her. "You told me once that there's a greater law than the ones written in a book someplace. I didn't believe you then, because I didn't know you and because I didn't understand the ugly, desperate world you had to live in for so long. But I understand now. And that's why I know it would be wrong, a greater wrong than anything I'd be doing, for you to go to prison for a crime you didn't commit."

A slow, captivating smile spread over his face, and his eyes warmed until they were twin pools of liquid silver.

"You really believe that, don't you?" He was so choked up he had trouble getting the words past his throat.

"Yes, because I believe in you. I'll always believe in you, Devlin Buchanan, because I love you." She said the words boldly, defiantly, daring him to accept them.

His shoulders jerked, and his eyes turned smoky as he lifted a hand to touch her cheek. His palm was warm and rough against her skin. She would always remember the sweetly gentle touch of those big hard hands, no matter how far away from her he might have to go.

"Then believe in this, too," he said in his wonderfully husky voice. "It would kill me to walk away and leave you to pay the price for my freedom." He bent swiftly to press a hard kiss onto her lips. "My brave Mandy."

"Buchanan? Are you in there?"

He dropped his hand and glanced toward the door. "Sounds like Cy's getting impatient. He never did like standing in the hot sun. Must be that thick Georgia blood of his."

His bruised knuckles protested as he pulled open the door and shouted, "I'm here, Cy. Santalucci and one of his buddies are coming out first. They're unarmed."

He shoved the door open wider and stepped back, keeping his body between Amanda and the two hoodlums. "You're on, George. Take a bow." He motioned toward the door with the .38.

Santalucci's face was twisted with hate as he moved past them. "You're dead, Buchanan. And so's your whore."

Devlin moved quickly, driving his fist into Santalucci's smirking face with so much force the heavy jawbone splintered with a loud sharp crack. Blood spurted from the Saint's slack mouth, and his snakelike eyes dilated in disbelief.

Devlin caught him by the collar before his head hit the ground, and with only the strength in his arm and his wrist, hoisted him to his feet. Before the bigger man could react, Devlin spun him around and pushed him out the door into the arms of two impeccably suited men in dark glasses.

White-faced and shaking, Keller followed his boss without a word.

"Don't tell me he didn't deserve *that*," Devlin challenged in a harsh voice. He'd probably busted his hand, but it was worth it. More than worth it.

Amanda grinned. She wondered how he would react if she threw her arms around his neck and refused to let go. "It was perfect. I couldn't have done better myself."

Gently she lifted his bleeding hand to her lips and kissed the ballooning knuckle. "You'll need ice for this."

He slanted her a scowling look. "You mean you're not going to lecture me?" He let his hand rest in hers. The fragile fragrance scenting her hair had gradually overpowered the musty smell of the small bunker, reminding him of the perfect hours he'd spent in her bed. He wanted to drown himself in her freshness, in her beauty, but Cy was waiting for him.

"Nope. No lectures." Her grin was endearingly pert. For the first time since he'd nearly killed her on his front stoop, she looked carefree, even cheerful. But why not? She had her daughter back, and all would soon be right in her world.

Devlin forced himself to withdraw his hand. This was the end of the line for them. No sense prolonging the agony.

Ruthlessly ignoring her, he unloaded the revolver and tossed it onto the table, along with the shells and his Derringer. He was preparing to give himself up.

"I'll testify," she asked quietly. "I'll get Pamela Devereaux to defend you. We'll fight this."

Devlin brushed her hair away from her face with hands that shook slightly. "I think that's when I first knew I was in deep trouble, when I found out what a tough little lioness lurked inside that sexy body of yours."

His thumbs massaged her jaw. "I knew you would never give up until I did exactly what you wanted." He grinned, his cheeks creasing into those beguiling male dimples that she loved. "Take good care of your cub, Mama. You're part of the reason she's still alive."

Her smile was wobbly. "It was you, Devlin. Only you. I would have done all the wrong things, I know that now. You saved my baby's life." She touched his face. "You know what that means, don't you?"

He shook his head.

"That she belongs to you. And since you saved *my* life in La Placita, I belong to you, too."

He pulled her into his arms and buried his face in her neck. "No, Mandy. I wish it could be, but...no."

His muscles clenched as though in pain, and then he raised his head and deliberately set her away from him.

But Amanda refused to let him go. "Yes, Devlin. I don't want to even think about a future without you." Her lips trembled, and she clamped her teeth down to still them.

Devlin tried to swallow the lump in his throat, but his muscles were too tense. He felt paralyzed, frozen, unable to move.

"Be reasonable, Mandy," he said impatiently, his stormy eyes imprisoning her. "I'm carrying some heavy-duty history with me. And it isn't over yet. The DA was burned badly by my acquittal; this time he's going to be out for blood. I can't drag you and Jessie into my mess. I...care too much to subject you to that kind of ugliness." A harsh line formed between his brows. "Forget it. Forget me."

Amanda let her love show in her eyes as she reached up to caress his hard cheeks with her palms. "What was it you told me not so long ago?" She pretended to ponder, and his face assumed a look of wary expectation. "Oh yeah, I remember. That I couldn't get rid of you if I wanted to?"

Her hands on his face were seductively warm and caressing, and the glow in her eyes was filling him with light. Could he risk it? Did he have the courage after all he'd seen and heard to start over? With Mandy?

Her lips curved into a soft, inviting smile, and her voice throbbed with all the love that filled her. "Well, Mr. Buchanan, here's my bottom line. I'm buying into your trouble just like you bought into mine. You couldn't get rid of me, even if you tried."

She stood on tiptoe and kissed him hard. "Take it or leave it."

Devlin was shaken by the instant enormity of his need. His heart, his soul, his body reached out to her in one violent surge of longing. He fought to breathe. God, he wanted her. He *needed* her.

Maybe life did give second chances after all, he thought as he found himself lost in the love shining in her beautiful eyes.

Devlin had to clear his throat three times before he could speak. "I'll take it. And you." His gaze drifted toward the wide-eyed little girl looking at him with her mother's eyes. "Both of you."

Epilogue

Five months later

"Mommy, what's that big building over there?"

Jessie hopped out of the Volvo and ran over to the tall chain-link fence screening the visitors' parking lot from the main grounds.

Amanda turned up the collar of her cashmere coat to protect her neck from the brisk winter wind and followed Jessie to the fence. Her boots echoed hollowly on the frozen ground, and her breath showed white in front of her.

"That's the state prison, sweetie, where they lock up men who break the law."

Less than a month ago George Santalucci had been sentenced to life imprisonment here. Amanda had been a witness in his trial for kidnapping.

She looked up at the forbidding walls and tried to imagine what it would be like to be shut away behind them. But the thoughts that surfaced were too painful, and she forced them from her mind.

Jessie picked up a stone and tossed it toward a nearby lamppost. She was wearing her furry white parka and her new red beret, the one Amanda had bought her to wear to the Christmas party tonight at the courthouse. She'd been overexcited and nervous since Amanda had received the surprise phone call from Mexico just after breakfast.

"But why are we here, Mommy? We're going to miss the party." Jessie's tongue poked through the new gap in her front teeth, testing the empty space where her tooth used to be. "The ice cream will be all gone by the time we get there."

"We're here to pick up Devlin, sweetie. I told you that." At the mention of her husband's name, Amanda's heart began to pound, just as it did when he was near. After nearly four months of marriage she still felt like a bride.

"But why's he here? Devlin's not one of the bad guys."

"No, he's—"

"He's the new head of the governor's drug task force, that's who he is."

Amanda and Jessie turned eagerly toward the sound of a husky male voice behind them. Devlin raised his thumb and grinned. "I got it, Mandy. I got the job." His gray eyes glinted with triumph, and his crooked grin spread across his bronzed features.

"Oh, Devlin," she cried as she launched herself at his broad chest. He crushed her in a strong embrace, his lips finding hers. They exchanged a long, thirsty kiss, then bent down to include Jessie in the loving embrace.

"Are you going to have to wear a suit all the time, Devlin?" the little girl asked with bright-eyed curiosity. "With a tie and everything?"

Devlin chuckled even as his fingers tugged on the perfect Windsor knot of his silk tie. "'Fraid so, Punkin. Does that mean you won't love me anymore?"

His grin was teasing, but his eyes carried a faint doubt.

"'Course I will. You're my daddy now."

Sometimes she called him Devlin, sometimes she called him Daddy, depending on her mood. She was as independent and as definite in her opinions as her mother. Frequently Devlin felt as though he were barely holding his own with the two feisty women in his life.

Grinning, he gave his daughter a hug, then stood up, his arm automatically going around Amanda's shoulders. He liked to have her close to him and felt unbearably lonely when he had to be away from her.

"Maybe someday I'll get used to it," he said in a low voice next to Amanda's ear, "but every time she calls me Daddy, I feel it right in my gut. It's like Christmas and New Year's and my birthday all rolled into one.''

Amanda pulled his head down for another kiss. His lips were warm and moist and molded fiercely to hers, exciting warm prickles of anticipation in her veins.

Desire shot through her, hot and insistent, just as it always did when he touched her. Tonight, after the party, she would ease the ache his kiss was exciting in her.

With a reluctant sigh, he released her. ''Easy, woman, I've been on the hot seat since nine this morning. Answering questions is damned hard work. I'm worn out.''

''I'll drive. You take one of your catnaps.''

He gave her a disgruntled look. ''No speeding. A man's not safe with you.'' His remarkable eyes shone with affection as he draped his arm possessively around her shoulder.

''Did they ask you a lot of questions about the Grimes trial?'' Amanda asked as they piled into the Volvo.

''Some. But most of the congressmen had read the transcript. A lot of them even wondered why it ever came to trial, especially since Lola had already changed her story several times by then.'' His lips thinned in disgust. ''I can't believe the DA wasted taxpayers' money on a trial that lasted only two days.''

Smiling gently, she reached over to smooth the frown from his brow. His skin was warm and erotically smooth against her fingertips.

''That was my fault, darling. Because you and I were romantically linked, he didn't want to risk an accusation of favoritism.''

Devlin's eyes sparkled as he buckled his seat belt. ''Romantically linked,'' he mused, his husky voice lingering over the words. ''More like besotted, smitten, hooked.'' He leaned his head against the seat and sighed heavily. ''I never had a chance.''

Amanda laughed and rummaged in her purse for her keys. She checked that Jessie was safely belted into the back seat, then started the engine.

''Better take that nap, darling. Jessie and I have a surprise waiting for you at home, and I want you to be sharp.''

Devlin eyed her suspiciously, a grin hovering over his hard lips. ''Another surprise? I hope it doesn't turn out like the cat you bought me for my birthday. You remember, the one who had her kittens in the middle of *our* bed.''

She giggled. ''It wasn't so bad, sleeping in the guest room for six weeks, was it?''

''Damn straight it was. That bed's too small for two.''

She gave him a warmly intimate look as her voice lowered into a suggestive purr. "Not the way *we* sleep, darling."

He flushed and glanced over his shoulder. Jessie was busy playing with the small family of bears she'd brought with her. As always the panda he'd given her was included, and she was badgering him for a larger version. A mama bear.

Feeling as though he was about to burst with happiness, Devlin rested his eyes on his wife as she concentrated on backing the Volvo out of the narrow space.

Her silky brown brows were drawn in concentration, and the pink tip of her tongue was caught between her small white teeth. She looked intense and utterly desirable.

Beneath the conservative pinstripes his body quickened with primitive force. Amanda was his. His woman. His wife. Sometimes, though, he found it hard to believe that she belonged to him, in spite of the matching gold bands they wore.

Many nights, lying beside her as she slept, he actually shook with the fear that his happiness would suddenly be taken from him. Maybe that's why he'd never been able to say the words that she said to him so often and so lovingly. He sighed and closed his eyes. Maybe someday.

There was an unfamiliar blue sedan parked in front of their house when Amanda pulled into the driveway. As always, the moment the engine died Devlin was wide awake.

He yawned and stretched, his eyes studying the Chevy absently. Probably belongs to the people across the street, he decided, climbing out. His long legs, encased in charcoal wool, were stiff from sitting most of the day.

Thank God, his job involved a lot more than simply working behind his desk. He would be training undercover agents all over the state, preparing them for the war on illegal drugs that had been part of the governor's campaign platform.

"Let me open the door, Mommy," Jessie pleaded, jumping up and down on the front porch. "I want to go in first."

Amanda smiled and tossed Jessie her key ring.

"You guys didn't pick out a tree without me, did you?" Devlin asked suspiciously. It was his first Christmas with his new family, and he wanted it to be perfect.

Amanda shook her head and linked her arm through her husband's. She started to step across the threshold, but Devlin suddenly reached around her to pull the door closed. She started to protest, only to be stopped by his lips taking hers. This time she didn't struggle, instead meeting his hungry lips with a fiery intensity of her own.

He groaned and tangled his hands in the shimmering hair brushing her shoulders. The roots tingled with a sweet urgency as he threaded his fingers through the thickness, and a flow of heat enveloped her from head to toe, heightening the sensitivity of her skin with each pulsing wave.

She parted his lips with her tongue, inviting the invasion of his. He accepted, exploring the sweet secrets with eager delight. Electrically charged blood warmed her skin, exciting the need to be touched, to be stroked, to be loved.

Her hands kneaded his broad shoulders, loving the rounded contours that hid the latent force of his upper arms. Her palms itched to feel his warm, smooth skin against hers, and she fumbled with the middle button of his crisp blue shirt, then slipped her fingers through the opening.

Devlin inhaled sharply as her cold fingers slid past the V of his T-shirt to brush his skin. Even through the layers of clothing covering his magnificent chest, she could hear the sudden gallop of his heart.

"I missed you today," she whispered, her lips following the hard line of his jaw. "I wanted to spend my day off in bed with you."

Buchanan groaned and closed his eyes. "Is this the surprise you have for me, because if it is, I have to tell you I love it already." He looked deep into her eyes, desire blazing with raw shuddering power between them.

His hands slipped beneath her coat to caress the enticing swell of her breasts, the callused texture of his fingertips roughening the expensive silk of her blouse, but she didn't care. The faintly raspy sound was surprisingly erotic, a caress that awakened the promise of what was to come.

But that would have to wait, and Devlin's sigh told her he was as impatient as she was. His lips found hers in an urgency that she shared.

"Later, my Mandy," he whispered against her lips.

"Later, my darling," she answered.

They were both breathing hard by the time the kiss ended.

Amanda wiped the lipstick from his mouth with her hand. "Ouch, stop it," she ordered in mock outrage as his teeth gently trapped her fingertip.

He chuckled and captured her hand with his. Side by side they walked through the door.

Jessie was waiting just inside, her eyes glowing with anticipation.

Amanda held her breath as the grinning little girl caught Devlin's big hand and tugged him toward the living room.

He went willingly, but beneath the perfectly fitted suit coat Amanda could see his back muscles bunch in anticipation. He was tense, wary. His old habits were still very strong.

Sometimes she'd catch him looking at her, a bleak, watchful expression in his eyes, and she'd known that he was remembering the empty, lonely life he'd led for so long. And sometimes at night, the bed would shake with the terrors he relived in his sleep. But the nightmares were gradually fading, and the dark brooding looks came less frequently.

One day, they would be gone for good. One day, the past would have no power over the strong sensitive man she loved so much, and then she'd know he was really hers.

Amanda almost crashed into Devlin's back as he stopped short, his head jerking in surprise. "Matt! Pepito! What...?"

The priest beamed in welcome, his hand releasing Pepe's as Jessie possessively put her arm around the boy's thin shoulders.

"This is my new brother, Pepe. He's going to have the room next to mine 'n' I'm going to teach him English, 'n' we're going to go to the same school 'n' everything." She nudged the wide-eyed, open-mouthed boy next to her. "Right, Pepe?"

But Pepe's eyes were fixed on Devlin's white face. "Señor Dev?" he said hesitantly.

Devlin dropped to his knees and wrapped the boy in his arms. His big hand pressed Pepe's face to his chest, and he lowered his head as though in prayer.

Father Garza discreetly withdrew a snowy handkerchief to wipe his eyes. Amanda simply let the tears flow unimpeded.

Finally Devlin stood, the boy still held in his arms. Pepe smiled in shy pleasure as he held on to Devlin's shoulder, his big brown eyes wide with excitement.

With his free hand Devlin pulled Amanda closer. "Why didn't you tell me?" His husky voice was ragged with emotion.

Her grin was triumphant. "Merry Christmas. Father Garza helped cut through some of that blasted red tape that was giving us fits, and the adoption papers are finally ready. Pepito is ours."

Jessie tugged on his arm. "Put him down, Daddy. I want to show him his room."

Devlin translated swiftly for the boy, then set him gently on his feet. As Devlin straightened, he inhaled slowly, trying to get a grip on the violent emotions shaking him. Next to him the children he never thought he'd have were trying to communicate in a mixture of Spanish and English that was probably hilarious if he could have heard it over the pounding of his heart.

He looked down into the upturned face of his wife, the feisty, uncontrollable, utterly adorable woman who'd given him back his hope, his heart, his life.

Tears shimmered in her eyes, and her lips were smiling sweetly in that special way she reserved just for him. Her face blurred slowly as his own tears welled hotly in his eyes.

He reached for her and crushed her against his chest. Just before his lips found hers, he whispered softly, ''I love you.''

* * * * *

If you've got the time...
We've got the
INTIMATE MOMENTS

Passion. Suspense. Desire. Drama. Enter a world that's larger than life, where men and women overcome life's greatest odds for the ultimate prize: love. Nonstop excitement is closer than you think...in Silhouette Intimate Moments!

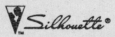

WAYS TO *UNEXPECTEDLY* MEET MR. RIGHT:

♡ Go out with the sexy-sounding stranger your daughter secretly set you up with through a personal ad.

♡ RSVP yes to a wedding invitation—soon it might be your turn to say "I do!"

♡ Receive a marriage proposal by mail— from a man you've never met....

These are just a few of the unexpected ways that written communication leads to love in Silhouette Yours Truly.

Each month, look for two fast-paced, fun and flirtatious Yours Truly novels (with entertaining treats and sneak previews in the back pages) by some of your favorite authors—and some who are sure to become favorites.

YOURS TRULY™:

Love—when you least expect it!

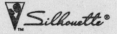

SILHOUETTE® Desire®

Do you want...

Dangerously handsome heroes

Evocative, everlasting love stories

Sizzling and tantalizing sensuality

Incredibly sexy miniseries like **MAN OF THE MONTH**

Red-hot romance

Enticing entertainment that can't be beat!

You'll find all of this, and much *more* each and every month in **SILHOUETTE DESIRE**. Don't miss these unforgettable love stories by some of romance's hottest authors. Silhouette Desire—where your fantasies will always come true....

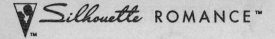

What's a single dad to do when he needs a wife by next Thursday?

Who's a confirmed bachelor to call when he finds a baby on his doorstep?

How does a plain Jane in love with her gorgeous boss get him to notice her?

From classic love stories to romantic comedies to emotional heart tuggers, **Silhouette Romance** offers six irresistible novels every month by some of your favorite authors! Such as...beloved bestsellers **Diana Palmer, Annette Broadrick, Suzanne Carey, Elizabeth August** and **Marie Ferrarella,** to name just a few—and some sure to become favorites!

Fabulous Fathers...Bundles of Joy...Miniseries... Months of blushing brides and convenient weddings... Holiday celebrations... You'll find all this and much more in **Silhouette Romance**—always emotional, always enjoyable, always about love!

SR-GEN